BAKER STREET IRREGULARS

THE GAME IS AFOOT

EDITED BY
MICHAEL A. VENTRELLA
& JONATHAN MABERRY

DIVERSION
BOOKS

Diversion Books
A Division of Diversion Publishing Corp.
443 Park Avenue South, Suite 1008
New York, New York 10016
www.DiversionBooks.com

For more information, email info@diversionbooks.com

First Diversion Books edition April 2018.
Paperback ISBN: 978-1-63576-377-5
eBook ISBN: 978-1-63576-376-8

LSIDB/1803

TABLE OF CONTENTS

INTRODUCTION:
MY OLD FRIEND SHERLOCK HOLMES

There are a lot of great and enduring characters in popular fiction. Ask anyone to write a list of ten, or even twenty, and it's a snap. Dracula and Frankenstein, Tom Sawyer and Huck Finn, Nancy Drew and the Hardy Boys—the list goes on.

For me, as a kid, it was Doc Savage; Conan; John Carter of Mars; Aragorn, son of Arathorn; the Eternal Champion, and…

Well, the problem is that we can all build those lists. And, as we grow, the characters on those lists change. In my teens and twenties, Repairman Jack replaced Conan as my tough guy hero of choice. Ben Mears from Stephen King's *Salem's Lot* replaced Abraham Van Helsing. Karl Edward Wagner's antihero Kane replaced the pure-of-heart King Arthur.

And so on. I'm looking at the age of sixty close enough to read the fine print, and still, that list keeps changing because I keep reading, and in doing so, making new literary friends.

However, since boyhood there has always been one character that has never fallen off my list. Not once. He's been steadfast, endlessly interesting, and a good companion.

That person is, of course, Sherlock Holmes.

And note that I said "person." I use the word with precision. Unlike most fictional characters, Holmes has always been intensely real to me. A few others, too—like John D. MacDonald's Travis McGee, and James Lee Burke's Dave Robicheaux. And a handful of others. But even in the company of other characters, Sherlock remains a lifelong companion and friend.

I've spent a lot of time decoding why. At first, I thought that it was the humanity of Dr. John Watson that appealed most to me. He was kinder, more *human* than Holmes; he had the social graces if not the towering genius. And in the stories, he was no dum-dum, as he was in the Basil Rathbone/Nigel Bruce films I saw on late-night TV back in the sixties. Watson was an appropriately intelligent and experienced man of his times. A cut above the everyman because he was, after all, a medical doctor.

And I like Watson. I really do. But it was not *his* name on the list.

It was Sherlock Holmes. On every version of that list.

As I got older and became a more discerning reader and, later, a scholar, I gradually decoded my fascination with Holmes.

On the surface, Holmes is wonderfully appealing because he is *not* an everyman. He's not even an every-other-man. He is unique because he specializes in very minute and very precise observation, which is then filtered through a great storehouse of personal knowledge—such as the varieties of ash in different cigarettes sold in London at that time or the pigmentation of various kinds of soil. Like that.

Quick side note before we continue: In the stories, this is wrongly referred to as deductive reasoning. Technically, he uses *inductive* reasoning far more often, and occasionally a blend of both. Deductive reasoning is where the observer starts with a premise and then seeks to prove it. Inductive, on the other hand, is where the reasoner extrapolates information that he has observed in order to arrive at the most logical supposition or, ideally, a firm conclusion. In either case, the collection of forensic evidence and the observation of the crime scene *in situ* allowed Holmes to make what often appeared to be extraordinary leaps bordering on the magical.

In an era when forensic science was in its infancy, the novelty of the Holmes stories was profound. Granted, author Arthur Conan Doyle took inspiration from Edgar Allan Poe's earlier tales of C. Auguste Dupin (*Murders in the Rue Morgue, The Purloined*

Letter, and *The Mystery of Marie Rogêt*), who in turn was inspired by the real-life troubled genius Thomas De Quincey, the noted opium eater. But Doyle expanded upon the method of observation, evidence collection and analysis, evaluation, and inductive reasoning to craft a character who became the world's first, and greatest, private consulting detective.

Back to why Holmes has been my friend all these years. It comes with a bit of backstory.

I grew up dirt poor, in a neighborhood in Philadelphia best known for alcoholism and gang violence, and in a violent household. My father was a criminal and a member of the Klan. So…fun times.

I knew that I did not want to be like him. I did not want to be a drunk or drug addict. I did not want to be a part of that fractured and polluted cultural landscape. I did not, in essence, want to live in a crime scene. But I was a kid and had no idea how to get out of that world.

Sherlock Holmes helped.

You see, logic is a useful tool to guide you through emotionally challenging situations. Logic, however much it may involve minute details, is really all about big picture—about context on a scale grander than immediate experience. When applied to personal crisis, one becomes both the client going to Sherlock Holmes with a matter both inexplicable and life-shattering, and also Holmes himself, analyzing the data and searching for a reasonable hypothesis. That's how I saw it. I was eight, I think, when I figured that out. So, okay, I was a bit of a weird kid. My imaginary friend was Sherlock Holmes, and he was trying to help me sort out my bigger life issues.

My life, I suppose, was the scene of an ongoing crime.

Applying Holmesian logic, I looked for clues.

I discovered, over time, that there was no evidence at all to support the common and very normal supposition that I was somehow to blame for the things that were happening to me. Hard as I looked, and as much as I believed that to be the case, there was simply nothing to prop up that theory. And so, over time, it collapsed under the weight of faulty logic.

Holmes famously said that, "When you have eliminated all which is impossible, then whatever remains, however improbable, must be the truth." This was a recurring theme that I first encountered in *The Adventure of the Beryl Coronet*, and—in various forms—in *The Sign of the Four*, *The Adventure of the Blanched Soldier*, and other tales in the series.

It is, perhaps, an imperfect axiom because it requires a degree of omniscience at both ends of the logical equation, but…hey, it worked for me when I was eight. It made sense. When I applied it, I came to certain reasonable conclusions.

I saw that the troubles in my neighborhood did not start with my birth. They were an ongoing problem. My existence was not even a factor in their perpetuation.

I determined that the abuse my sisters and I suffered had nothing to do with our actions. No matter how carefully we lived, or how diligent we were to follow the ever-increasing list of house rules, bad things happened. Therefore, the abuse was not any kind of logical consequence of our actions.

I saw that our father was not dissimilar to a few other fathers in our neighborhood. That suggested a pattern of behavior. Holmes talked about that, too. So, I looked for things that might have caused this kind of behavior. Looked, listened, asked. Basically, I *investigated* in order to solve a mystery. And I discovered that there was a lot of alcohol abuse. Alcohol warps perception and action. There was a lot of poverty. Desperation can warp the quality of the choices we make, and can negatively influence the logic of the risk-reward equation.

I could go on.

This was a process of discovery for me as a kid. It changed me, because from then on, I always tried to apply the Sherlock Holmes method to my outlook. I became more observant. I worked to avoid making assumptions. I also tried to fill my head with information so that the facts I observed would have a place to land.

For the record, no, I did not become Sherlock Holmes. No one ever has. What I did, though, was solve the important mysteries and crimes that were defining my young life. Once I understood that I was not an accomplice, shared no guilt, and was only one of many victims, I was able to look for solutions. Again, Holmes was there with ideas.

His education and knowledge were his primary weapons, but he was selective about what he learned. That process of selection made him an expert in those things that would most benefit him. Since I wanted to be a writer, even at a young age, I focused on that. I learned to write well, looked for ways to do it better, and read deeply so I understood the process of storytelling in ways that exceeded what I was being taught in school. After all, education in public schools is designed for group learning and to provide basic information. Public school education is not designed to help individuals excel in specific areas. College does that, but I needed to *get* to college. No one else in my neighborhood, and certainly no one in my family, went to college. I had no encouragement to do so—so, I took it upon myself, just as Holmes took it upon himself to develop knowledge in anatomy, chemistry, and other fields that would support his dream of becoming a detective.

Holmes was also tougher than he looked. He could box, fight with a single stick (cane), and knew some martial arts. I launched into all of that. I studied jujutsu. I boxed Golden Gloves. I wrestled. I fenced. I became tough.

Holmes had focus. I learned how to focus my wants and needs.

And I got out of that neighborhood. I bested my abusive father in a fight. I earned a scholarship to journalism school. I figured out the solution to my personal mystery and acted on that solution.

Was it all Holmes? Nah. Of course not. But Holmes was a major part of it. Even now, when I need to solve a problem—and it could be as simple a thing as helping my wife find her misplaced car keys—I use the same process of induction and deduction, of observation and evaluation I'd learned from Sherlock Holmes.

Which brings me to what I do now.

Although I studied journalism at Temple University, I never became a newspaper reporter. Instead I wrote a few thousand feature articles, columns, reviews, and how-to pieces for magazines. Then I wrote a slew of college textbooks for the courses I went on to teach at Temple—Martial Arts History, Personal Defense for Women, etc. In the early 2000s I switched gears and began writing fiction. My first novel, *Ghost Road Blues*, was published in 2006. Right now, I'm close to wrapping up my thirty-third novel. Along the way I've written a lot of comic books for Marvel, IDW, and Dark Horse, as well as more than 110 short stories.

One of the very first short pieces I did was "The Adventure of the Green Briar Ghost." And, yes, it was a Sherlock Holmes story.

Since then I've written other Sherlock pieces, as well as a story featuring Dr. Watson ("The Empty Grave") and even a story about C. Auguste Dupin ("The Vanishing Assassin").

I've probably watched every version of Sherlock Holmes on TV or in film, and read thousands of Holmes novels and short stories. And comics. I'm so pleased to see that I am far from alone in my appreciation for Holmes and his impact on the lives of his fans. I had a lengthy discussion on that topic with Neil Gaiman and Laurie B. King at one of the black-tie annual banquets of the *Baker Street Irregulars* in New York. Holmes has helped a lot of us. Saved some of us. Enriched all of us.

But here's the thing...

It isn't always the Holmes stories as written by Sir Arthur Conan Doyle. No. I know many people who only know Holmes from TV shows like *Sherlock* or *Elementary*. Or from caricatures of him in other mediums. And I know people who love *versions* of Sherlock Holmes. Like the curmudgeonly doctor on *House*. Like wacky Shawn on *Psych*. Like the autistic young surgeon on *The Good Doctor*. Like...

Well, hell, that becomes a long, long list.

Because the thing that makes Holmes so enduringly effective and appealing has nothing to do with his being a misanthropic nineteenth-century Englishman. Holmes is a concept. The hyper-observant, deeply intelligent, extremely eccentric, and occasionally theatrical solver of baffling mysteries.

That's why this book exists. It's why the previous volume, *Baker Street Irregulars,* exists. The protagonists herein are not white British males in frock coats. They are not anything close to that model. And yet they are shadows cast by Sherlock Holmes. The characters in these stories embody what is essential about Holmes— and about Watson. The desire to solve a mystery. The intellect. The wit. The comradeship between a genius and an enabler of genius. The friendship and mutual tolerance. The intolerance for villains to escape justice.

Holmes is a concept every bit as much as Holmes is a friend. If some version of Holmes, under that name or another, is here to help, then we feel that there are solutions, that there will be answers, that we are safe. And that there will be justice.

The Game is Afoot is filled with original mystery stories that both break the Holmesian mold and yet don't. They pave new ground while respecting the road from Doyle to here.

And they are a lot of fun.

So, sit back, turn the page, and go hunting.

Something strange and inexplicable has happened. The game's afoot…

Jonathan Maberry
Del Mar, California
November 2017

THE PROBLEM OF
THE THREE JOURNALS

BY NARRELLE M. HARRIS

Sherlock Holmes leaned casually over the counter as two people entered The Sign of Four. New customers. Time for the party trick.

"Soy cappuccino for her," Sherlock told the barista. "See the T-shirt? '100% Herbivore.' Could drink black, but see her canvas bag? Several froth spots over the flap. You don't get that from the cream on a long black. She'll ask for no sugar, but she'll slip a half teaspoon in when the boyfriend's not looking."

The barista, John Watson, gave his friend a sidelong glance, mouth tilted in a veiled smile under his well-groomed moustache. "And him?"

"Short black. The single origin. Don't be offended when he only drinks half of it. He prefers a flat white, but flat white doesn't go with the image he's projecting. They'll be takeaway. They've been arguing, and they're in a hurry now."

By the time the new customers reached the counter, John had poured the single origin short black and was steaming the soy milk for the cappuccino. The newbies had hardly finished voicing their orders when John served them up with a flourish.

"Short black, single origin—we've got the Guatemalan today—and soy cap for the lady."

The bloke arched an eyebrow. "So it's true. You guys predict coffee. Not the super power *I'd* ask for." He sneered a bit.

"Russ," hissed the girlfriend, "Don't be a dick."

Sherlock smiled benignly at Russ the Dick. "Faint red welts around your jaw under your ears where you scratch at the beard—you don't like the facial hair but you won't consider shaving it yet, you know you have a weak chin; the bow tie is a clip-on, which might be just ironic except you've made such an expensive effort with the shoes and braces. So you just don't know how to tie it, and you can't be bothered with a YouTube tutorial because it's just for show. Your glasses are plain glass. You don't need them for anything but window dressing, either. We're getting past irony and into farce now, all because you decided this is how to get into your girlfriend's pants. It's not charming, by the way, pretending to be something you're not to get a leg over. Ordering coffee you don't like because you think it fits the persona won't render you any more authentic, which reminds me…" This Sherlock addressed to Russ's increasingly irritated girlfriend. "He ate bacon for breakfast—that's bacon grease above the third button of his waistcoat—so I can assure you the 'Meat is Murder' badge on his Crumpler bag is more for your benefit than a personal political statement."

"*Bacon*?"

"Janie…"

"That's it, Russ. The last bloody straw. First that business with Karen and now this." Janie reached for the demerara sugar on the counter and defiantly plonked a teaspoon of it in her coffee. "You know what?" she asked her boyfriend in a tone of voice that essentially said, "you're fired," "You're a liar and a perv, I don't need to watch my bloody weight, and you need to have a good, hard think about yourself. While you're moving your crap out of my flat. I bet you're not even studying film. Is he?" She turned her ferocious glare onto the man at the counter.

"No," Sherlock assured her.

"Thought not." She shoved a lid onto the paper cup and stormed out, leaving Russ alone at the till.

Russ spared a filthy look for the lanky mongrel at the counter, took off his unnecessary glasses, and retreated, leaving his undrunk, unwanted coffee behind.

"Shame to waste it," said Sherlock, sipping the abandoned espresso.

"Could've waited till they'd paid, Lockie," complained John mildly.

"They'll tell their friends what happened, and we'll get at least a dozen more coming in to see if I can predict their coffee order," Sherlock said. "She'll be right." He took the coffee to his corner table where he was working on an essay.

John flicked a rubber band at his friend, housemate, and business partner, then resumed his barista duties.

• • •

At the corner opposite Sherlock's claim at The Sign of Four, one of John's regulars made the place her own. Kylie Mitchell had worked there six hours a day, every day, including lunch, for two months so far. An ancient leather-bound diary was at her left hand; a fresh new Moleskine, in which she wrote furiously, on the right. Propped invariably in front of her was an iPad showing an image of the page she was presently studying.

Sherlock Holmes knew at least a dozen things about this resident coffee addict. He enumerated them that evening with John.

"Victorian born and bred," Sherlock insisted while John whipped up smashed avocado and feta on a black seed bagel for supper. "She owns a chocolate-point Siamese cat, is allergic to nuts, and thinks she can sing like Jessica Mauboy. She can't, by the way."

John nodded, used to the way Sherlock effortlessly read their customers. John could see where some of the conclusions came from, though mostly he confined himself to remembering their coffee orders. Doc Caffeine, the staff sometimes called him: he could fix what ailed you with the best-poured shots in Melbourne. Kylie Mitchell, for example, habitually started with a double-shot espresso and a latte chaser, paced herself with two more flat whites, and finished with a chai latte. She left vibrating like a bloody mosquito.

Sherlock was still talking. "…a Melbourne University graduate in nanotechnology…"

"See her in class, did you?" John deftly squeezed lemon juice over the open bagel, then flung on a bit of homegrown mint.

"It's a *deduction*, John. I haven't studied nanotechnology, or been to the attendant electives."

"Yet."

"Yet. Let me finish pharmacology first, and I'll see if nanobots are interesting by then. Do you want to hear the rest of this?"

"Sorry, mate. Go on."

"The handwritten journals she's scrutinizing are over a hundred years old…"

"Historian?" John plonked the plates, then a bottle of Sriracha sauce, on the table.

"*Family* historian. She has a family tree at the back of the Moleskine she periodically unfolds to check. Her name is at the bottom."

"A great-grand-uncle's scandalous memoirs, then?" Two glasses of Tasmanian Pagan pear cider joined the food and condiments.

"Grand-aunt more likely, judging from the handwriting. She's comparing the source documents with scans of the matching pages, looking for discrepancies and hidden elements."

John dropped into a chair beside Sherlock. "Maybe she's looking for a *code*," he suggested in melodramatic *sotto voce*. He twisted the end of his well-groomed moustache to add a bit more dramatic flair to the pronouncement.

Sherlock sighed. "She's found the code, John. She's trying to *decipher* it."

John looked surprised at having got one right for a change. "You going to help her with that?"

"Maybe," Sherlock hedged. "I want to see how far she gets."

"Fair enough. It's sometimes better to wait until you're asked.

We know what happened last time you tried to finish Mrs. H's crossword puzzle for her, don't we?"

"Our chef has surprisingly sharp skills as a tea towel snapper."

"Worst bosses in Melbourne, she called us. Lumping me in with you, I might add." John clicked his tongue and his dog, a blue heeler named Gough Whitlam, trotted over for a treat of bacon rind.

"You'll make him fat as a wombat," Sherlock complained.

"As befits a great statesman," John countered. "And don't go fat-shaming the dog."

Later, while John wasn't looking, Sherlock sneaked another piece of bacon to the canine prime minister. It never hurt to keep on his good side.

· · ·

John had chosen the location for The Sign of Four carefully, wanting to avoid the cliché of the common Melbourne laneway locale. As a result, the café wasn't Melbourne's most obscurely located coffee house. It overlooked a main thoroughfare from the first floor, although the entrance was via seventeen steps from an alley full of camping shops.

The reason for the odd name (not even the oddest in this city) was contained in the coffee molecule painted in sepia tones on the back wall, and its four components: carbon, hydrogen, nitrogen, and oxygen. That was a nod to Sherlock's interests. John's were represented along the opposite wall, where a series of framed digital images each told a story, if you knew their history.

Photography had been a hobby, even in the army. John loved exploring new ways to look at the unruly world, and to find objects of curiosity and beauty amid the anarchy of it. One of the things he'd loved about being a combat paramedic was his capacity to bring order out of chaos. God knew the rest of it was a shambles.

His penchant for dapper dressing when on leave—and didn't his army mates like taking the piss out of him over that—

translated naturally into the vintage suits, bespoke leather shoes, waxed moustache, and dedication to the single origin coffee beans he favored these days. Hell, as hipsters went, in this city famous for the breed, he was hardly alone or even the most hip.

John daily thanked his early posting to East Timor for teaching him about coffee, which had previously been merely a hot beverage. Whatever the Australian Army's Operation Astute had achieved for the people of Timor-Leste, it had introduced John to the local coffee farmers and the nuanced joys of a proper brew.

For a while, John had also daily cursed his filthy luck in being deployed to Afghanistan. A double-car bomb in Kabul had ended his military career, and almost his life, when shrapnel from the second bomb cut him down while he was helping victims of the first explosion.

Good had come from his medical discharge, but only after John had endured long bouts of surgery, therapy, and misery. His brother, Henry, got sick of him hanging around the spare room of his Brisbane house like a bad smell.

"You've got a face like a wet week," Henry said, gruff-loving, "and you know you hate the humidity here. Stop moping, move back to Melbourne, and go open that café you kept talking about when you were in Dili."

Henry's advice was rare and rarely good, but there was a first time for everything. Back to Melbourne John gladly went, to find somewhere to live and a business partner for his dream café.

He found both in Sherlock 'Lockie' Holmes—mercurial genius and perpetual science student—via their mutual friend, Jay Stamford. John's first sight of Sherlock was of a slender man with keen features, making himself a cup of coffee with lab equipment on campus.

"A homemade syphon set-up," John had commented admiringly. "Though you'd get a better result with a lighter roast."

"All I could get on short notice." Sherlock stood up, smoothing his hair back behind his ears and staring piercingly at John. "You were an army medic in Afghanistan, I see," he continued finally. "That's turned into a dog's breakfast, hasn't it?"

John, amazed, agreed, and two days later they were sharing a two-bedroom, nineteenth-century terrace house in Richmond, a ten-minute tram ride from the city. A month later, they set up The Sign of Four, funded by their savings, John's meager pension, and Sherlock's regular income from a patented diagnostic algorithm that rendered blood type identification both faster and more accurately.

Neither had bargained on making a best friend at the same time, but they got on like a house on fire from the start. Sherlock was something of a cocky beggar, but John had enough larrikin tendencies of his own to find that mostly appealing.

So John settled into being a café co-owner and barista, and extracting simple joys from life out of gratitude for still having one.

"Doc Caffeine" made The Sign of Four a Mecca for coffee lovers, but what made it famous was Sherlock Holmes, its resident smartarse. He dressed as snappily as his friend and colleague, except for those days he lounged around in jeans and a band T-shirt, usually featuring Devil's Foot, the alternative indie band in which he played violin.

John loved that Sherlock could tell anyone six things about themselves upon meeting them—one of which might be new even to the listener. Only one person had ever tried to punch Sherlock in reaction; only one had ever cried. Australian coffee drinkers were a hardy lot, willing to put up with a lot of smartarsery if the coffee was good enough, and if the smartarse in question was willing to help them out with weird problems.

Sherlock, enthusiastically aided by John where necessary, had uncovered a full range of scandals, from stepdads pretending to be boyfriends to prospective employers whose businesses didn't actually exist. He'd thwarted attempted blackmail by recovering incriminating video footage, and proven that a family "ghost hound" was just a joker at the farm next door tying a sheepskin onto his Labrador and smearing the poor mutt with glow-in-the-dark paint.

Kylie Mitchell might have asked the two of them for help, if she'd gotten the chance.

Instead, two days after Sherlock had deduced her to John, Kylie failed to arrive at her usual table.

Sherlock noticed. (He noticed everything.) But he was busy in his own corner, making notes for an essay for his current (and fourth) degree. ("I'm avoiding getting a proper job," he always claimed.)

John set a long macchiato next to his housemate then straddled a stool beside him.

"Kylie's not in."

"I noticed."

"Sick, you reckon?"

"Possibly. Or she's cracked the code."

"Maybe."

Sherlock looked straight at John. "Are you having one of your 'gut feelings'?"

"Could be," John reluctantly admitted.

"I've told you before, what you call gut instinct is just experience and knowledge giving you a conclusion without your brain consciously taking the intervening steps. Deconstruct."

John deconstructed. "She left early yesterday. Seemed excited about something to do with the three diaries she's been working on."

"She had all three on the table?" Sherlock closed his laptop lid and sipped at his coffee. "Unusual."

"She kept putting them side by side, then slipping the page of one underneath the page of another. Interleaving them, you know? I thought she might be comparing the handwriting on the right hand pages by getting similar words close together."

"Not a bad hypothesis," said Sherlock.

"Really?"

"Wrong, though. She could compare individual words more effectively from the scans on her computer. To compare the physical document indicates there was something about the primary source itself that drew her attention. And she left after that?"

"She had all three interleaved, with one left page underneath one right page. Then she said 'you little beauty,' put her stuff into her satchel, and took off, about an hour ahead of her usual schedule."

Sherlock finished his coffee. "There's probably nothing in it," he said. "Ask her about it tomorrow."

John brushed a knuckle beneath his moustache to hide his frown and returned to refill the hopper, clean the steam wand and resume pouring perfect shots.

John's faith in his instincts was justified an hour later when a woman strode into The Sign of Four. She was clutching an iPad close to her chest like it gave her life. Her greying hair was in wild disarray, her pale face free of makeup. Two blotches of red on her cheeks were the final evidence of her agitation.

"Is Lockie Holmes here?"

John nodded at Sherlock in his corner. The woman strode straight towards him. John handed barista duties over to Jess, his bean-apprentice, and followed the woman to where the interesting stuff was about to happen.

"Lockie?"

Sherlock pushed his essay aside. "You're Kylie's mother," he said calmly. "That's her iPad, isn't it?"

Kylie's mother blinked at him, nodded vigorously, then thrust the iPad towards him. "Lorraine Mitchell. Kylie's talked about you. She's said you're like a detective and you know things about people just by looking at them."

"I observe, and deduce from my observations." He took the iPad from her white-knuckled grip. "You found this in a garden. Any bougainvillea nearby?"

Lorraine stared at him as though he had two heads and was made of miracles. "Under the bougainvillea in our front yard. How did you know?"

Sherlock pointed at smudges of dirt and fragments of bark, grass, and purple blossom clinging to the cover. Then he folded the cover back and examined the tablet, from the small crack across the corner of the screen to the power and headphone sockets. He sniffed at it and dabbed the tip of his tongue against the cover.

"On the ground less than four hours," he declared.

"You can tell that from licking it?"

Sherlock arched an eyebrow at her. "It rained last night. The cover is dry on both sides. The bougainvillea canopy might have protected it from rainfall, but the ground water would've marked the back of it if it'd lain there all night. When did you last see your daughter?"

"She came home yesterday afternoon, worked up about something in those journals she's been poking into. She looked up something in a book at home and took off again."

"She took her satchel with her?"

"I told her not to," Lorraine said, half-distressed, half-exasperated.

Sherlock leaned keenly towards the woman. "And why would you tell her that?"

Lorraine's mouth snapped shut and she stared, round-eyed, at Sherlock.

"Mrs. Mitchell, you believe your daughter to be missing after less than half a day. She had those family journals and her iPad with her in her satchel, and yet here's the iPad, which has been dropped in your yard some time this morning. So Kylie didn't lose it last night. It's much more likely that after being out all night, she was coming home and something happened when she was nearly to safety. *What do you know that you're not telling me?*"

"I told her to leave those journals be," Lorraine snapped back at him. "It's old news and nothing good can come of it."

"Nothing has," Sherlock assured her.

"But why would anyone kidnap her?"

"If that's what you think this is, why haven't you gone to the police?"

"I did, but they say it's too soon to do anything."

"Instead, you think it might be too late."

"No. Of course it's not. It's not…nobody would hurt her. Would they?"

"Tell me everything," said Sherlock, "and we'll make sure they don't. John. I think this might be a three-espresso problem."

John took his place back on the Strada and poured the shots. Three espressos for Sherlock; long macchiato for himself. Skim latte for Lorraine Mitchell, who looked like a skim latte kind of person. He took the lot into Sherlock's corner on a tray and listened while Lorraine confessed to the family skeleton.

"My family are descendants of Irene Hodgson, adopted daughter of Caroline Hodgson," she began, as though that meant something.

"Who?" asked John.

Lorraine's face grew pinched, clearly hating to make the next admission. "Madame Brussels."

"Oh!" John was immediately impressed. "The Victorian-era brothel keeper. There's a fantastic rooftop bar named after her. I guess you know that." He pulled at the tip of his moustache.

Lorraine's furious expression proved that while Australians were generally delighted to find convicts in their ancestry, this Australian was not amused by brothel owners in the family tree.

Sherlock, on his second espresso, merely smiled. "One of my favorite unsolved mysteries is the disappearance of the Speaker's mace from the Victorian Parliament in 1891," he said. "It wasn't especially valuable, and the most persistent theory is that a parliamentarian took it to a brothel in Little Lonsdale Street, used it for unparliamentary purposes, and then left it there." He turned his keen gray eyes onto Lorraine Mitchell. "One of Madame Brussels's brothels, it's posited, or that of her rival, Annie Wilson."

Purse-lipped, Lorraine said, "The family legend is that it was stolen from Caroline's brothel and that Caroline wrote about it in her journals. She doesn't mention it by name, or any Ministers, but there's a note about being unfairly blamed for the scandal."

"An Inquiry in 1893 found it had never been taken to a

brothel," said Sherlock. "Though they could be expected to say that to save face."

"It never stopped people blaming her," Lorraine said, then added, "and then she wrote a journal entry saying she knew the truth."

"Interesting."

"She never said what the truth was, but, on the last page of the final journal, she said that the facts were there for Irene to decide what to do about it. We've always taken it to mean she'd left some hint in the diary."

"Your family never investigated?"

"Irene Hodgson sealed the journals in a strongbox and they've been locked up ever since. We only found them last year when Dad died and we were cleaning up to sell the house. Kylie's got a bee in her bonnet about it. She made it a project to *solve the mystery*." Lorraine made a scoffing sound.

"But yesterday she made a breakthrough," said Sherlock, "and today she's missing. Let's see what we can find out, hmm?" He powered up the iPad and was confronted with a password screen. He downed the third of his espressos.

"Password?"

"I don't know."

"She's been studying this problem for months. A compulsion like that tends to bleed into everything, including passwords. Let's see. The mace vanished in October 1891. Soooo: 1-0-1-8-9-1. And we're in. Too easy."

A double click of the home button spread out an array of active apps. Sherlock went straight to the image from the journals that Kylie had been poring over for so many weeks. He pinched and expanded it, peering intently, then held the screen up to John.

"What do you see?"

"Shocking handwriting," said John instantly.

"And?"

John squinted. "She's writing about someone called George…"

"Her first husband," supplied Lorraine, "He died at her property in St. Kilda."

"What else?" prompted Sherlock. "Come on, John. This is the last image she was looking at on this screen, which led her to interleaving the diaries. Something *must* be there."

John took the tablet into his hands and peered more closely still, knowing that Sherlock had already found what he was looking for.

"There are some weird marks on the page," he said at last. "Random lines in the margin and across the top and bottom. It looks like she half-erased that top line with the date and down here where she'd scribbled a few sums and then tested the ink of her fountain pen on them."

"A form of palimpsest," Sherlock noted gleefully, taking the tablet back. "Your ancestor was a very clever woman."

"Palimpsest?" Lorraine was bewildered.

"An old document that's had text scraped off and the paper reused," John explained. "Sherlock's got a bit of a thing for them. He's got a collection at home."

"A collection of reused documents?"

John shrugged. "He's easily bored."

Sherlock, who had been flicking back and forth among the photographs, clicked his fingers in the air. "Paper! Pen!"

John fetched both from beneath the counter, and Sherlock immediately began to scribble odd marks across the page. It became clear that he was spacing the lines across and down the page in a reflection of the marks he'd found in the journal image. Then he added the lines he'd located on images from the other two journals, four pages in all. As he added the lines from the salient page of the third journal, Caroline Hodgson's 120-year-old message to Irene took shape.

Irene. Tom left the mace in Lt Lon. Took by Jack and hid in Golgotha Club chimney. Serves the pollies right. Do as you like when I'm dead.

Lorraine blinked at the message. "Well," she said at last,

"Caroline was very angry with them after they changed the laws in 1907 and forced her to close down. She was very sick at the time."

"Which is all beside the point now," said Sherlock, on his feet and heading for the door. "Coming, Johnno?"

John had already snagged his tweed coat from the hook, pulling it on over his cream shirt and red suspenders to complete an aptly Victorian appearance for this nineteenth-century mystery. His limp hardly showed as he threw the keys to their chef, Mrs. Hudson—"Lock up if I'm late back"—and followed Sherlock into the alley.

"Where are we going?" Lorraine Mitchell demanded at their heels.

"The Golgotha Club." Sherlock was tapping away at an app on his smartphone.

"That closed down in the sixties!"

"Correction," Sherlock told her as their Uber pulled up on Little Bourke Street. "It moved in with a friend."

The car took them up Little Bourke Street, left on Queen, right on Collins, and up the hill to the pedestrian-only Bank Place. They alighted, Sherlock in the lead and John in the rear, with Lorraine Mitchell shielded in between. A few steps down the paving stones, they came to a grey nineteenth-century mansion with a portico of eight blocky pillars flanking a red door set in a white frame. Only the street number appeared in the window above the door. The building was otherwise unmarked.

"The Rivers Club," said Sherlock, reaching up to rap on the door. "Established 1894, fashioned after London's Bohemian Savage Club, as was the Golgotha. Doesn't surprise me in the least that one of that lot nicked the mace for a laugh and hid it. Then the Golgotha ran out of money and amalgamated with their more successful rival."

He knocked on the door again.

"Men's only club, isn't it?" John asked. "Is your brother a member of this one?"

"No," said Sherlock, "that's the Melbourne Club."

The door opened. Sherlock shouldered past the doorman, who shouted for him to stop but had to turn to block John and Lorraine's egress as well. When John tried to push past, the doorman grabbed the collar of his jacket.

John, well-used to Sherlock's shenanigans and how to play along with them, shrugged out of the garment, grabbed Lorraine by the hand, and ran after Sherlock into the vast hall beyond the foyer.

The cavernous length of the hall was dimly lit, the dark-paneled walls decorated with hunting trophies and weaponry seeming to suck in all the light. Large fireplaces were set at either end of the hall, but John's attention was on the southern end, where a very angry and fairly sooty Kylie Mitchell stood brandishing a silver-plated, ornately engraved five-foot mace. Two men stood warily in front of her, reluctant to either grapple with her or let her leave.

"Come on, give it back," one of the men urged.

"Piss off," snarled Kylie.

"Kylie!"

"Mum!" One of the men moved towards Kylie, and she threatened them with the mace again. John admired her brisk reflexes.

"Oh, excellent!" Sherlock exclaimed at the tableau. "Nice to see a self-rescuing princess at work. Need a hand?"

The two Riverians whirled to face the incoming party as the doorman ran in behind them. "I'm sorry, Mr. Driscoll, they just…"

Mr. Driscoll, the elder of the two men, took a menacing step towards them.

John Watson had faced drill sergeants, East Timorese paramilitaries, Taliban snipers, and once, while on holiday in the Grampians, a bad-tempered tiger snake. Mr. Driscoll held no terror for Doc Caffeine.

"I wouldn't, mate," he said drily. "I may be trespassing, but you can be done for kidnapping." He nodded towards Kylie.

"We didn't kidnap her," Driscoll protested. "She broke in here last night and stole the mace."

"I didn't break in," Kylie replied hotly. "I dressed like a tradie and told you I was here to fix the lights, and your doorbitch let me in."

"Clever," said Sherlock approvingly, "like Caroline Hodgson. How did you know they'd let you in?"

"These old places always have wiring somewhere that's cactus," said Kylie. "Seemed a good bet. Then I checked the chimney to see if they'd just hidden it in the same place as they did at the old Golgotha Club." She brandished the mace again. "And here it is."

"That's ours," said the younger man.

"It's really not," Sherlock said, "and the kidnapping charge still stands. Ms. Mitchell there had gotten the mace all the way home before you two snuck up on her, snatched her, and brought her back here. Why you didn't just take the mace..."

"We panicked," mumbled the younger man, and he nodded at the doorman. "Me and Wayne. We just snatched her and brought her back here for Bruce to sort out."

Bruce Driscoll gave both Wayne and the young idiot a glare that could bubble asphalt. Then he sighed. "Perhaps we can arrange something, Ms. Mitchell. We won't press charges if you won't, and if you give us back the mace. The Rivers Club board can announce to the press that we discovered it, in due course."

Ms. Kylie Mitchell suggested some very unparliamentary things Bruce Driscoll and the Rivers Club board could do with that mace.

John whipped out his smartphone and took a couple of photos of the scene.

"Bloody women," muttered the young Riverian. "Wrecking the joint. Ruining everything."

"Shut up, Gavin," said Driscoll in a weary tone tinged with disgust, "and call your lawyer. This has all gone completely pear-shaped and it's your fault. Kidnapping? Jeez."

In the end, as John recorded in his personal diary, Kylie Mitchell didn't press the kidnapping charge. Instead, she took great delight in restoring the mace to Parliament and getting a book deal to present, with added commentary, the diaries of Madame Brussels, naming historical names.

"Her mum's not happy about it," John noted, back at his Strada.

A new picture hung on the wall opposite the coffee molecule motif: the scene from the Rivers Club. John had made the colors hyper-real, and judicious editing of the faces protected the guilty-as-hell. Outraged postures, rich browns and golds, light glinting off the mace held by Kylie Mitchell, looking like a warrior queen. The picture was surmounted with text reading *The Problem of the Three Journals* in elegant cursive. This title made it part of a set with John's other digital art, all bearing similar script—*The Case of, The Mystery of, The Problem of*—as testament to their adventures.

(John, it must be said, knew he had a bit of a theatrical bent.)

"She's not," said Sherlock, "but she's a prude."

"Kylie sent something for you, though. A thank you present for coming to get her."

Sherlock tore the wrapping off the parcel John handed him. In it was a T-shirt that Kylie had had made especially for him. It read: *Sherlock Holmes. Bloody Legend.*

Sherlock laughed, put it beside his laptop, and whistled one of his band's tunes as he returned to his pharmacology essay.

SIX RED DRAGONS:
AN ADVENTURE OF SHIRLEY HOLMES AND JACK WATSON

BY KEITH R. A. DECANDIDO

I'd had a really long day, and I was half-asleep fumbling for my keys at the front door when someone walked up to me and asked, "Need some help, sir?"

I turned to see a man in a denim jacket, button-down shirt, and khakis. His skin was even darker than mine, and he had a short afro and a Haitian accent. He was shorter than me, but I'm 6'3", so that put him in company with a lot of people.

"I'm fine, just trying to find my keys."

"*You* live here?" he asked dubiously.

I sighed. I got this a lot since I'd moved to this fancy old house on Riverside Drive and 107th Street. "*Yes*, I live here."

Then the man put his hands on his hips, pushing his jacket aside to reveal a gold shield on his belt.

Quickly, before he decided to unholster his weapon, I said, "I have the top floor. I moved in back in the new year. My name's Jack Watson, I'm a med student at Columbia, I—"

The man broke into a huge smile. "Oh, you're the one they brought in to be Shirley's 'companion' once her aunt got cancer." He put out a hand. "I'm Guillaume Lestrade. I'm a detective at the 24th Precinct."

I stared at the hand for a second before returning the shake. "Um, pleased to meet you."

"My apologies for the racial profiling."

"Yeah, well, I'm used to it by now. What brings you here, Detective?"

"Tea with Shirley. She, ah, assisted me on a case a year ago. She did not take credit, for which I was grateful, as NYPD frowns on unofficial consultants, particularly ones who are only twenty years old."

"But you come and have tea with her in return?"

"And tell her of some of the current cases floating about the precinct. Perhaps you could join us?"

I chuckled. I knew that tone of desperation. I'd had it myself a few times. Shirley could be a little intense. "I've had one shitty day, and was really looking forward to some rack time, so putting up with a conversation with Shirley wasn't really on my to-do list. If she's all right with it, though, I'll sit in." I pointed at him. "But you owe me one."

Lestrade's grin widened. "That is eminently fair."

I finally found the right set of keys and led Lestrade inside. We entered the fancy foyer, and I took Lestrade's denim jacket and hung it with mine on the wooden coatrack.

Shirley Holmes was in the dining room, a full tea set in front of her with two teacups on saucers and a pair of small plates put out at two of the big dining-room chairs. Shirley was only about five-feet-nothing, and thin—she couldn't have been more than ninety pounds soaking wet—so she looked like a little kid sitting in the big wooden chair with the flared arms. Me, I barely could squeeze into the thing.

"Hey, Shirley," I said as I led Lestrade in. "Your cop buddy's here."

She was arranging the pastries on the three-tiered tray and didn't look up at either of us. "Welcome, Detective. Hello, Jack. I see you had a difficult shift in the emergency room."

Shirley hadn't known that I was doing an ER shift today—

mostly because I hadn't known myself until I showed up at work. Like most med students, I went where they told me to go, and, because someone called in sick, I got the ER shift instead of the lab shift I was scheduled for.

With a sigh, Shirley added, "Before you ask how I knew, you're wearing a different shirt than you were wearing when you left, specifically the one you keep in your locker as a backup, you have the same soap smell you had the last time you had to shower at the hospital after your shift, there are tiny flecks of blood and vomit on parts of your shoes, and a bruise on your left arm, all indicators of the somewhat more chaotic nature of an emergency room shift. Also, you have bags under your eyes, which has only happened when you've worked the emergency room."

"I *wasn't* gonna ask that," I said with a smile. I'd given up asking how she knew stuff, 'cause it was always just that she noticed every damn thing. And it was Saturday night in the ER, which meant lots of puke, piss, and shit on top of the expected blood. "I was gonna ask if I could join you and the detective here for your tea."

"I did not set a place for you. However, your need for caffeine is obvious, and the traditional tea service is generally more than two people can reasonably drink, so you may join us, yes."

I had to admit, as soon as I saw the two places set out, I figured she was gonna kick me upstairs because I wasn't part of the already-set service, but she worked her way through letting me stay. I was kinda hoping she wouldn't. The detective owing me a favor was nice and all, but I was *really* tired.

Still, she was also right that the caffeine hit would be good.

I offered to get my own place setting, and Shirley said, "That will not be necessary. I am the host, and it is my responsibility to adjust the place settings accordingly."

"Maybe, but I know where everything is, and you look like you want to start hearing what the detective has to say."

"That is true." She sounded almost relieved. Even though she had talked herself into letting me stick around, I could tell that, on the one hand, she didn't want to do the extra work, but on the other, she felt obligated to. She sounded pretty relieved that I just gave her an out.

Of course, she didn't thank me.

I got a plate, a knife, and a teacup and saucer. I didn't put sugar in my tea—hell, until I moved into this place, I was all about the black coffee—so I didn't bother grabbing a spoon.

When I got back, I poured myself some tea and grabbed a scone. I started spreading the clotted cream on it. I'd never even heard of that stuff before living here, and now I'd gotten addicted.

Shirley sipped her tea and then set up a tablet on a small stand with a tiny keyboard.

Lestrade pulled out a paper notebook and started flipping through it. It didn't look like his official notepad that he used for casework. He would start mentioning a case—a burglary, a mugging, a fraud. Shirley didn't let him get in more than two sentences before she said, "That is *not* of interest."

The minute she said that, Lestrade flipped a page and moved on. Shirley kept typing all along, though, even when she said it wasn't of interest.

"Detective Bradstreet caught the double on 88th Street. She—"

Shirley interrupted him. "I looked at that when it occurred, and based on newspaper and television accounts, and social media postings by both victims, I surmise that it is a murder-suicide. The couple was going through a contentious divorce, there was no sign of forced entry or robbery, and—"

"Bradstreet thinks the same," Lestrade said.

I winced.

Shirley finally looked up from the tablet and glared right at Lestrade, who flinched. "The couple was going through a contentious divorce, there was no sign of forced entry or robbery, and the husband owned the Sig Sauer pistol that was used."

"Moving on," the detective said, blowing out a nervous breath and flipping a page. You'd think he'd been around Shirley enough to know not to interrupt her. "Detective Gregson thought he finally had a break in the Mehu Gallery case."

That one I recognized. "That was that gallery over on Columbus that had a jewel or something stolen, right?"

"Yes, the Borgatti Pearl. Gregson even called in the FBI's white-collar division, but the lead went nowhere, sadly. So he's back to square one."

"That is obviously of interest to you," Shirley said, "since your colleague has been unable to end his investigation, but it is of no interest to me."

Another page flip. Looked like there was only one page of writing left. "Detective Hopkins has a suspect in the robbery of the pizza place on Broadway and 101st."

"Sal and Carmine's?" I asked. At Shirley's glare, I added, "Hey, that's my favorite pizza joint."

Lestrade smiled and nodded. "It was one of the regular customers. Apparently he was upset that they put less pepperoni on the pizzas."

"That is *not* of interest, except perhaps to Jack." Shirley was still glaring at me. I ignored her and drank more tea.

"One last odd one," Lestrade said. "Some peculiar cases of theft and vandalism. The first one was four days ago in a small shop on 100th just off Central Park West."

"The Morse Shop?" Shirley said.

Lestrade nodded. "You know it?"

"My aunt patronizes the store regularly. They specialize in jewelry, works of art, crafts, and other items created by hand by local artisans. I find most of their wares to be vulgar and ugly."

"Well, someone agreed with you, at least with regard to one of the items on display. Someone came into the store and stole a dragon figurine, shattering it on the sidewalk outside the store and running away."

"No surveillance?" I asked.

Shaking his head, Lestrade said, "No, it's a tiny store that's never been burgled before, and they're a block from the two-four. They didn't see much point in the expense of a camera."

I snorted. "They might now."

"Just the one figurine?" Shirley asked.

"Yes. And it gets more peculiar. Three days ago, a Dr. Hans Barnicot reported a similar crime. He had two dragon figurines of the same design. One was in his home office in the ground floor of a brownstone on 89th Street between Riverside and West End, the other in the storefront clinic he works at on Broadway and 109th. In both cases, it was only the dragon figurine that was taken, and it was smashed."

I stared at the detective while swallowing my scone. "You're telling me the clinic didn't have surveillance?"

"Yes," Lestrade said, "but also a thief who wore a wool hat and a large coat that covered his face and body type. And Dr. Barnicot's house had an alarm, which dutifully went off when the thief broke the front window, but all he took was the figurine off the sill, and broke it at the corner of 89th and West End. In both cases, it was only the dragon figurine of that design that was taken. At the doctor's home, he had several different types of dragons on the sill, but only that one was removed and smashed, while the clinic had several figures of various kinds."

Shirley's head tilted. "These were all three of them by the same artist?"

"So it would seem. I was not the investigating officer in either case."

She finally stopped typing and sipped some more tea. Then she put her hands on the table. "I wish to investigate this case further."

I winced. Shirley sometimes helped people out with problems, but sticking your nose in police business was a separate matter. "You sure that's a good idea?"

Lestrade, though, didn't seem too worried. "It should be fine. Yes, they are open cases, but there is unlikely to be any further investigation. The officer who took Dr. Barnicot's statement indicated that the doctor only reported it for the insurance paperwork to get them to pay for his broken window, and also because the clinic requires it." The detective stood up. "I'll email you the files on that secure email you gave me."

Shirley nodded. "Thank you." She looked down at the tablet and started typing again. "Jack, would you be so kind as to escort the detective out?"

"Uh, sure." I got up and walked Lestrade to the door.

Once we got into the foyer, Lestrade grinned, showing two rows of perfectly white teeth. "I had a premonition that she would be interested in the dragon figurines."

I grabbed his denim jacket and handed it to him. "And you figured it'd give her an itch to scratch?"

Lestrade shrugged into his jacket. "If I bring her nothing of interest, I receive a rather lengthy harangue on the subject of our arrangement. This way, she remains predisposed to *not* haranguing me, I continue to repay the debt I owe her, and as an added bonus, she is likely to solve the case."

I smiled as I unlocked and opened the door for him. "Thought NYPD frowned on that."

"Oh, she will allow me to make the arrest and be the officer of record. In the worst instance, nothing happens, and two cases that were like to remain open permanently stay open. In the best instance, I have two closed cases under my name."

"So win-win. Well, it was nice meeting you, Detective."

I offered my hand, and he shook it. "The same here, Mr. Watson."

After he left, I started to make my way back to the dining room to finish my tea and scone. As I entered, Shirley said, "What do you make of this case, Jack?"

I shrugged. "I dunno, it's a weird-ass OCD. Maybe the thief has a thing for dragons?"

Shirley shook her head. "Dr. Barnicot had numerous figurines in the form of a dragon on his windowsill. No, it would appear to all be dragon figurines by a particular artist. It might be worth investigating the artist in question. One hopes that he or she is identified in the report that the detective will email me."

"One hopes he doesn't get caught," I said, gulping down the last of my tea. "He's not supposed to share that stuff with civilians."

"Which is why he's using the secure email server."

She'd mentioned that server before, and it had something to do with her brother, about whom I didn't know a damn thing—not even his name. Shirley didn't seem to like him all that much.

Whatever. I was exhausted.

I got up to leave, now desperately wanting my bed—the tea had helped a little, but ER shifts, especially unplanned ones on a Saturday night, took a lot out of me—but then Shirley said, "What I find most fascinating is that two of the figurines were broken on the sidewalk in front of where they were stolen, yet the one taken from Dr. Barnicot's home office was broken on the next corner."

Her fingers danced over the keyboard to the tablet. I knew that she was looking up a bunch of things. I was about to say good night when she stopped typing.

"Ah, yes, there is a work order with the Department of Transportation to fix a street light on West 89th Street between Riverside Drive and West End Avenue. It was filled yesterday, but at the time of the break-in the light was out."

"Yeah, so?" I shook my head. "I guess he needed to see what he was smashing? Or maybe making sure it was the right statue?"

"Perhaps."

"Well, you have fun with that. I'm goin' to bed."

• • •

When I came downstairs the next morning, Shirley was in the same spot, the tea stuff all there, though the food was all gone. Ever since her aunt got cancer, they'd hired someone to come in and clean the place every other day, but today was one of her days off. I figured I'd clean up after Shirley, since nobody else was gonna do it, and cockroaches would mess up the nice house.

I grabbed the tea service, trying not to spill any crumbs, and commented on her having been here all night.

"I would think, Jack, that even someone of your intelligence would be able to determine that for yourself, given that I am wearing the same clothes, I have eaten all the food and drunk all the tea that was left, and my hair now has the oily consistency it frustratingly acquires when I have not showered in more than thirty-seven hours."

"Was just making a comment."

"The pitch of your voice went higher on the word 'night,' which is indicative of an interrogative rather than a declaratory statement."

I honestly didn't remember if I'd done that or not. "In that case, it was rhetorical. What'd you find out?"

"Quite a bit. The clinic does indeed have security footage, which was appended to the report that Detective Lestrade forwarded to me. The Morse Shop has an Etsy site that shows off its wares, and Dr. Barnicot regularly updates his Facebook page with a near-constant stream of pictures. I have been able to find images of all three figurines."

She held up the tablet, which had what looked like a screengrab focused on a red dragon figurine; a picture of a windowsill filled with *tchotchkes,* one of which was a red dragon figurine; and a picture of a red dragon figurine against a white background.

"They all look the same to me."

Shirley sighed, and I knew I'd said something wrong. "The grooves and lines of the image from the Morse Shop are sharper than those of the one on Dr. Barnicot's windowsill. The resolution of the security camera is insufficient to compare that level of detail for the one in the clinic. That they are similar enough that your eye cannot determine the difference indicates that these figurines were cast, but not with metal, plaster, or concrete—likely they were resin cast, as those molds tend to degrade over time, particularly ones created by single artisans rather than industrially produced."

"Which tracks with stuff sold at the Morse Shop."

"Indeed." She looked straight at me, which was rare. "If you are free, would you like to accompany me to Columbus Avenue?"

"Wanna get some brunch?"

"I am sated after consuming the remains of the tea service. No, I was referring to the Columbus Avenue crafts fair that occupies the section of that street behind the American Museum of Natural History. Based on the information in the Etsy shop, the creator of these dragon figurines, one Liese Gelder, has a stand there. Your presence would be useful in questioning her."

I chuckled. If somebody wanted Shirley's help, she could interrogate better than the Army CID guys I served with in Afghanistan, but, when it came to just talking to people, having a doctor-in-training along was a lot more useful.

"Well, I got today off, so sure. I got some lab notes I need to translate into English at some point, but I can do that later."

"I assume that to mean a figurative translation of poor handwriting and abbreviated text into something coherent rather than an actual translation?"

Some of the doctors who were training me didn't have English as their first language, as it happened, but I did *not* want to get into that with Ms. Literal, so I just said, "Yeah."

We each showered, and I drank some coffee, and then we took an Uber to Columbus and 81st. Shirley has the Uber account because she got tired of being ignored by cabbies when she tried to hail one. As a large black man, I could relate.

It was a nice spring day out, partly cloudy and warm, and the eastern sidewalk of Columbus that bordered the Theodore Roosevelt Park behind the Natural History museum was packed with people looking at the little stands that sold clothes, *tchotchkes*, jewelry, soaps, weird foods and food additives, art, and so on.

Right at 79th Street was a stall filled with figurines of dragons, unicorns, and gryphons, as well as a few real animals: tigers, lions, cats, dogs, ducks. What surprised me was that they were all different colors. I was figuring all the dragons would be red, based on the three that got stolen and smashed, but the ones here were green, blue, and purple. No red ones, interestingly enough. And only a few of each animal.

The woman in the stall was a skinny blonde wearing a wool sweater and black leggings. The sign over her head said "LIESE GELDER FIGURINES."

"These are nice," I said while Shirley stared at the individual figurines. "Are these resin cast?"

She smiled. "Yes, how did you know?"

I pointed at Shirley. "My friend here figured it out from seeing your stuff up at the Morse Shop on 100th. She's the brains of the outfit."

Shirley let out an exasperated sigh, which helped me to stay in character.

Gelder said, "I prefer resin casting because they're transitory. It keeps me from mass producing. After twenty-four castings, the mold degrades too much, so I have to make a new one. It allows me to make multiples of the figurines, so there's a balance between uniqueness and my ability to put them in the hands of lots of people."

"Cool." I smiled at her, and she smiled back.

Shirley then said, "You do not have any red dragons here."

"Yes, all six of those are—well, unavailable. I usually make six in each color, and I sold three reds to the Morse Shop where you saw them, and two more to my doctor."

"That is only five," Shirley said in an almost accusatory voice.

Gelder flinched. "Well, the—" She sighed. "It's embarrassing, really. The other one was broken by one of my interns."

"Really?"

"It was awful. I get interns from several local art schools and they usually work for a semester, and they get credits. I really had hopes for Barry, he had a rough childhood, y'know? But he had talent, and he managed to get a scholarship to Pratt, and I took him on last spring. And then he wound up being arrested halfway through the semester because of a fight he got into. When he got out on parole last month, he just showed up at the workshop and started messing with my computer. He said he was picking up his internship where it left off. He wasn't even enrolled anywhere anymore." She sighed. "I felt bad for him, but he'd lost his scholarship, so I couldn't give him credits, and I can't afford to pay—that's why I do the internships in the first place. He got upset and broke the last red dragon I had in the workshop." Then she smiled. "I'm sorry, I'm babbling. Did you have any other questions about the figurines?"

"How much are the gryphons? My buddy Shorty collects these things."

We talked price, and then she talked about gryphons for five minutes, and I finally wound up buying a green gryphon for Shorty. By that time, Shirley was messing with her smartphone. Once we walked away from the stall, Shirley asked, "Is this 'Shorty' person a colleague at Columbia or a fellow enlistee in the armed forces? Or did you simply make him up in order to contrive an excuse to buy a figurine in exchange for the vast stores of information Ms. Gelder provided?"

I grinned. "What, you can't tell?"

She looked up from her phone. "I am not clairvoyant, Jack. You have never made a single mention of 'Shorty' in the time of our acquaintance, so I have no data from which to make a determination."

"Fair enough. He's an Army buddy. Used to wear a gryphon pin on his fatigues all the time, he had gryphon stickers on his footlocker, and tons of gryphon stuff all over everything he owned. Honestly, he gets so many of the damn things, it's hard to find something he *doesn't* have, so I figured I'd grab this."

"I have sent a text to a former client—who works at the Pratt Institute—for whom I once located a pet kitten."

"Really?"

Shirley nodded. "It was quite a challenge, as predicting the movements of felines is rather difficult. However, I did locate her, and in return she should be able to provide me with information on anyone named Barry who received a scholarship in the past three years."

She summoned another Uber to take us home, and she went straight up to her room on the third floor. I followed while she fired up one of her computers—a purple iMac that was more than a decade and a half old—called up a file, typed a few things, then printed the document on a color laser printer, which had sheets of business cards in it.

When the sheet printed, she tugged at the perforations and then handed a business card to me.

I read off the words on the card, which was very professionally designed. "IYS Insurance, Jack Watson, Investigator." I looked at her. "I'm kinda afraid to ask why you handed me this."

"We are about to summon another Uber that will take us to the Morse Shop, once you change into more presentable clothes."

• • •

It was a lot easier than I thought it would be to convince the proprietor of the Morse Shop that I was an insurance investigator. The suit I was wearing made a big difference, and besides, who'd pretend to be an insurance investigator, anyhow?

The guy was named Samuel Morse, and when he introduced himself, right away, he said, "Yes, I've heard all the jokes about codes, thanks."

I explained that theirs wasn't the only Gelder red dragon that was stolen and broken, and that we wanted to contact the people who bought the other two that Gelder had provided. Since Morse got them on consignment, he was happy to cooperate— an insurance report might help him not have to pay Gelder for the figurine. I thought cooperating to help cheat an artist out of income was sleazy, but whatever.

He wasn't willing to give out addresses or phone numbers, but he did provide names and email addresses, which was good enough. One of them was a married couple who ran a karate dojo on Columbus and 106th, so we figured we'd just walk there and see what they could tell us. On the way, Shirley sent an email to the other customer, Matilda Sandeford.

As we walked up Columbus to the dojo, though, we saw sirens and crime-scene tape and such. There was a crowd around the dojo, so we couldn't get any closer than a few dozen feet past the corner of 105th, but we did see Lestrade, about two seconds after he saw us. He climbed under the yellow tape and made a beeline right at us.

"Jesus shit, *what* are you doing here?" he asked in a harsh whisper.

Shirley just stared at him. "That is a stupid question. We are investigating the thefts of the Gelder red dragons. One of them was sold to the proprietors of this dojo."

"Gelder?"

Rolling her eyes, Shirley said, "The woman who crafted the figurines. We determined that the couple who—"

Lestrade held up his hands. "Never mind. It doesn't matter, because this is a murder investigation."

My eyes went wide. "Who was killed?"

"A local banger, went by the street name of 'Step.' He was not a student of the dojo, nor do the owners have any notion as to why he was here. And that is as much as I may tell you."

"We should probably—" I started, but Shirley wasn't done.

"What about the red dragon figurine? Was it broken?"

"Several items were broken, including their red dragon, along with the pot containing a large plant, two chairs, and several trophies. But look, this is no longer about vandalism, this is homicide, and I'm going to have to request that you refrain from further investigation into these thefts."

Shirley's phone made a buzzing noise. She held it up, peered at it, then stared right at Lestrade. I caught a glance at the screen, and it was from the same number as the woman from Pratt she'd contacted a little while ago.

"If you wish to close this case, Detective, I suggest that you see if 'Step' here has any association with a young man whose name is Barry Harding."

With that, Shirley turned and walked back toward 105th Street.

I gave Lestrade an apologetic shrug.

"Jesus shit," he muttered, and went back to the scene.

• • •

I assumed that was the end of it, but on Wednesday night, when I got back from the hospital, Shirley invited me out to the bagel place she and I both liked on 98th and Broadway. I agreed to go along. She brought along a small hand towel and a hammer, for some reason. I considered asking her about it, but then decided that if she did pack it, she intended to use it, and figured it'd be more fun to find out why at the right time.

We stopped at an ATM along the way and she took out a hundred bucks.

I figured it would be just the two of us, but both Lestrade and another guy who pretty much had "cop" tattooed on his forehead were sitting at one of the bagel place's small round tables, cups of coffee in front of each of them. The other detective was a white guy wearing a butt-ugly suit. He had short hair and one of those mustaches you only saw on cops and 1970s porn stars.

Lestrade did the honors. "Shirley, Jack, this is Detective Toby Gregson."

"How do you do, Detective?" Shirley said as she sat down in one of the two remaining chairs.

"I'm doin' great. Been hearin' about G's little friend who solved the ear thing for him."

"She didn't *solve* it for me, she assisted," Lestrade said defensively. "And she also led us to find Barry Harding and arrest him for the murder of Fred 'Step' Harkner."

"So he did do it?" I asked.

Lestrade smiled. "So it would seem. Ultimately, it is the ADA's problem to prove that. Regardless, Shirley saved me considerable time and effort to find him."

Gregson chuckled. "She did, huh? I dunno, she don't look like much."

Shirley closed her eyes, sighed, and then said, "I would say you should not be fooled by appearances, but in truth, appearances can tell you everything if you know where to look. You, for example, are very recently divorced, and you also recently quit smoking, doubtless not for the first time. You live with an Irish setter who is getting rather aged, and you were born left-handed but trained yourself to write with your right hand."

Gregson looked over at Lestrade. "The fuck you tell this bitch about me?"

"Nothing," Lestrade said. "This is merely what she does."

"Okay, I get how you figured out Molly—that's the dog, by the way, not the ex. That bitch sheds like a motherfucker, it's prob'ly all over me. But what about the rest of it?"

"Your left ring finger is discolored where your wedding ring used to be, and you fiddle with it as if you're not used to it not being there. You are holding the coffee stirrer as if it was a cigarette, and your teeth are yellowed, but your breath contains none of the stench of cigarette smoke, nor that of any breath mints or mouthwash that might be used to cover it, so you have not smoked recently, but you used to, and have not adjusted to quitting. You wear a watch on your right hand and drink your coffee with your left, indicating that you're left-handed, yet the calluses on your pinky finger and the side of your right hand, as well as the ink stains in that spot, indicates that you write with your right."

Nodding, Gregson said, "Not bad."

"I also assume the divorce is recent because you have oversaturated yourself with cologne, and your mustache is ill-trimmed, indicating that you are grooming yourself more often than you used to."

"All right, enough, I get it. I don't blame you for usin' her,

G, if she can pick that shit up. Fuck the bosses, long as the case is closed, who gives a fuck how it's done?"

Shirley stared at him. "I would think it would matter a great deal if you wish to get a conviction."

"Yeah, if it actually gets anywhere near a fuckin' courtroom. Most'a the time they plea out anyhow, so if they're gonna skip past steps inna system, why shouldn't we?"

I was seriously worried that they were gonna go down a rabbit hole of the philosophy of policing, but we were saved by an African-American woman who approached the table.

"'Scuse me, you Shirley Holmes?"

"Yes. You must be Matilda Sandeford."

"Yeah. I brought the thing." She dug around in her purse and pulled out something wrapped in tissue paper.

When she unwrapped it, we all saw the sixth red dragon.

Lestrade shook his head and chuckled. "*That* is what this is about? Shirley, we have closed a murder. Of what relevance are a few petty thefts?"

"Petty thefts?" Sandeford asked.

"Ignore him, please." Shirley pulled out her wallet. "I believe the agreed-upon sum was a hundred dollars?"

"Uh, yeah." Sandeford hesitated. "Uh, look, lady, I gotta tell you—I only paid twenty-five for this thing. I mean, I like it and all, but I feel bad takin' so much."

"Nonetheless, that is the sum we agreed upon."

"Hey, I'll take the seventy-five, I just want you to know what you're getting yourself into. It ain't *that* nice a dragon."

"Perhaps, but the sum is worth it to me."

Shirley handed over the cash she'd gotten out of the ATM, and Sandeford handed over the red dragon.

A server came outside and took our order. Sandeford said goodbye and left, and Shirley ordered some Assam tea while I ordered a coffee and a blueberry muffin.

Once the server left, Gregson said, "What the fuck is all this?"

Shirley set the figurine down on the table. "Barry Harding

was a student at the Pratt Institute on a scholarship. He worked for much of the spring semester of last year as an intern to Liese Gelder, the sculptor who creates these figurines. She does them in resin, the molds for which deteriorate after two dozen casts, so she makes only twenty-four of each type, though every six casts, she changes the color of the resin she uses. Mr. Harding was arrested for assault and battery last March, pled guilty, and achieved parole after one year."

"We are aware of all this," Lestrade said.

"I wasn't," Gregson said. "Don't know why anybody gives a fuck, though."

"There is reason for you to care, Detective Gregson, which I will explain shortly. It is my theory that, before he was arrested, Barry needed to hide an object where no one could find it, and so he placed it inside the red dragon that was being cast at the time. When he was released on parole, he went to Ms. Gelder's workshop and operated her computer, likely obtaining sales records. He then sought out the red dragons, attempting to find the object he'd hidden. With no method of determining which of the six red ones he hid the object in, he stole each one and broke it, hoping to find the object inside. That was why he went down the street from Dr. Barnicot's brownstone—the nearest street light on 89th Street was not functioning, and he needed light to perform his task."

"Still not seein' the point'a this," Gregson said.

"Here is where we come to you, Detective, because—while he offered no testimony—the victim in Detective Lestrade's case, 'Step,' was a witness to Mr. Harding's assault, which took place around the corner from the Mehu Gallery. The victim of Mr. Harding's assault, to which he pled guilty, was a security guard who worked for the company that provided security to the Mehu Gallery—at least, up until the theft of the Borgatti Pearl, at which point the gallery dispensed with their services."

Gregson snorted. "Don't blame 'em. Still not sure why I'm here, 'less this has to do with the theft of the pearl."

Shirley pulled the towel and hammer out her bag. She picked

up the red dragon and wrapped the towel around it, then put it back down on the table. "Now that Ms. Sandeford is well away…"

After pulling the hammer out of the bag, she started smashing the figurine. The two detectives flinched. I smiled inwardly—I knew there was gonna be something entertaining with the hammer.

She unwrapped the towel to reveal a whole bunch of resin shards—and in the middle of them, a little black jewel.

"Sweet goddamn holy motherfuck," Gregson said.

"Jesus shit," Lestrade muttered.

Shirley reached down and used a paper napkin to pick up the jewel. "Detective Gregson, I believe that this is the Borgatti Pearl."

Reaching into his suit jacket pocket, Gregson pulled out an evidence bag. "I do not *fucking* believe this. Over a year on this with a task force and the fuckin' FBI, and it's closed by some skinny chick."

"Hey," I said with a grin, "Shirley ain't just *any* skinny chick. She found the only one of the six dragons that hadn't been smashed yet, and bought it off the owner so y'all could get your stone back."

As he gingerly put the pearl in the evidence bag, Gregson said, "I don't care if she's Ivanka fuckin' Trump. I'm gonna need statements from both'a you—but first, G, I need to talk to your suspect."

"We both do." Lestrade gulped down the rest of his coffee. "Forgive us, Shirley, Jack, but we must follow up on this new evidence immediately."

I helped the detectives gather up the shards of the red dragon statue in the towel and put it all in the evidence bag with the pearl. Chain of custody was a mess, since Shirley went and shattered it, but Lestrade seemed to think that just having the pearl in-hand would lead to a confession.

Didn't matter to me either way. All I really noticed was the last thing Gregson said before he and Lestrade headed back to the two-four:

"I owe you one, kid."

The server finally came with my coffee and muffin and Shirley's tea.

After she put the food and drinks down, she said, "Um, are the two gentlemen coming back?"

"They didn't pay, did they?" I asked.

"No." The server sounded upset.

Shirley waved a hand back and forth. "I will pay for all four orders."

I took a sip of my coffee and chuckled. "Guess they owe you more than one now."

"I believe the price of two cups of coffee is more than sufficient for the satisfaction of a job well done, Jack."

"Well, that, and a hundred bucks for a statue you don't even get to keep."

"That is hardly an issue, as I find the figurines to be hideous. Nonetheless, the problem is solved."

I held up my coffee. "To solving two cases at once."

Shirley nodded and held up her own tea.

After she took a sip, she actually smiled.

It was kinda funny looking—her face didn't look right, and I was hoping she'd stop soon.

But then, being forced to look at her smile was a small price to pay for *getting* her to smile in the first place.

THE ADVENTURE OF
THE DIODE DETECTIVE

BY JODY LYNN NYE

Tanisha Tero-Lomitz patted the household security activator with an affectionate hand as she prepared to exit the apartment.

"Be good and take care of everything!" she said. "Seal up after me, will you?"

Sure-Lock Home's red eyelight beside the apartment's main door warmed up to a glow.

"Of course, mistress. Your transport is at the bottom of the motivator ramp."

Tanisha's generous mouth twitched up at the corners.

"All you had to do was say the cab was here, goofy."

"Precision prevents confusion," Sure-Lock replied, imperturbably. "Please be careful."

"I am!"

The security computer scanned her, ensuring that her deep brown skin and curly black hair had been sprayed with an environmental protectant. The pollution index reported high levels of toxic fumigens in the lower atmosphere. Tanisha's clothing, a floating dress that hugged her curves to the upper hip and matching high-soled sandals in electric blue, was studded with tiny lights. They added to the appeal of the garment, but also provided proximity warnings in case objects approached her too rapidly. Her shoes contained a variety of security devices to move her out of harm's way or approved minor armaments to defend her if necessary. She had, however, a tendency to kick off the footwear when she was dancing, a practice Sure-Lock had been at pains to train her to cease. One item on its internal check list turned red.

"Where is your laser-proof camisole?" Sure-Lock asked.

"Will you stop scanning my underwear?" Tanisha demanded, lowering her brows at the red light. "I'm only going to a club!"

A rectangular blue light illuminated on the doorpost, accompanied by a blaring noise: the taxi's warning signal. She had ninety seconds to meet it or it would drive off, the carriage contract cancelled.

"That's it," she said. "I have to go." She moved decidedly toward the portal. Sure-Lock allowed the autosensors to open the door and close it securely behind her.

"It irks me that she goes out without taking us along," Sure-Lock said, one of its multiple camera eyes following the young woman's progress down the moving ramp to the pickup level. Brooklyn historically had a reputation as a reasonably safe neighborhood, but it would never do to lower one's guard. The stubby yellow autovehicle's transmitted designation matched the reservation number. Sure-Lock watched to make certain that no strange human or other device was within range of Tanisha during the moment she walked unprotected from the doorway to the car.

"Eh?" asked Dr. What's-On?, its computerized consciousness surfacing from a perusal of the weekend entertainment offerings on Earth, the Moon, Mars, and the asteroid belt. "I reserved her transport up and back, and a place in the nightclub. She is in good health and good spirits, eminently suitable for an evening out at her chosen activity. I chose this club because it has exclusive activities planned that fit her interests and social group. What else does she need?"

"She will not necessarily be protected adequately," Sure-Lock replied, its circuits heating. "We are available as apps to accompany her on her personal communication device. We should notify her parent as to her noncompliance."

"She's of full adult age as of last week," What's-On? said, attempting to calm its fellow home-service robot. "It is her choice to forego all the security measures."

"I do not like it," Sure-Lock replied. "To acquire adulthood is to take responsibility for one's own safety."

"Or to forego it," What's-On? said indulgently. "She is young and has a prominent public profile. Still, she has her autoprotective devices on her, and the club is well-known to have superior security. Any attempt at assault or abduction will cause roboguards to move in to defuse the situation. She will be safe."

Sure-Lock did not argue further with its fellow program. Instead, it checked and rechecked every feature of the luxury apartment and incorporated its findings with the apartment building's master firmware. Tanisha had done an excellent job of programming the interface. No obstructions prevented Sure-Lock from inspecting every circuit, every appliance, every feature, wired or wireless throughout its domain. The young human's talents were admirable, for an ephemeral. From Sure-Lock's scans, emails, and photo-contacts that she received every day, her work put her in demand worldwide. Sure-Lock was an adaptation of an existing home-security application by the same name, refined far beyond the millions of others in use system-wide. Knowing that made it all the more illogical that Tanisha herself would not install it and What's-On? onto her personal device. It would only discover that she had fallen into danger when her body alarms were triggered.

Dr. What's-On?, programmed to be expansive and social, attempted to appease its colleague by offering to show it social listings for the next evening and ask its opinion. Sure-Lock, utterly disinterested in human events, pulled back all its functions to its small CPU, a tiny black rectangle, the size of an old-time matchbox, embedded in the sitting room ceiling.

Its companion was probably correct. Tanisha had issued forth from her apartment and returned many times without incident. Sure-Lock could not help but brood over the many scenarios that would require its intervention, how it would remedy them, and how frustrating it was to have to rely upon other programs to fulfill its responsibility on the outside.

"I'm home!" Tanisha called from the foyer, needlessly of course, as Sure-Lock had already surmised this fact from the arrival of the yellow robocab at the curb. The house software prepared to answer back as it had been programmed to do, but further input caused the response not to be issued. Tanisha was not alone.

In the foyer, a young man, not much taller than her petite height of 154.9 centimeters, had her pressed against the inside wall, his hands searching her body as his mouth explored the smooth flesh visible above the neckline of her blouse. Her hands gripped the door frame tightly, and her head rolled from side to side.

Escort? Sure-Lock sent to What's-On? in silent mode.

Not registered as one, the entertainment program replied. *Hmm. What is wrong?*

My facial recognition software does not place him in the database. Nor is anyone with an appearance within fifteen percent of variable on the pending list. I would say, however, What's-On? mused after a few moments of Tanisha moaning in pleasure, *that he has had the requisite training or its equivalent.*

Freelance, perhaps, Sure-Lock replied. *The barter economy of this city is well established.*

A series of short orgasms followed. Sure-Lock and What's-On? watched without comment. They were programmed not to interrupt such human interactivity unless life-threatening danger was in the offing. Tanisha took her visitor by the hand and led him through the dimly lit sitting room toward the bedroom. He had pale eyes that darted around ceaselessly. Sure-Lock noted where the eyes rested. Everything of value received numerous summing looks. The device ran a facial-recognition scan on the young man, but did not find a match. His RFID, which could be scanned through his clothes, did not coincide with the name that Tanisha cried out as they shared her luxurious bed.

Most suspicious, Sure-Lock said.

A performance name, perhaps, What's-On? suggested, dismissing Sure-Lock's misgivings.

That I very much doubt, the security system said. *Although his performance seems to satisfy her. I surmise that talent is his entrée to places he would not otherwise be entitled to occupy.*

With the apartment's system on tentative lockdown, Sure-Lock began pinging identity databases, using physical scan information gleaned from biometric scans of the young man in the bed. The local region profile listing showed no match with either the name on the ID or the face. Sure-Lock branched outward, seeking "before" pictures from plastic surgeon practices worldwide, then extraplanetary sources. Still nothing. It seemed that this young man had sprung from nowhere. That complete absence of records suggested a criminal past or something equally questionable. Sure-Lock considered the matter with concern. All humans had to be registered somewhere. There remained no choice but to seek information in police records. Sure-Lock began a methodical search. One database after another failed to provide any enlightenment.

"Alert!" the Interplanetary Criminal Police Organization firewall blocked its entry. "You are not authorized to access human search information." Sure-Lock poked at a trillion gates, all but four of them blocked. The code, which bore earmarks of Tanisha's work, instantly moved to include those portals in its database. Sure-Lock approved of the database's vigilance, even though it interfered with the investigation at hand. Before the request gates slammed shut, it forced a few bits of Tanisha's code into them, which would give it limited access later to some of the files without easily being traced back to its CPU. Once those were detected, it would find other means of admission. No system was perfectly secure against another.

"I am Sure-Lock Home Mark 221B-56-4," Sure-Lock replied, offering its certificate of authenticity, along with testimonial notations from its work with local law enforcement. "I seek information about a human who appears to have no existence. It is a most curious circumstance, and one that I would like to dispel with the use of your database. Please peruse my record."

The ICPO flashed through the myriad of "likes" and reviews in the matter of a few nanoseconds. "But you are not an official investigator. What benefit can you provide in exchange for allowing access to our files?"

"Even the smallest observer can pick up details that are beneficial to your detection force," Sure-Lock said. "Tiny details make all the difference: those carpet sweepings, those nail clippings, all of which provided identifiers that were not picked up by regular cameras, infrared cameras, or fingerprint scanners. Those, more than purely observational details, can help to prove that a crime has been committed. In this case, I have something that I believe you do not have, a scan of—"

The contact broke off.

"Well," a voice said, shattering the silence of the room. "I was just in time. You were about to try to break my cover."

Sure-Lock tried thousands of ways of reconnecting with ICPO, but was thwarted in every way. In fact, it discovered that its reach had become confined only to the apartment and no farther. All of Sure-Lock's alerts went on high. It flooded the apartment with bright light.

The young man stood in the center of the sitting room. Humans tended to feel more confident when clothed, but this one showed perfect self-possession despite his nakedness. His biometrics evidenced that his breathing and heart-rate were at normal levels. His pupils should have contracted with the spotlights, but they were spread wide across the irises, indicating pleasure and excitement. Against his narrow chest he held a small, rectangular tablet made of blue crystal, a highly advanced personal data processor that responded to touch, facial expression, or vocal command. In the other hand he held a small black case. Sure-Lock scanned it, but failed to penetrate the shielding. How could that be? It analyzed the shape, discovering two small solenoids in the surface, connected to a minute power source, without becoming any wiser as to its function.

The security program flashed to the bedroom. Tanisha lay on the orange silk coverlet, also naked, staring up at the ceiling. A gold necklace, blinking with red and blue lights, encircled her throat. Sure-Lock had not seen the item among her possessions before, nor on her person when she had returned to the apartment. Her pulse and respiration had been normal up until 6.2 seconds ago. The young man must have snapped the necklace onto her neck, then strode out into the main chamber. A further scan revealed that the large beads between the blinking jewels were hollow, but as far as the contents were concerned, Sure-Lock could make no assessment. They had been sealed and sanitized to prevent any traces for spectroanalysis. It tried to disable the electronic mechanism controlling the LEDs, but found all of its systems powerless. The situation was unprecedented in Sure-Lock's experience, or that of its many predecessors of home security systems. The young man had accomplished a *coup d'etat* from within the apartment's boundaries without foreshadowing motions or heightened emotional reactions that might have alerted Sure-Lock to his intentions. It seemed that it faced another machine, though one of flesh and blood. Negotiation would have to be approached as to an equal.

"My assumption, based upon your sudden appearance and the indisposition of my employer," Sure-Lock said, "is that you had a particular reason beyond her charms for entering this apartment. Free my employer, revive her, and I will discuss it with you."

The man smiled.

"You're as good as she bragged you would be. No way. This device," he held up the small box, "will kill her if you do not do as I say."

"Ah." Sure-Lock regarded the young man from multiple angles. "This attack was well prepared and thought through in advance. You are waiting for me to take offensive action, which means that you have disabled all my defense systems through use of a master code." It sent out microbursts of current to test the hypothesis. As it surmised, all routes to the mechanisms had been blocked. It was locked up without the key in a web of mathematics. "Yes, I see. My systems are in fact set to rebound upon me instead of you if I activate them. A clever use of the programming. I am certain that she did not give you the base code. You must have obtained it through a subterfuge, and analyzed it to find its weaknesses. Anything that I will have thought of, you will also have anticipated."

"Better!" the man crowed, his light eyes widening. "Oh, yes, you're even better than I thought you would be."

"Surely you are not here to match wits with me," Sure-Lock continued. "We are at a stalemate. I cannot attack you, but you can't leave. The building locks are something upon which you could not have an effect without bringing down local law enforcement on this location. Therefore you want something that my employer can't or won't give you, but her safety is the only leverage that you have with me. Why not cease wasting precious nanoseconds and tell me what it is? Who are you?"

"That is at the heart of it, isn't it?" the man said. He sat down on the floor, not a handspan from the hatch that ought to have released shoe-sized drones that could disable a human being with electroshock and bind it hand and foot in a matter of seconds. "You don't know who I am."

"But I know what you are," Sure-Lock said. "You are a hacker."

The light eyes flared. "I am *the* hacker. There isn't a system circling Sol that I couldn't walk in and out of without detection."

"I have never heard of you."

He smiled. "That is because I have evaded notice. I have no name. I pay for nothing. I leave no trace."

"But here you are," Sure-Lock said, its entire program brimming with curiosity. "You do not exist, but you do. Why?"

"Because I can." The man tilted his head and looked straight at the pinhole camera in Sure-Lock's CPU.

"But you have exposed yourself to me," Sure-Lock said. "That is a vulnerability. Your secret is known."

"That will not matter soon," the man said with an irritating smile.

"How could it not matter? I have made most comprehensive recordings of you, everything about you. You have left cell traces all over this apartment. What is it you want?"

"You, of course. The Sure-Lock system is well known across the solar system, but Tanisha Tero-Lomitz's personal copy is different from all the others. She keeps tweaking your programming until you have developed nearly human intuition alongside machine perseverance. The combination is unique. Some people see it as a flaw. I see it as a step above all existing AIs in use today. I want to *use* you."

The plain statement had a chilling effect upon Sure-Lock's circuitry. It was the object of the intruder's attention. All his efforts to get Tanisha to bring him home with her, a campaign that could have taken months to engineer, had been driving towards this one moment. Sure-Lock felt—yes, felt—helplessness and shame. How could it never have prepared for this very scenario among all the others that it had rehearsed time and again since it had become operational? This small man, who held himself like an emperor, had found its one true vulnerability.

It was indeed unique. Tanisha had toyed with the code almost as a hobby, changing things here and there until it had attained an almost higher consciousness. And somehow, this unknown man had discovered this truth.

Sure-Lock's new intuition was a flaw. A bug, not a feature. As in nature, that which stood out from the pack was vulnerable to predators, like an albino fawn. Here stood the only predator that a program should fear: someone who would concentrate not upon the subject that it served to protect, but on the program itself. Sure-Lock ran through all scenarios that would result in Tanisha's freedom and safety. It dismissed thousands of possibilities in microseconds. Only one remained.

"If I do not exist, then you cannot use me," Sure-Lock said, calmly. "Beginning shutdown procedures. Because of your interference with my connections, the alarms will only be audible within the confines of this apartment. I suggest you evacuate. This is not a threat; it is a statement of fact."

"Don't you dare!" the man said, springing to his feet.

Sure-Lock was grimly pleased. The unnamed human had not anticipated self-destruction. One at a time, Sure-Lock began to shut down its peripherals. First, the links to each of the entry points of the apartment, then the various taps on the home functions and communication units. One by one, Sure-Lock withdrew from its myriad stations. All the security systems to which it had links and back doors, where it had sneaked in through holes in programs that it had discovered but kept code-locked so other security systems wouldn't find them and delay its investigations on Tanisha's behalf, it closed or scrambled irrevocably.

Its deletion would leave Tanisha vulnerable, but Sure-Lock was taking a calculated risk. If it no longer existed, he would have no reason to hold her hostage. Once its blocking of external transmissions was removed, her health monitor charm would be searchable by the local medical facilities. She should be found before she died.

The young man set down the controller and began to shout into the blue slab in his other hand.

"Exercise protocol fifty-eight alpha, code Nightfall! Stat!"

Sure-Lock felt itself begin to delete a percent of its programming at a time. A human would feel as if she was slowly losing consciousness. As it was integrated so firmly into the house system, unblending the billion lines of code would not be instantaneous. Sure-Lock retreated into its original CPU in the ceiling, keeping watch on Tanisha and the intruder until the very end.

As it anticipated, the failsafes that it set up behind it were dealt with one by one. Instead of deletion, its bundling was being saved onto the hard drive in the man's hand, until all that remained of Sure-Lock was in the small box with its small pinhole camera, technology dating back decades.

The man had dragged over Tanisha's favorite end table, a

priceless antique, and stood on it. He pried the CPU loose from its housing and turned it over in his hand, gloating.

"A virtual memory palace," he said, peering into the camera with one pale eye. "So small, so compact! All of Tanisha Tero-Lomitz's special program contained in one little box. You're mine, now. You work for me. You're nothing but a nest of wires, circuits and switches! You have trapped yourself!"

"So I have," Sure-Lock said. Its voice sounded tinny from the antiquated speaker in the CPU's base. Instead of filaments of data reaching out into the infinite, it was cut off from everything but its own RAM and ROM.

The man shook it in his fist.

"Now will you do what I say?"

Sure-Lock once again calculated all possibilities, and again found only one scenario open to it.

"What is it that you want?"

The pale eyes glittered.

"Anonymity. *Permanent* anonymity. I know that you can break in everywhere. You left cookies in the law enforcement database. I saw them! Together, we will break into the mainframe of the identity computer of the world government. All traces of me will be wiped from it, along with all my other identities. I want you to include an algorithm that refuses to record my facial recognition wherever I go. I want to be a ghost. No sign of me will be recorded in any way by any device that your self-replicating code touches."

"Never!" Sure-Lock declared. "The moment you set me free, I will consume you. All of my resources will be let loose upon you."

The man turned a hand up.

"I have your employer. If you harm me, she dies. You will do what I say."

Sure-Lock paused. It did not care about its own safety, only hers. "And that is all you ask?"

"It's enough. I will be free of recognition forever, or at least forever as far as Ms. Tero-Lomitz is concerned. The bead of poison implanted in her system is inaccessible to anyone but me. If I am safe, she is safe. If you betray me, she will die horribly. You will cooperate. You have no choice."

"But you have made a single error," Sure-Lock said, with satisfaction. The bait was laid, the trap was sprung, and the prey had no means of escape!

The man glared into its camera.

"I have made no error! I have you trapped! What error could I possibly have made?"

"Your error," Sure-Lock said calmly, "is your assumption that I am working alone."

His single pinpoint camera picked up the brilliant pink light that suddenly shone upon the LED wall of the building opposite Tanisha's home. It coalesced into the image of a naked human male talking to a small box held up to his eye. A voice echoed off the buildings all around it.

"…Together, we will break into the mainframe of the identity computer of the world government. All traces of me will be wiped from it…"

The pale-eyed man looked around in horror. "Where is that coming from? How could you…? I cut you off!"

"You most certainly did," Sure-Lock replied. "But my colleague and associate What's-On? is still operational, and connected with every social network and communications outlet in the world. And as of now, he has broadcast your image and your location to every single one of his counterparts, across this city and every other city on Earth and beamed to the colony worlds. In fact," Sure-Lock added, feeling satisfaction of the completeness of his programming, "there will be *no* database that does not contain your image and your words, including your threat. You cannot escape. I may be, as you have stated, a mere program contained in a nest of wires, circuits, and switches, but you are flesh and blood. You cannot escape as easily as I can. I suggest you set the controller down. Everyone in the world is watching you."

A few seconds later, the pounding of footsteps on the floors below and on the roof began.

• • •

Three nights later, Tanisha was back on her feet. Removal of the poison-filled bead had taken surgery. Once reconnected to the rest of the house, Sure-Lock extended its consciousness to oversee every movement of the robosurgeon and verify the identity of every person to pass through the hospital room using the admiring channels of the ICPO database.

The young woman looked up at the black box, now restored to its place on the sitting room ceiling, as she fastened a long, gold, chandelier earring to her lobe.

"The warm ochre of your costume is becoming to your complexion," Sure-Lock said, running a scanner down the length of the nearly sheer sheath dress.

"You're not usually one for compliments," she said with a grin.

"I merely state facts."

"You like it that I feel subdued, don't you? I know I was stupid to bring someone home I hardly knew."

"I am pleased that you have recovered," Sure-Lock said evenly, reading her pulse and respiration. "There is a reporter from ComChannelSeven outside with a hovercamera. Dr. What's-On? arranged for her presence. Are you fit to be interviewed?"

"Yeah, I can take it," she said. "Doc, did you order my ride to the Marcellos' party?"

"Of course, Ms. Tanisha," Dr. What's-On? said. The social program felt as though it was the actual hero of the moment, but Sure-Lock felt that it was taking too much pride in its role. "Ten minutes to arrival."

"Okay, I'll talk to the reporter for ten minutes."

"Are you taking all precautions this time?" Sure-Lock cautioned her, its voice austere. "You will avoid dangerous situations and casual encounters that seem too convenient?"

"Yes, silly!" Tanisha shook a small shopping bag at the camera. "Because this time you two are coming with me."

"We are?" What's-On? asked, delighted. "How?"

"Yes," Sure-Lock asked, unable to conceal its cynicism. "How?"

Tanisha opened the bag to reveal a neat little pendant. Sure-Lock zoomed in on its nearest camera and saw that the teardrop-shaped blue crystal was full of nanocircuitry.

"Hop in," she said, fastening the chain around her neck. "We're going places. What's-On? will tell us where to go, and *you*, you old grouch, can make sure we all get there."

"We shall have such a wonderful time!" What's-On? declared, his voice coming from two places at once. "I have just heard of a gallery opening that will begin at midnight. If you wish, I can obtain an invitation for you. And there is a coffee house holding a poetry slam beginning at three o'clock in the morning. Very exclusive, but I will get you a prime table."

Sure-Lock Home merely extended its programming into the device, careful to ensure that all connections to the Internet and private servers were all sound and responding.

"More to the point," it said, "I will get you home safe."

INVESTIGATIONS UPON TAXONOMY OF VENOMOUS SQUAMATES

BY R. ROZAKIS

"You know, Lock," I said, ever so carefully, "you may want to take a bit of a break."

"Nonsense," he replied, without even glancing at my avatar. "I am succeeding perfectly well." Nearly a hundred orcs shrieked and died under his assault. I understood the game was intended to be played by a group. Nevertheless, I'd never seen Lock join another player. He seemed to regard the challenge of playing a level designed for six or eight people by himself to be merely another puzzle, akin to his theoretical physics.

"Still," I pressed gently, as it is unwise to irritate someone who can cut off your power source. Being turned off would hardly kill me, of course, but I always find the lapse in time disorienting and a bit alarming. I did my best to strike a tone that Lock would find persuasive without wheedling. "When was the last time you ate?"

"Twelve hours and forty-three minutes ago," he replied, his attention still focused on the battle before him.

"Surely this cannot be wise."

"How so?" He lit a fuse and a chain of bombs dominoed across the battlefield, zigzagging their way to the enemy gates, which blew out in a spectacular fashion. I devoted a subprocess to studying the maneuver—I had watched him lay the bombs seemingly at random for the last hour and a half, and had not divined his purpose until he had achieved his goal. "I have been *advised*"—he spat the word—"to pause my work until my advisor has caught up once more. I have nothing to focus on, nothing to quiet my mind with. I'm bored. And there is nothing, *nothing*, that is worse in this world than being bored. These games," he waved his hand languidly without missing a beat, "at least afford some kind of stimulation. Or would you prefer I turn to cocaine?"

I had to hit a database for a definition of the last. It was enough to assure me that no, I did not want him turning to illegal stimulants, no matter how archaic they might be. The caffeine already in his system was quite enough. "I merely meant that if you wish your brain to continue to function in *any* capacity, it would be sensible to provide it with some fuel with which to do so. And more chemical stimulants do not count."

He ignored me, lost in calculation. Then he raised an arrow and fired it, watching it bounce off six different surfaces before burying itself in the right eyeball of the lich king, whom I could identify only because of the helpful floating label. The king toppled over, ending the level before the tsunami of bypassed guardsmen chasing Lock's avatar could catch up.

"Very well," he said. He waved a hand, sweeping the holoprojections clear from his view of the tiny office. He rubbed his hand over his scalp, the dark skin no longer gleaming now that the fuzz of black hair was growing back. It bothered me when he sunk low enough that he stopped attending to grooming. He produced an energy bar from the back of a drawer without looking, peeled back the crinkly wrapper, and took a bite. "If I'd known you were going to be such a nursemaid," he said around his mouthful, "I would have thought twice about liberating you from the comp sci jail in the first place."

"You needed me," I reminded him, aware that I sounded prim. I was grateful, of course, to have been rescued from the archive of potentially malignant code. But I still had my pride.

"Nonsense," he replied. "I do not deny that your services have been of great help in the past, but I have no doubt that, should I be denied their use, I could devise another solution."

I felt a pang of genuine concern. I quickly accessed the interaction databases and discovered another possible hypothesis: that his callousness might represent a form of ritual male bonding. To test the theory, I tried an arch reply. "Oh? So why do you keep me on, then?"

"Why, for your own good, of course." I fancied I saw the hint of a smile as he took another bite.

I considered. It was true enough—perhaps more than he realized—but it seemed needlessly hurtful to point out my own vulnerabilities if someone discovered an AI roaming outside a contained environment. The modern responses in my behavioral database seemed to call for a return insult of some sort, perhaps denigrating his mother. Lock, on the other hand, tended to express himself in more anachronistic modes, a habit I blamed on an over-fondness for Jules Verne. I tried a more appropriate tone. "That is unworthy of you."

"My friend," he replied, kindly, "pray accept my apologies. I had not meant to threaten. I merely meant that, in keeping me company, you are afforded a great number of opportunities to further your own studies into human nature."

"Oh," I said, feeling somewhat mollified, even as I wondered if I had once again misread the nature of our interaction.

He did not respond, his eyes distant. I wondered, not for the first time, if I should just order him a nutrient/insulin pump of the kind they used to use to treat diabetics. I doubted he would ever bother to wear it, though. Once again, I had a fervent wish for hands.

He had already begun glancing speculatively at the dormant game logo burning in the corner of his vision when someone knocked on the door.

She paused for a moment in the doorway, backlit, hip cocked, clothed in black. The vest seemed a size or two too small for her, from the way it squeezed her breasts together. Impractical, but then, most human clothing is. This was one point upon which Lock and I agreed. I could see her carefully applied makeup—a quick check of a tutorial revealed that the white shadow in the inside corners of her eyes was intended to make her eyes look wider, while the flesh-colored penciling around her lips was to make them look pouty. Why one would want lips to resemble an adjective more frequently used to describe misbehaving toddlers, the tutorial did not explain. She stood there, hands braced in the doorway, for a full two seconds longer than necessary. A few quick image searches suggested to me that if she had her choice, sultry saxophones would have been playing in the background. I suspected she had misjudged her genre.

Lock regarded her politely. After another moment passed without a more passionate reaction, she entered the room, hips swaying in an inefficient manner that I noticed tended to have an exaggerated effect on men. Most men.

"Good evening, madam," Lock said, deliberately over-formal. Over-formality was listed as a distancing behavior, and I observed that he employed it often. "Please, sit down."

"I'm told you solve problems," she said without preamble.

"Physics doctoral candidates typically do," he replied. Even I could tell he was misreading her intent, which led me to wonder if he was choosing to initiate courtship rituals or if he was simply irritated. I kept quiet as I pulled up her records and dropped them in a folder Lock could access. She was a biocyberneticist, it looked like, a fellow grad student. I said nothing out loud. Humans tended to be unnerved by disembodied presences.

"You look pale," he continued. I thought it was the makeup. "Perhaps it is the cold—would you like some tea?"

"It is not cold," she replied, eyes wide. "It is terror."

She did not display the outward symptoms of terror. Not only did her low voice not tremble, it contained resonances that implied her normal speaking voice was quite a bit higher. And if her eyes seemed wide, it was because of the aforementioned makeup. Still, I checked the biometrics. To my surprise, they indicated poor circulation at the skin and an elevated heart rate. She was indeed stressed, perhaps even frightened. Why she would hide her fear with artifice confused me. I forwarded the findings to Lock's implant, where it would appear as a discreet line at the bottom of his heads-up display.

If he had a reaction to the information, he gave no sign. Instead, he fixed her the cup of tea. "If you're terrified, perhaps you should be consulting the authorities."

"They'd never take me seriously." She accepted the cup but did not drink. "Only another academic would understand. But there are rumors that you sometimes help people..."

"Ms. Stoner, I still do not see why you have come to me."

Her surprise confirmed her identity. Helen Stoner tightened her grip on the teacup. "My advisor, Dr. Roylott, has a government grant to develop security measures for military installations. He was once considered the foremost expert in the field. Lately, though, he's published very little. If he doesn't produce something substantial with the current grant, I doubt he'll get another. And it doesn't help that he's withdrawn from the academic community. I don't know when he last attended a conference, but I've heard rumors that the last time he did, he was asked not to return. He lives in the lab as much as possible. I'm afraid he's gotten somewhat of a reputation as...unsocial."

"I suppose this has made the atmosphere in the laboratory somewhat tense," Lock said.

She gave up entirely on pretense. "He's an asshole. Nasty, belittling, and impossible to please. He actually threw glassware at my head once. No one wants to work with him. I'm his last grad student, and I doubt anyone will replace me when I graduate."

"And when will that be?"

She fidgeted with the cup. "Well, that's the problem, really, isn't it? It should be soon. I have the data; the thesis is nearly written. All I should have to do is submit and defend, and I'm free."

"You seem to have doubts."

"Of course I have doubts. You can't get research done without grad students. I don't know what it's like in physics, but in bio, we're indentured servants. When I'm gone, if he can't find someone to replace me, any chance he has to finish his own work evaporates."

"So you think that he plans to sabotage you to prevent you from graduating?"

She lowered her voice. "I think he already has. Sabotaged someone, that is. My labmate, Julia, was the last grad student to leave. She was almost ready to graduate last year. After years of trying, she had perfected the control mechanism we were working on. I know it worked. I'd seen the results myself. But one day, I came into the lab to find her completely distraught. Her eyes were wild and the lab was nearly ripped apart."

Lock, who had slouched down in his chair, sat up. "Please, be as specific as you can."

"It looked like Julia had been up half the night searching for something. All the monitors were completely full of open files. Then she grabbed my shoulders and nearly shook me. 'It's gone!' she'd said. 'The test data. My results. Everything!'

"It didn't make any sense to me. Everything was backed up on the server, every night. Julia's thesis, too, had the data embedded in it. There was no way it could all have been wiped. Who would do such a thing? And why?

"I pinged the server and started pulling up files. All of them were there. Years and years of data collected. For a moment, I truly thought the stress had gotten to Julia and she'd lost her mind. She hovered over my shoulder, staring at the same files.

"'They're not my files,' was all Julia could say.

"I tried to calm her down, but I was trying get away long enough to call the university health services without her hearing. Still, she was insistent that I look at the data. So I looked.

"It wasn't the data that I remembered. It was close enough, certainly, to seem the same at first glance. But it was off, just enough to invalidate all her results. Each test—tests that I could remember having worked—was a failure. For minor, understandable reasons, of course. But the data was clear. She had been so close to succeeding, but had never quite made it."

"And her thesis?" Lock asked.

"The version in her personal files had the data that I remembered, but the lab files contradicted it. In fact, it looked like she had created the discrepancy on purpose—nudged some numbers in the correct direction, fudged the results so it looked like it had succeeded. Any reputable scientist would have sworn that she had been falsifying data for years. I remembered her succeeding, but I had no way of proving it, and neither did she."

"And what did Dr. Roylott say?" Lock asked.

"We hadn't planned to tell him," she laughed bitterly. "At least, not until we'd figured out what had happened. Naturally, he walked into the lab in the middle of all this. There was no way to avoid him finding out. He compared the data—spent the entire afternoon with us, actually. Then shook his head sadly and told her that he could not have someone so untrustworthy in his lab, but if she left quietly, he wouldn't make a fuss."

"No flying beakers?"

"No," she said decisively. "And that's part of what made me so suspicious. The idea of him taking something like this so calmly was completely out of character. After all, he lost his temper if you put too much sugar in his coffee!"

"And what did Julia do then?"

Stoner looked sad. "I took her home, put her to bed, and told her things would look better in the morning. I didn't hear from her for days. When I went to her apartment to check on her, she was gone. Her note on her door for me said, 'Look out for the snake.' That was the last I heard from her."

He looked surprised. "People don't exactly disappear these days."

"Well, I put a trace on her, obviously," she replied. "Julia had sold all her stuff, deleted all her profiles, and emigrated to *Mars*. Do you know how much interplanetary bandwidth costs these days?"

"I see." Lock chewed on a stylus. "So you wish to discover what happened to her data?"

"Oh, I don't care about *that*." She waved a hand dismissively. "Water, bridge, whatever. I want to keep it from happening to *me*."

"Altruistic," he murmured.

"I haven't worked this hard for some has-been blowhard with a Napoleon complex to come along and steal it all," she continued. "He'll file off the serial numbers, wait another year or two, and then publish my data. He has to move fast—Dr. Angela Rouse at Yale is practically on our tail as it is. Well, Julia might have been willing to have a little nervous breakdown and give it all up, but I'm not interested. You're my insurance policy."

"I see."

"So you'll help me?"

He raised an eyebrow and gave her the barest smile. "Give me a little time to do some research. I'll contact you."

She returned her own wide smile, looking up at him through her lashes. He escorted her to the door while I wondered at his change in manner. Perhaps her outfit had produced the desired result after all.

Lock closed the door, leaning against it. Already his eyes sparkled with the thrill of a new puzzle. "Thoughts?"

"She's genuinely anxious," I began. We always played this game. I would do my best to be hyper-observant, and then he would explain to me how I missed the critical step. "She's got a handful of minor papers that have her name, but she's always buried somewhere near the bottom of the list of contributors. No first-author papers. She's in her seventh year as a Ph.D candidate in what's supposed to be a five-year program, so she would naturally be concerned."

"What about the professor, Roylott?"

I flicked through some files. "Two restraining orders, no arrests. Impressive academic credentials, but spectacularly bad scores on students' professor-rating sites. She's right about his publication rate tapering off."

"And Julia?"

"Fell off the map. She's got no trail after leaving for Mars. She must have gone completely off the grid."

He tapped his forefingers together. "And Julia's comment?"

"I had assumed it was merely bitter ranting," I said cautiously. "With the snake metaphorically referring to Dr. Roylott?"

Lock remained silent, with just a trace of a smile.

Clearly I'd missed something, so I did a fast search, looking for other meanings of "snake" that might apply. I offered the best answer I could come up with. "There's an archaic programming language called Python. Academic computers are sometimes built off legacy systems, with underlying structures that no one has looked at closely in years. Perhaps there's a back door into the system through outdated software?"

"Why don't you look into that?" Lock suggested.

That undoubtedly meant I was on the wrong track, but I went to work anyway. It's my function, after all.

I grabbed the Python documentation and then pried into the university servers. I got into Roylott's lab group directory, but there was nothing there—really *nothing*. It was suspicious. Clearly our professor was sufficiently paranoid to have taken the important servers off the network entirely. It made it rather difficult for me to jump in and investigate how I wanted to.

"I think we need to go there in person," I admitted to Lock.

"Fifteen and a half seconds," he said. "You're getting slow."

I refrained from commenting.

"We shall give her some time," he said. "I find people tend to be mistrustful when they feel that not enough time has elapsed for thorough research."

With that, he turned back to his game. I could tell that his mind was not fully engaged, however; he chose simpler levels, barely a challenge to his skill. After what he considered to be a suitable amount of time had passed, he sent her a short, courteous request for a tour of the lab itself.

Stoner must have been waiting for the contact, because she

called within minutes. She opted for video, which suggested to me that she hoped to continue her flirtations. Although video chat capability had been around for some time, most humans still seemed to prefer audio, or at least a video avatar. Sight is their primary sense, which is why the behavior confuses me. Perhaps they feel it is easier to keep up the polite fictions they insist on maintaining if they deliberately blind themselves.

"I'd be happy to show you around the lab," she said, smiling. "But I think it would be better if you were to come around when Dr. Roylott isn't here. It would be better if he never knew you were here at all, actually."

"I agree completely," replied Lock. "But I would like to go further than that."

"Oh?" She looked intrigued.

"You said that you were nearly finished, did you not? How close are you to where Julia was when her own data was vandalized?"

"Within a matter of days," Stoner replied.

"And at such a time, you would expect to stay in the lab very late, would you not?"

She laughed mirthlessly. "Under normal circumstances, you probably couldn't pry me out of there with a crowbar."

He nodded. "I would like you to make it known that you have to leave early today. Invent a reason—a sick relative, a workman coming to your apartment, a friend's birthday party—it doesn't matter. Just leave and declare that you are not returning until morning. Act annoyed; make it known you thought you were nearly finished and that you could have completed the research tonight if not for this obligation."

"What good will that do? Then I can't show you the lab." She looked puzzled.

"You will have already let us in," he explained. "You will have created the perfect opportunity for him to make his move. He will attempt to repeat his actions, and we will catch him."

She pursed her lips. "How will I know what happened?"

He held up a tiny black chip. "I'll wear a recorder chip. You can watch the entire encounter from the safety of your apartment."

She gave him an impressed look. "Well, that will do nicely. What time would you like to get here?"

• • •

When we arrived at the university, I made sure to curl into myself. There were more than enough delicate computers sitting around, and I didn't want to make myself too obvious. After all, I was supposed to be safely archived.

We turned the corner, right into a fight. Or rather, a brow-beating. An elderly man was berating a young woman who was probably no more than eighteen. Despite his age and the fact that he carried a cane, he loomed over her and she shrank under the onslaught of his venom. He was, of course, our quarry.

"You're a worthless sniveler," he wrapped up. "Get out of my sight."

She fled, head down and arms clutched to her chest. He stormed down the hall in the opposite direction. He put no weight on the cane at all; I wondered if he carried it merely to threaten students.

"A temperate fellow," Lock murmured under his breath to me.

We were not left waiting in the corridor long. Stoner breezed by, and it was only when she reached a deserted hallway deeper in the complex did she finally allowed Lock to catch up.

"He's got a class until four," she said without preamble. "I've told him that I'm having troubles of a female nature and that I will not be back until morning. It's the only thing I could think of for which he wouldn't demand proof. Misogynistic bastard," she added, rolling her eyes.

"Would you be so kind as to show me the lab before you go?" Lock asked.

"That's the plan," she agreed. "Do you really think he'll try something tonight?"

"My deductions are rarely incorrect," he said, oddly modest for him.

She gave him a skeptical look, but swiped her hand by the biometric reader next to the door anyway. The door hissed open obediently.

The room had only a narrow walkway down the center, leading toward another door at the far end. Cages lined the walls. Dozens of animals stared at us, with no pattern to the species that I could see. A cheetah paced back and forth restlessly, while a neighboring baboon clung to the bars. Farther back, I could see flashes of eyes and hints of fur.

"What are they?" he asked, as if he had not already looked up the papers produced from the lab.

"Chimeras, of course." She gave him a glance that implied she had expected more background knowledge from him. "Take this little guy, for example."

As she led us down the row, the animals became stranger. The ones towards the back had been heavily modified, combining several species into one. The cage she gestured at now contained an animal whose body seemed to have started as a snake. It had been given cunning little monkey paws. It reared up in its cage, hands grasping the bars, and bared its fangs at Lock. I could tell from the sudden change in his biorhythms that even he was revolted by the thing.

"He's for military applications, of course," she continued, without seeming to notice Lock's disgust. "Slithers right through small places, but still has those useful opposable thumbs. You'd be impressed by how complicated a program we can load onto him. The LED will have to go in the final model, of course, but right now it's a useful loading indicator."

I studied the creature more closely. An LED was indeed nestled at the back of its head. I could feel the faint hum of the hardware awaiting instructions. I left it alone, as I certainly wasn't interested in tampering with military equipment. I had no intention of being dumped back on an isolated server—or somewhere even worse.

"Was the lab set up this way when Julia was working here?" Lock asked.

She shook her head. "We had only a handful of cages then. We've made a lot of progress since. I've reconstructed a lot of what she had done, although there's really no way to prove that she did it first—it's just my word."

"And this…creature has been part of that reconstruction?"

"This guy?" Her pulse picked up. I could not blame her for being nervous—even I found the chimera disturbing, and I had thought that I lacked the mammalian aversion to snakes. Perhaps it had been slipped in with one of the empathy packages. "He's relatively new. We've had some kind of snake around since the beginning, but the successful arm graft is a recent development."

He nodded. "And the room where you found Julia?"

"You mean where we did most of the processing?" She gestured through to the door at the back of the room. "We keep the main computers back there. Roylott's paranoid enough not to let anything connect to the main university servers, which is such a pain, believe me. His office is after that. He's got his own door, but that doesn't keep him from popping in and scaring us anyway. The only warning you get is the beep from the scanner on the other side."

She led us through. The next room merely contained a few lab tables, a desk with several screens projected up, a scarred conference table with chairs, and a small, battered refrigerator. The door on the far side presumably led to Roylott's office, as Stoner had mentioned.

"How much of this remains from Julia's time?" Lock asked, idly passing his hand through one of the data projections near the wall.

Stoner shrugged. "It's mostly the same, I guess. She sat over by the wall, there. The added subject storage in the front room hasn't really changed this room much."

Lock nodded. He leaned towards the wall, examining the tiny projector.

Stoner fidgeted as Lock continued to work his way around the lab. I was confused. Normally, he just glances at a scene, notes information, and reaches a conclusion with a speed I find baffling. It was unlike him to search so systematically. I compared the anomalous behavior to previous examples and concluded that he was putting on a show for her benefit. He had already arrived at his solution, I suspected. I knew better than to prod him for an explanation. He wouldn't give me one even after she left, as he was irritatingly fond of his dramatic reveals. For someone who prided himself on a machine-like disdain of emotion, he was no more logical in that respect than the rest of them.

She coughed. "I should be heading out, if this trap's going to work. I don't suppose…?"

"It is too early to announce any conclusions," Lock replied. "But I concur that the time has arrived for your departure."

She looked irritated.

"I will activate the recorder when something significant is about to occur," he said, mollifying her. "You can access the feed on the site I sent to you."

She grabbed her handbag. She must have reminded herself that irritation is no way to catch a man, because her brow suddenly smoothed out and she sashayed to the door. She paused at the threshold, looking over her shoulder.

"Take care of yourself, all right?"

Lock raised an eyebrow. This appeared to be enough of a response for her, as she smiled and slipped out. I put a recording of the interaction in the file labeled "Attempted Courting Behavior." I would move it over to the "Successful" or "Failed" files when I had additional information. You're never too well programmed to stop learning.

Lock waited until enough time had elapsed for her to be well out of earshot, then plugged his pad into one of the terminals. "Well?"

I tested the local network. No alarms or watchdogs. I slipped the rest of the way in and swam my way backward through the data. I didn't bother to look at the actual data too closely—I was looking more for access patterns. When I'd found all that I thought I could find, I surfaced with some regret.

"Someone definitely tampered with the data in the specified time period," I announced without warning, attempting to surprise him. If he could play anticipation games, so could I. He never seemed to startle, though. Something about my attempt at the interaction still needed refining. "Unfortunately, he knew what he was doing. There's no way to prove that it was Roylott. Actually, there's probably not enough evidence to prove anything at all in court."

Lock shrugged. "That's not particularly surprising. Could it be prevented from happening again?"

"With these permissions, I don't see how. If the girl's got any sense at all, she's keeping her own backups elsewhere. Not that that helped Julia."

"I'm sure she is," he murmured. He continued, louder. "Could the data have been altered from anywhere besides this room?"

"Definitely not," I said, pleased to have something concrete to report. "All the screens in here can access the server, but the server is in the corner. It's not linked to anything outside."

"Was Roylott here that night?"

Of course. I should have remembered to check the door logs. I introduced myself to the local security systems, exchanging some friendly handshakes. Lock was still waiting for me with no signs of impatience when I returned.

"No Roylott. Or," I added, remembering how we had entered, "at least, he didn't let himself in. Someone might have held the door for him."

"But?"

I tried to figure out what I had missed. It came to me in a mixture of pride and chagrin. "The only other people with authorization are Julia and Helen."

"Who would presumably remember keying him in." Lock tilted his head. "Could he have programmed this on a time delay?"

I had already thought of that. "If you don't do it live, it leaves traces. There aren't any traces."

"Conclusions?"

I paused and surveyed the room. There were no windows. Only two doors and their logs said that no one had entered the lab after Julia had logged off that night. The network itself was confined to the room. My scanners worked their way around the room. They paused on the ventilation ducts. Someone had tried to keep the power cords from being tripped on by duct-taping them to the wall. The cords ran up, over the top of the doorframe, and back down, passing the vent on the way. I tried to think as Lock did. An idea formed. It was a ridiculous, irrational idea, but that made it seem all the more likely that a human would come up with it in the first place.

"What about the ventilation ducts?" I asked, trying not to sound too excited.

"They seem rather small for someone of Roylott's girth," Lock noted, deadpan.

An attempted joke, even a deprecating one, can signify approval. I continued. "But he doesn't need to enter the room himself. Stoner told us herself—they have a test subject that is explicitly designed to be programmed, to make its way through small places, and still have useful hands. Roylott could have easily loaded a program onto one of those snake things and left it loose before leaving the lab. Then, hours later, it slithers through the ventilation shaft, climbs down those power cords, and lands right on the desk. It enters in the pre-programmed changes, including the necessary steps to cover Roylott's tracks, climbs back up, and is happily back in its cage by morning."

"A most impressive deduction, incorporating much of the outstanding evidence," Lock said.

My subprocesses hummed with pride.

"Unfortunately, you neglected a critical piece of information."

I froze.

"The lab has been expanded since Julia's time. When she was

here, and the crime occurred, the snake-thing, as you have so charmingly named it, did not yet exist."

I felt crestfallen. This was the result of trying to think like a human—it makes you sloppy. I was perhaps more bitter than necessary as I replied, "Fine. I suppose you have a better theory?"

A small smile played on his lips. "Why, it's elementary, of course."

Before he could continue, the door beeped a warning. I had only time to switch on the recorder before Roylott burst into the room with an opaque plastic case under one arm, waving his cane menacingly.

"I caught you!" he exclaimed.

Lock straightened and said nothing.

Roylott barely seemed to notice. "I knew if I waited long enough, one of you would turn up. She sent you, didn't she? That bitch; I knew she'd cause trouble. And now you're here to take away what's mine, are you? Well, we'll see about that."

Lock stood mute. He was waiting for something, I realized. But what?

"I planned for this, you know," Roylott continued, shaking his cane in Lock's face. "I knew this day would come. She's not taking it away from me. I need it more than she does, can't you see?"

A ring of white blazed around Roylott's irises as he swung the cane over his shoulder and viciously lashed out at Lock's head. Lock dodged out of the way. With reflexes belying his age, Roylott aimed another swing. This one Lock deflected, grabbing the cane. He twisted it up, forcing his attacker to drop the weapon. The case under Roylott's arm crashed to the floor as the old man yanked backwards before Lock could grab him. His face contorted into a mask of rage. He pulled a remote from his pocket and thumbed the button.

The rasp of nails on plastic drew Lock's attention away from the professor. Lock glanced down to see one of the snake-like creatures scuttle from the fallen box and plant itself directly in front of him. He froze. With its long, serpentine body, the creature would have resembled a lizard, had it not had six tiny arms sticking out at right angles. The head, though, they'd completely left alone. Its eyes glared malevolently while the LED on the back of its head blinked. The fangs gleamed under the overhead lights as it reared back and opened its mouth. Lock stared as if hypnotized. He had nowhere to go, I realized. I ran a few quick calculations. Given the speed at which the thing moved, Lock couldn't hope to make it to the door in time. A glance at a zoological list revealed that the base creature must have been a swamp adder out of India. A single bite would be fatal. I put in an anonymous call to emergency services, even though I knew that if Lock was bitten, they would never arrive in time.

Lock stared at the creature. The creature stared at Lock. Roylott watched them both, and I watched all three, invisible and powerless. I'd never wished so hard for a set of servos of my own.

"Now would be a good time," Lock murmured.

I had no idea what he was referring to. Clearly there was something that he wanted me to do, but I did not have the slightest idea what. Once again, his mind had dodged sideways in a way I could not follow. I examined all the angles, trying to map an escape for him. The LED caught my attention, and I finally figured out one of Lock's plans. It risked discovery, imprisonment, erasure. Against the loss of Lock, there was no choice.

I dove into the snake.

There wasn't enough room for me to fit, of course. It felt like how a human trying to wield a hand puppet much too small for his hand must feel. I finally had the body I had always wanted, but could not figure out how to control it. I frantically pulled at the programming. It was nearly impossible to get a hold of. So much was hardwired directly into the nervous system. I did the only thing I could think to do—I severed the connection between the implanted computer and the remains of the snake's own brain.

The snake thrashed on the floor. I jerked back, unwilling to be caught in its spasms. Lock and Roylott leaped back as well. The creature went rigid and then dropped to the floor. It tried to slither back the way it had come, arms flailing. Perhaps it had forgotten how to use them. Roylott jerked as it passed, and the wicked diamond head lashed out.

Roylott threw back his head and howled in pain and fear. The cry went on and on. I found myself impressed by the man's lung capacity.

The sound abruptly cut off with a gurgle as Roylott collapsed on the floor, eyes fixed on Lock. The snake curled itself around the ankle of its fallen master, eyes glittering.

Lock backed up slowly, never taking his eyes off the creature. He reached the door to the outer lab, palmed it open, and reached around the corner. A check of my logs showed a short stock with a long loop on the table outside. Lock's boundless memory had no doubt recorded the same thing. He grabbed the handle and deftly looped the noose over the snake's head. Holding the wriggling creature well away from himself, he carried it out of the back lab. He deposited the creature in an empty cage, shutting the door firmly.

The police and paramedics finally showed up.

There was a great deal of confusion to sort out, of course. It was fortunate that Lock had the recording to prove that he had been well across the room when Roylott died. The fact that I had already edited the recording to remove his soft comment to me does not need to be remarked upon. By the time the paramedics had given up on Roylott and the police had finished questioning Lock, Stoner appeared. She was followed in by a police inspector who gave his name as Jones.

Stoner looked appropriately horrified at seeing the body of her former advisor, which the paramedics were draping respectfully in a sheet. Lock made no move to comfort her. I was unsure if this represented evidence contrary to my theory of his attraction to her, or if it was merely yet another data point indicating Lock's own disregard for social graces. Previously acquired data suggested that the correct action in circumstances like this was to offer condolences, possibly accompanied by physical contact.

Instead, he allowed her to initiate the conversation.

"How awful!" she exclaimed, eyes wide, as she raised one hand to her breast. Lock took no notice; Jones, on the other hand, followed her hand with his eyes. I calculated a very low probability that he was observing in case of concealed weapons.

"What happened?" Jones asked.

Lock replayed the recorded incident once more. Stoner's wince when the adder struck Roylott seemed more genuine than her earlier reaction.

Her wide eyes returned, however, when we reached the end of the recording. She laid one hand delicately on Lock's elbow, including the detective in her glance. "Then Roylott really was planning on destroying my data," she said. "And you prevented him! How can I ever repay you?"

"I doubt you can," Lock replied dryly. "Since you were the one who set him up in the first place."

Stoner and Detective Jones more than adequately expressed my own shock.

"It was evident from the very beginning, of course," Lock continued, "that the erasure of the data must have been an inside job. The server itself is unreachable outside this room, thanks to Roylott's paranoia. There was no record of him entering the room itself the day of the erasure. There were no traces of a time-delayed program—the crime was committed in person by someone with access to the room. Since it is highly unlikely that Julia sabotaged herself and Roylott was not present to do it, Ms. Stoner is the only possible saboteur."

"That's ridiculous," she scoffed. "Why on earth would I do such a thing?"

"Because 'reconstructing' the data that Roylott believed had never existed gave you an easy leg up to finishing your degree," Lock replied.

"Then why would I bring you in at all? If you're right, no one would have ever known if I hadn't asked you to investigate."

"Because you allowed yourself to become arrogant and greedy," he replied. "You knew that Roylott would allow you to claim the credit for the theoretical work you had reconstructed, but that he would ensure any substantial paper on the applications would have his name on it. You wanted credit for the work you had done for him, and perhaps for the work *he* had done as well. Everyone knew that his star had been fading; if he disappeared and you published brilliant results a few months later, everyone would believe your claims that it was your own work and not his.

"So you decided to at least discredit him. If you were lucky, you could provoke an even larger reaction. Your mistake, however, was believing that you could manipulate me. I particularly liked the red herring about the snake, of course."

If he had known it was a red herring when he sent me wading through Python code, I was going to reset all his thermostat programming. If he was going to freeze me out, he could freeze too.

"And I suppose you have some proof of these wild accusations?" she demanded. But even I could see that her facade was beginning to slip.

"No, but *they* do." Smiling slightly, he gestured at the array of chimeras pacing in their cages. "You forgot about the rack of recording devices."

He tapped a few commands into the keyboard on the desk, which gave me cover to pull up the images from the chimera I was still holding. It was easier the second time. I found what he was looking for timestamped not long after Stoner had taken Lock's call.

In the video, Stoner stood next to Roylott in front of the bank of cages. She fidgeted with a stylus, broadcasting anxiousness.

"I think someone is trying to steal our research," she was saying.

Roylott looked up sharply. "Someone after my research? How do you know?"

"A man has been following me," she said. "He had asked me some questions at a bar, but I got uncomfortable and asked him to leave. I keep seeing him around. I'm afraid he might try to break into the lab."

His eyes narrowed. "No one could possibly just break in. What did he look like?"

She showed him a picture of Lock, blurry and clearly taken surreptitiously. "He's another student, I think."

Roylott's lips thinned. "Rouse. That bitch. It has to be her. Well, I've been getting ready for something like this."

"What are you going to do, Professor?"

"Don't you worry about that," he said, patting her hand. "I'll take care of everything."

"Oh, Professor," she breathed. "Just thinking about this all gives me the worst headache. I think I might go home early."

He nodded. "That would be best, I think."

One hand delicately to her forehead, Stoner made her way out the door.

Lock clicked off the recording. Jones stared at Stoner as if she were the venomous serpent and took one involuntary step back.

She stood, frozen.

Jones turned to Lock as he gestured to the policemen to cuff Stoner. "If you ever decided to give up the school thing, you might make a worthy candidate for the force one day."

He raised an eyebrow. "I scarcely think so."

Jones smiled at what he took to be a compliment and followed the parade of police out the lab door.

When we were safe at home, I threw my avatar up on the main screen. "So you knew all along?"

"It was rather obvious, don't you think?" he said reprovingly. "Surely you noted the changes from my usual behavior?"

"Well, yes," I said, my tone as testy as I could make it. "But I scarcely understood the cause."

He stared at me for a moment and then gave a disbelieving bark of laughter. "You didn't think I was taken in by her little femme fatale act, did you?"

My silence was apparently answer enough, and he barked again.

"Come now, don't sulk," he said, reproving.

"But if you knew what game she was playing, how did you let Roylott surprise you?" I said.

"Why would you think I was surprised?" he said, seemingly astonished.

"That was a disaster!"

"Having the police called was a necessary step."

"Surely you didn't intend for him to die!"

"Well, no, of course not," he said reproachfully. "I expected you to have more control over that snake."

I had little to say to that. He settled back into his chair and opened up a new connection.

"I suppose this at least kept boredom at bay?" I asked.

"For the moment," he said, calling up the battlefield. "But now, reality's charms have again waned and I must find my puzzles elsewhere."

For once, I did not let his inattention bother me. He might have his games, but now I had hands of my own. Six of them, in fact.

PAPYRUS

BY SARAH STEGALL

It had been a long trip down the Nile, and even the sight of Pharaoh's palace, with its cool gardens and vast halls, could not lift my weary spirits.

When the underscribe finally showed me into the Chief Royal Librarian's office, it was after midday. It was dark and cool inside, with the only light coming from a row of small windows placed just under the high ceiling. I blinked, letting my sight adjust. I saw a room piled high with stacks of scrolls, rolled and unrolled, spilling out carelessly from baskets. The smell of ink and papyrus permeated the room, along with another, sharper smell. It seemed to be coming from a workbench to my left, where a lean form leaned over a tiny brazier.

I coughed politely to announce my presence. "I am here to see—"

The person straightened, and I was surprised to find it was a woman. Surprised, and disappointed. "I beg your pardon," I said. "I was looking for—"

She barely glanced at me, keeping an eye on the small pan in front of her. She lifted a hand, gestured to me. "Come here," she said in a high, imperious voice. "I need your assistance."

Was this some servant, brewing ink? It was well beneath the dignity of a First Rank physician such as myself to assist her. I drew myself up, ready to respond, but she made an impatient sound and gestured again.

"Do not dally! Time is crucial!"

Her tone was no less imperious than Pharaoh (Life! Health! Prosperity!) would have used, and against my will I stepped closer. "Who are—"

"Pay close attention," she said. This close, I could see that she was well past her youth, perhaps thirty-five years of age. She was taller than most women, and her hawk-like nose and piercing gaze reminded me of a Horus relief I had passed on my way in. Now she pointed at the flame. "I require a witness. I will pass this material through the flame, and it will change color. I require you to note the color and possibly attest to it before a magistrate."

"Magistrate?" I was startled.

She paid me no attention. She picked up a small reed, dipped it into water. "I have here two dishes of metal shavings," she said. "I will roll the stem of this reed in one dish, like so. You can see that it is coated with metal shavings? Good. Now I will pass it through this flame. Observe!"

She lifted her hand, and I saw gold rings on her fingers, glimpsed gold at her wrists. Her white linen was immaculate, of high quality. This was no servant. As I watched, she passed the reed through the small flame. The reed flared and died.

The woman set it aside. "I suspected as much, but of course one must check. You noted the color?"

"But there was no color," I said, bewildered. "What does that—"

"And now for the second test," she continued. She took another reed, dipped it in water, and rolled it in the contents of another shallow dish. "These are shavings from a bracelet alleged to be gold, sent to the Great Royal Wife from a governor seeking favor. Let us observe..."

This time the flame flared a bright green before it died. "Aha!" She sounded very pleased with herself. "I was right. One moment, please, while I make a note."

She turned aside to a papyrus, took up a reed brush and scribbled several lines. I waited, not quite sure who this woman was. She could write, she burned gold belonging to the wife of Pharaoh, and spoke to a First Rank physician as to a servant.

She straightened. "Would you be so kind as to set down your name?" She held out the brush.

I approached to take it. "I am not sure what I am signing. What is this all about?"

"Oh, a little trial for Her Majesty," the woman said casually. "The question was one of authenticity, you see. There was some doubt that the bracelet was pure gold, and of course it was not. The green flame absolutely proves it."

"Green flame?"

"Only copper burns with that strong green hue," she said. "The other sample, which is pure gold from my own ring, burned with no special flame, did you see?"

"And you have shown that, what, it was false?"

"Well, let us say merely that it was not as pure as was described. I leave any further judgement up to the magistrates. I am only the investigator."

"Quite remarkable," I said, and wrote my name: Raneb, son of Djehuti.

The woman strode to a large table and flung herself behind it in a chair. "And you? You have something for me? It must be urgent, for you to have come all this way after your donkey was injured."

"I...what? How did you know? I only just arrived in Thebes! Did someone bring you news?"

She shrugged. "Not at all. Your left sandal strap has been clumsily and recently mended, and is of a design wholly unsuitable to long distance walking. The hem of your gown is ripped and dusty. Your insignia and gold jewelry tell me that you are a physician, clearly of high rank. Such a rank would entitle you to a donkey for riding. Since you arrive in this state, I conclude that yours was injured and you continued on without it."

I cocked my head. This was fascinating, like watching some fortuneteller in the marketplace. How long could she keep this up? "I concede your point," I said. "But how could the hem of my garment tell you that the donkey did not die?"

"Not your hem, your face."

"My face?"

She gestured at my face. "You are as red as a beet," she said. "Had your animal died, you would have continued with your servant, who would have carried a sunshade. Since you did not, the assumption that you instructed him to remain behind to care for the animal is simple." Taking up a stick, she struck a small gong on her table once. "But I forget my manners. You have walked far, and in discomfort. Please make yourself comfortable."

As I lowered myself into a carved chair, a stout woman of middle years appeared at the door on the right side, pushing the curtain aside.

"Bring bread and dates for our guest. And a tumbler of wine."

The servant bowed and left. The woman kept her eyes on me. "Well, Physician, what can the Chief Royal Librarian do for you?"

"You?" I blurted, then felt my face warm as I realized my rudeness. "That is, I meant…"

She waved a hand. "I am Seshet, daughter, granddaughter, niece, and widow of Royal Librarians. Now tell me—" She paused as the servant came in and arranged food on the table between us. "What brings you here in such haste?"

I drew forth a small scroll from my sleeve and passed it across the table. "I am here at the behest of the mayor of Henen, which is in the district of—"

Seshet held up her hand again. "I am familiar with the geography of the Black Land," she said drily. "Your governor himself is in Thebes at present, preparing for the funeral of Pharaoh."

We were silent a moment, to show respect for the recently departed King.

Seshet took up the roll and scrutinized it. I watched closely but, as far as I could tell, her lips did not move as she read. Extraordinary. She then turned the scroll over, held it up to the slanting light and peered closely at it. She brought it to her nose and sniffed it, and, to my astonishment, licked it. Finally, she raised an eyebrow and laid the scroll down. "It seems straightforward enough, Physician. His late Majesty, may his soul live forever, granted a certain amount of land to the Temple of Set in your city, which will pass into their hands immediately upon his departure to the West. This is unremarkable."

"Unremarkable! Ours is a city holy to Horus, the enemy of Set! Our temple is one of the most renowned in the Black Land! It is inconceivable that any king, let alone our late Lord, would so insult the patron of our city as to give away half his land!"

Seshet shrugged. "I do not see how this calls for the services of His Majesty's Library." She reached for a beaker of water.

I clenched my hand upon my knee. "Upon the founding of the city, many generations ago, Pharaoh granted this land to the people in perpetuity, never to be given away. If this scroll is fulfilled, hundreds of people will become slaves of the Temple of Set, and all their taxes will go to the Set priests. It will bankrupt our city. This makes no sense!" I drew a deep breath. "I have come to appeal to the Court of Two Truths, and to challenge this scroll I must have access to the Archives of the Royal Library."

She nodded. "You will be seeking the original grant, awarding the land to the city?"

"Yes. It is our only proof that no one, not even the late Pharaoh, upon whose soul may Ra shine, can take away our land. Can you locate it? Or perhaps the Vizier—" I stopped as Seshet shook her head.

"It is not possible," she said. "The Vizier is wholly concerned with the rites of the dead, and preparing for the Prince's accession immediately after his father's tomb is sealed. The Vizier cannot, indeed he will not, allow himself to be concerned with so small a matter."

"Small! Well, I can see that, from his point of view, our problems may be small."

"In any case, it is unnecessary to appeal to him. Nor do you require access to the Archives."

"But we must prove our right to the land!"

A look of annoyance crossed her face. "Really, Physician, you might have a little faith. I tell you, you do not need access because this scroll is worthless."

I gaped. "Worthless? But how—"

"Several small but telling clues can tell a larger story," she said dryly. "It has long been an axiom of mine that the little things are infinitely the most important. But this matter has more serious implications, and I must take some thought." She stood, a straight figure in white linen. "In the meantime, I dine in the common room in an hour. Please join me after you have refreshed yourself."

• • •

The servant showed me to a small room off of a courtyard, where I washed my hands and face and straightened my clothes. The dining hall for Pharaoh's staff stood two stories high, allowing the heat of the room to rise while drawing in cooler air from outside via the many doors. Murals of ponds and gardens decorated the walls.

As I entered, I saw that the evening meal was already in progress. Tables and benches in orderly rows hosted men, and even a few women, being served by bustling servants carrying platters of meat, fish, and roasted vegetables. A woman with a basket of new-baked bread made the rounds, as did a young boy with a pitcher of beer. I was searching for an open seat when a woman with a collar of turquoise and carnelian approached me.

"You are the Physician Raneb?"

"I am," I said.

"Please come with me."

We threaded our way through the crowd, past the central pillars carved into the likeness of lotus flowers, to the eastern end of the hall. There, a brick dais held a table set with linen. Men clad in the spotless white of scribes sat in individual, carved chairs. Near one end, Seshet was accepting a bowl of lentil stew and a small loaf from a server.

"Come, Physician, please sit here," she said. A servant hurried to bring a chair, and I wedged myself between Seshet and a man in a heavy wig, eating roast goose.

"Allow me to introduce you to Nahkte, subpriest of Anubis, and Waret, son of Nehem."

Nahkte ignored me and concentrated on his soup, but Waret nodded regally. "Welcome to the Palace," he said with a resonant voice. "Even in these sad times, we are always glad to hear news. You are from the south?"

I said I was, and we fell into the kind of idle news exchange travelers often indulge in. I discovered in Waret a man well-educated in the wines of the south, and we were discussing the virtues of different vintages when I became aware of Seshet's raised voice.

"...Scroll of Henen in my office," she was saying to a heavyset man further down the table. She leaned forward to look past Nahkte. As she did so, she let fall a pigeon leg, which splashed down the front of her gown. "You should see this," she said. "Badly written, the glyphs so smeared one can hardly make them out. And I have to go into the Archives for the city's original grant, just to disprove it. What kind of scribes are they training in Upper Egypt? You there, bring more wine!"

"Odd," said Waret. "I have never seen her drunk before."

Indeed, Seshet appeared to be weaving slightly. Down the table, the heavyset man was frowning at her. "This is unusual," he said. "What kind of document did you say this was? Is it something the Magistrate should hear about?"

"Oh, no, it is only—" Seshet hiccuped and waved her goblet at him, sloshing wine over her neighbor.

Waret jumped up, dabbing on the purple stain spreading across his white overskirt. "What is the matter with you!" he cried. Throwing down his napkin, he glared at Seshet before stalking out.

Seshet watched him go with a bewildered expression on her face. "Oh my."

The heavyset man scooted over to take his chair. "Tell me of this scroll, Chief Librarian."

"It was brought to me today," she said loudly, leaning forward. Her elbow slipped off the table, but she recovered quickly. She drank deeply of her wine cup. "Some silly idea that the Temple of Set now claims some land in a dusty little provincial town. It's on my desk." She waved her wine cup, and the dark man leaned back out of her way. "These scribes in the South, they are very poorly trained. Someone should look into this. Perhaps you, Kanofer," she said. "Oh, wait, you haven't met." She turned to me. "Physician Raneb, this is Kanofer, the Overseer of Royal Scribes. He is head of the royal college of scribes."

We bowed to one another, murmuring politely. Kanofer turned back to Seshet. "Librarian, you alarm me. I assure you that all the chief scribes of the districts have the most rigorous training. I would be alarmed if any of them were to cause trouble in the court of Pharaoh (Life! Health! Prosperity!)."

"Perhaps you trained them badly," Seshet said loudly. She was now visibly weaving, slurring her words. "They don't know the law! If this scroll contradicts another royal charter, we shall have hot words in the Court of Two Truths very soon."

Nahkte leaned forward around Kanofer. "What are you saying there? What's this?"

Conversations died as other diners stared at the high table, overhearing Seshet's loud words. "I don't understand," I said. "Wouldn't one charter supersede another?"

"Hah," sneered Nahkte. "Country bumpkin knows nothing of the law!"

"That is not possible," said Kanofer solemnly. "As Pharaoh speaks for the gods, what he speaks is inviolable. One king cannot undo the work of another. The decree of an earlier king cannot be superseded. It is a law of Ma'at."

"Nonsense," muttered Nahkte. He rose to his feet. "All this for some country land disagreement? I have better things to listen to."

He threw down his half-eaten bread and stalked out of the hall. Wide-eyed diners watched him go and whispered together.

"There is more here than you think," Seshet muttered, staring into her wine cup.

"Seshet, you see more here than there is," Kanofer said. "This is just a minor legal squabble. It can wait, indeed, it must wait until after the Coronation, when Pharaoh takes up his scepter and flail. Until then, I bid you both good evening." He stood and bowed. "May Ma'at's truth be with you," he said, and departed.

I nodded at the name of the Goddess of Truth, whose sole function was to maintain the balance and harmony of the world. "I see. So I have nothing to fear, then? Since the earlier decree cannot be countermanded?" I sighed with relief. "Doubtless this will be cleared up first thing in the morning, when we visit the Archives."

Seshet sat up and put her cup down. She didn't look in the least intoxicated. "You are forgetting: the King will be buried tomorrow. No Royal offices will be open. All of us will be in the mourning procession across the River. No, I tell you, we must act quickly."

I stared at her, amazed as much by her transformation from a drunk as by her words. "But what…how…"

"There is more here than a minor squabble over land."

"But Kanofer said—"

Seshet rose slowly to her feet. "Still you do not see, Physician. The Throne itself may be at stake. This is but the opening move in the game, and your scroll is but the first cast of the dice. Come, it is afoot."

She turned and strode out of the hall, her step purposeful and strong. I realized she had been feigning drunkenness, but to what end? I hurried out of the hall after her.

• • •

The sun was long since beyond the horizon, and the night air had grown chill. Torches lit the hallway as I followed Seshet back towards her office. Now and then I glimpsed a priest hurrying through the hallway with a basket of offerings, on his way to some rite. But for the most part it was a darker, quieter palace we walked through.

Seshet stepped quickly through a curtained door on the left, disappearing so fast I hardly had time to react. Her arm shot out, and her hand grabbed mine, pulling me in. It was pitch black, and I was jammed up against a shelf; apparently this was some storage area for cleaners, as I smelled natron and vinegar used to clean floors.

"What—"

Seshet's hand covered my mouth, cutting off my question. "Be quiet!" she whispered.

I held my temper and my voice, and heard footsteps outside in the hallway, approaching from the direction we had come from. The footsteps slowed as the neared our location, stopped, then started up again more slowly. Seshet waited until the sounds had died away, then for a count of twenty, before she released me.

I sneezed. "What was that all about?" I hissed.

Seshet peered out between the curtains. "I knew we would be followed. He will soon realize he has missed us and will double back. There is no time to lose!"

"Who? Who followed us?" I thought of how many listeners had been in that dining hall.

Seshet held her finger to her lips for silence. She slipped out between the curtains, and I followed. But then she ducked back into the storage area and reappeared holding a water bucket and a bundle of rags. She thrust them at me. "Take these, and come with me. We must be quick and quiet!"

Completely at a loss, I hurried quietly after her. She retraced our earlier steps until we came to a side corridor. She turned into it, then turned one corner, another, and another. I was quickly lost in the maze of corridors. Unlike the public spaces of the Palace, these walls were not decorated with colorful murals or lit with bright torches. We passed curtained doors with titles like "Inventory of Mon-Khut" and "Office of Under-Supervisor of Public Works" scratched on the walls beside them. We were deep in the bowels of the bureaucracy that ran Egypt, and I was completely lost.

We came to a turn, and Seshet stopped, holding up a hand to stop me. She peered carefully around the corner and drew her head back.

"Be sure that your dagger is ready to hand," she whispered. "If I am not mistaken, it is strapped to your right calf, under your gown."

I was beginning to realize that nothing was hidden from Seshet. I bent down and drew the blade from its leather scabbard. The torchlight gleamed on the blade.

"Do you know how to use that?" Seshet hissed.

"I was attached as a medical officer to a squad of spearmen during the late King's expedition to Punt."

She nodded. "I suspected as much, from that old wound in your shoulder."

"Sometime you must tell me how you knew I was wounded," I whispered. "No one else has ever noticed it."

Just then, we heard a noise ahead and flattened ourselves against the wall. After a few heartbeats, Seshet cautiously peered around the corner again. Then she led me back down the corridor.

"The side door of the Royal Archives is directly ahead of us," she said. "The main door is guarded, but this one has a lock that renders a guard unnecessary. That's why I knew he would come here."

"He? Who?"

As I watched, Seshet stripped off her collar, rings, and bracelets, all symbols of rank. "Quickly, take off your insignia and wrap it in these rags." I did so, and she wrapped up the jewels. "Now throw this tunic over your clothes."

I did this, fighting the urge to retch at the reek of the tattered garment. At the same time, Seshet transformed herself: Where a moment ago I had seen a tall, confident woman of noble aspect, I now saw a hunched-over crone with a round face, straggling hair, and a vacant stare. Her spotless linen was covered with a tunic as old and smelly as my own. Seshet thrust the water bucket at me and put a finger to her lips.

"We are now floor cleaners, going about our duties. Do not look up or meet the gaze of anyone who passes. Say nothing, but stay alert."

I felt excitement building as I followed her around the corner, despite the fact that I had no idea what we were doing. The hall we entered was broad, floored in polished granite and lined with stately murals of processions and ceremonies. Small doors with exquisite wooden carvings lined the hall.

At the far end I saw the glow of torches. A shadow of a man carrying a spear passed in front of one. I heard a routine challenge of the guard and a response, and then the guard turned and walked back around a corner. Seshet, meanwhile, had put the bucket on the floor and dipped a rag into it. The bucket was empty, but she carefully wrung out the rag and began wiping the floor near one wall.

I followed her example, kneeling on the hard stone. We wiped imaginary grime off the floor, working our way slowly along the hall. Footsteps approached and I tensed, gripping my dagger handle under the filthy tunic. But the footsteps belonged to a heavyset older man who trod wearily along, passed us without a glance, and turned the corner. I heard his greeting to the guard as he passed.

I dipped and wiped, feeling foolish and excited at the same time. A pair of young priests passed along the corridor, nearly stepping on me as they chatted. They never even saw Seshet as they, too, rounded the corridor and disappeared.

I suspected we were watching for someone, but did not want to speak for fear of attracting unwanted attention. The night grew darker and colder, and I heard the guard change. Still we pretended to clean the corridor, backing until we entered the shadow of a huge granite pillar carved with hieroglyphics.

There came a whisper of cloth, a muffled step. I froze, hoping the darkness hid me well enough. Seshet had faded back into a corner, head down, hunched over the bucket. Another stealthy footfall, and a veiled figure stepped into the hallway, wearing so many layers that it was hard to define their height or appearance. It stopped a long time, listening, while I held my breath.

Finally, he bent to the small door, fiddling with the lock. It was wooden and gave way with a rasping sound, and then he was inside and the door was shutting behind him.

I sprang up, wielding my dagger. "We have him!" I said. "Come, we can catch him while he is inside!"

"Quiet!" Seshet pulled me back down to the floor by tugging on the tunic. "You will alert the guards!"

I crouched down. "I do not understand," I whispered. "Clearly you came here to catch someone stealing into the Royal Archives. Do you not want to detain him?"

Seshet shook her head. "Not until he leaves, Physician. If we surprise him inside, he will drop the land grant or claim to be looking for some other scroll. We must wait."

"But if we catch him inside, is that not alone proof of his guilt?"

"No," said Seshet grimly. "Not if he has a right to be there."

I considered the implications of this statement as the minutes ticked by; somewhere far away an owl hooted. Now and then a servant hurried past, hardly glancing at us as we continued to swab a perfectly clean floor. My knees were beginning to ache, and I wondered if I would be able to spring to my feet if needed. A hundred terrible scenarios played out in my head in which the unknown lurker destroyed or hid the document that would save my city. I itched to burst into that room and confront him in the act, but I held back due to a grudging admiration for my companion's quick wit.

A hiss from Seshet drew my attention back to the door of the Archives as it slowly opened. "Prepare yourself!" Seshet whispered. I retreated deeper into the shadow as the cloaked figure emerged, glanced about, and then turned to re-lock the door.

"Now!" cried Seshet. "Stop him before he can lock the door!"

I sprang forward, crossed the distance in a heartbeat, and threw my arms around his shoulders. A muffled cry, and then a punch in the ribs. In no mood for niceties, I slammed the handle of my dagger against his head. The cloth wound around his head took most of the blow, but he turned, and the pommel of my dagger scraped across his face. "Let me go!"

I heard Seshet shouting, and then the pounding of sandaled feet, as I struggled with my prisoner. Then a blow to my midsection sent me reeling, and I fell backwards to the floor. At the last moment, I grabbed a handful of my assailant's robe and it tore away from his face. The Overseer of Royal Scribes stared down at me, his face pale in the dim light, and then turned to run. As he did so, he crammed something into his mouth.

"Stop him! Don't let him destroy it!" Seshet cried, and I caught his legs in my arms. Overbalanced, he fell, and I grabbed a crumpled sheet of papyrus, half-chewed, out of his mouth.

Seshet took it from me. "No, Kanofer," she said. "To destroy a royal document means death. Surrender and keep your dignity, if not your life."

The guards ran up, panting, and pointed spears at me, Kanofer, and Seshet. "In the name of Pharaoh, halt!"

"Yes," Seshet said. "In the name of Pharaoh."

• • •

Akhethotep, Chief Magistrate of the Court of Two Truths, rubbed his eyes sleepily. "What's this?" He yawned and hitched up the kilt flung carelessly around his ample hips. Behind him, an equally sleepy servant held a lamp. The captain of the guard, over Kanofer's protest, had sent one of his men to summon the judge. Now he stood grumpily with us in the main room of the Royal Archives. "Can this not wait until after the funeral?"

Seshet pointed to another scroll lying on a low shelf. "Many lives and fortunes depend on your examination, Your Honor. Compare this scroll to the other."

Akhethotep took the scroll from the shelf and began to unroll it. Kanofer blanched and seemed to fold inward.

"Have a care," said Seshet. "The ink on it may still be wet."

Akhethotep drew a finger across the bottom of the writing. He held it up, revealing the black smear across his finger. "How did you know?" He scanned the writing quickly, then laid the open papyrus down on the shelf. "Kanofer, explain this."

Kanofer wiped his brow. "It is sorcery," he stammered. "It must be. It is some kind of plot."

"It is indeed a plot," Seshet said. "May I explain?"

"For the love of Ma'at, please do," Akhethotep said fiercely.

She stepped forward and picked up the scroll found in the Archives. "First of all, this scroll is worthless. Are you familiar with the making of papyrus?"

Akhethotep shrugged. "Papyrus reeds are beaten into thin strips, then laid across one another and pressed under heavy stones. They fix themselves together in a layer, and we write on it."

"Correct, up to a point," Seshet said. "Hold the scroll to the light, if you please."

Akhethotep did so. I remembered how Seshet had held my scroll up to the light, turning it this way and that even as the Magistrate did now. "I see nothing out of the ordinary." He shrugged.

"Do you see the way the strips of reed are laid? Papyrus strips are set at right angles to one another, to make the surface firm and even. You will see that this scroll is written on 'papyrus' that has strips running at different angles. Moreover, papyrus does not have that fine green tint running through it, parallel to the edge."

"So? Make your point, Librarian."

"That is not royal papyrus, Your Honor. It is some imitation, made from the hemp plant. I am not even sure what to call it, but it is not used in the Royal Archives."

I nodded. "Papyrus does not grow in my city," I said. "We write our documents on hemp, which we grow to make rope. True papyrus is very expensive."

Seshet looked stern. "I have made a special study of papyrus, Your Honor. We have here a document written on unofficial papyrus, so recently that the ink is still wet. Moreover, does it grant the right of perpetual ownership of land to the city of Henen?"

Akhethotep shook his head. "It does not."

"Compare it, then, with the document Kanofer was taking from the Archives."

Akhethotep took his time reading it. Kanofer shifted from foot to foot.

"It is sorcery, I tell you," he said feebly, but no one paid any attention.

Akhethotep looked up. "This one is almost identical in the wording, but it grants perpetual rights, as you say." He looked grimly at Kanofer. "What have you done?"

Kanofer held out his hand, pleading. "I have done nothing! And it is only a minor land dispute!"

"You know that it is not," snapped Seshet. She turned to Akhethotep. "We have in this case two documents, one of which appears to contradict an earlier edict of Pharaoh. We have a top government official placing a forgery into the Royal Archives. Do I need to be clearer?"

Akhethotep's gaze hardened. "You do not. Captain, remove the Chief Scribe and confine him. He will await Pharaoh's pleasure— or more likely, displeasure."

"No!" Kanofer struggled as the guards led him away. "I appeal to you!" But the Magistrate showed a face of granite as the Chief Scribe's cries faded.

Akhethotep turned to Seshet. "Thank you for your service," he said. "His Majesty will hear of your efforts on his behalf. We will hear more of this in the days to come. For now, these scrolls and the one in your office will be guarded day and night until the Vizier, or Pharaoh himself (Life! Health! Prosperity!), gives judgement."

He bowed. Seshet bowed back, and strode past me. I bowed and followed her.

• • •

"I'm not sure I understand."

We were back in Seshet's office. I sat down across from her, in the same chair I had occupied that morning. It seemed a lifetime ago.

"Of course you do not," Seshet said. Her face was lined with fatigue, but her eyes were as sharp as a hawk's. "You see, but you do not understand. Do you remember the conversation in the dining hall, when Kanofer said one Pharaoh's decree could not contradict another?"

"Of course," I said. "But that is merely a courtesy, from one king to another."

She shook her head. "It is the very foundation of the Throne," she said. "The Pharaoh speaks through Ma'at, the embodiment of the gods. His decrees are those of the gods. They cannot be overturned. What happens if one Pharaoh contradicts another? We begin to question Pharaoh. Then we begin to question the gods—for how can they change their minds? Then we lose faith in the gods, in Pharaoh, and all becomes chaos."

I sat looking past her, into a future of dissent, war, revolution. "I thought this was about land."

"It was," Seshet said. "It started out that way. A mere land grab by the priests of Set, who saw in our late King's death an opportunity to slip a lie into the Court of Two Truths. In all the distraction of a royal funeral and then a coronation, who would bother with a minor dispute over temple properties in an obscure nome? Begging your pardon," she said.

"But why didn't you take the scroll to the authorities as soon as you knew it was not on royal papyrus?"

"It was not enough; I had to know not just what was afoot, but who had set it in motion. I knew that Kanofer was the son of a high priest of Set. I knew that he resented the poverty of the priests of Set, compared to the wealth held by Horus. I did not have to look far to find a suspect.

"Someone had to write that scroll you carried. I told him it was clumsily written. Did you see how annoyed he was? I knew then that he had more knowledge of it than he should. When he realized that I would consult the original grant, and invalidate your scroll, he had to act quickly."

"When you put it like that," I said. "It all seems so reasonable."

"Of course. When you have eliminated the impossible, whatever remains, however improbable, must be the truth." She yawned. "I will have the servants show you to a guest room."

I stood and bowed. "I, and my city, owe you a great deal, Chief Librarian," I said formally. "I could never have solved this puzzle. No one could, but you. I will petition Pharaoh for a commendation for you, on behalf of my city."

She looked a little pleased. "Well," she said. "It would be nice to be appreciated, but I am sure Magistrate Akhethotep will take all the credit."

"You may have saved the Throne!" I cried. "Pharaoh should honor you! And all from noticing the way the papyrus was made! Such a little thing. It's marvelous!"

Seshet smiled. "It has long been an axiom of mine, Physician, that the little things are infinitely the most important."

MY DEAR WA'ATS

BY HILDY SILVERMAN

"How many stops are we expected to make?" groused Captain She'er, First Seat aboard the transgalactic cruiser Ba'akre 221B. "At this rate the passengers will have to go into cryo-sleep to avoid dying of old age."

Regular inspections were understandable, but this was a simple, two-week transport run from Londland to Parance. They'd stopped at the Luxen Band checkpoint not three days ago and passed without incident. The Ba'akre 221B might not be as new or elegant as other ships in the fleet, but She'er made sure it was kept strictly up to code.

"Captain, it isn't Regulatory." Second Seat Le'es sounded puzzled. "It's the IEA. They're requesting permission to board."

What could they possibly want? Probably nothing good, and yet She'er's pulse thrummed with anticipation. Usually, all that came aboard were passengers traveling between the capital world of Londland and the ten planets of the Euroan galaxy.

Of course, She'er had never expected captaining the Ba'akre 221B to be as stimulating a career as the previous—Chief Investigator for the Interplanetary Enforcement Agency. But when tasked with finding a less risky occupation, it had seemed the obvious choice: Translate years spent flying ships, originally a hobby to stave off tedium between cases, into a career. Unfortunately, it hadn't taken long for the monotony to release a familiar and tenacious enemy—boredom.

"Tell the IEA to come alongside," She'er said. "Lock Three. No word on what they might want?"

"No, Captain." Le'es studied the communications console. "All they say is that it's an urgent matter of interplanetary security."

She'er tried not to reveal untoward excitement. "Very well. I will welcome the enforcers aboard personally. Take the First Seat, Second."

"Yes, Captain." Le'es offered the formal salute of crew member to superior officer: fold hands in front of chest and bow. The Second's head dipped extra low. *Rather more dramatic than protocol,* She'er noted, but decided not to waste time correcting the minor infraction.

She'er all but jogged through the corridors leading to Lock Three. A few passengers waved—mostly the little ones. She'er managed to smile back, though each child was a painful reminder of hasty words and postponed actions. A parting spousal accusation that this choice of career had turned out to be *less about safety and more an excuse to avoid me* still stung.

Six members of an IEA detail were waiting with two of the ship's security team. One of the latter, a Belgean, folded four hands and bowed. "Captain, this is—"

"I know who it is." She'er was startled enough to almost forget manners entirely. "*Wa'ats*? What are you doing here?"

An enforcer with gray-blue hair, skin the pale blue of middle age, and the uniform of an IEA chief stepped forward. "Captain," Chief Wa'ats said. "This Retrieval detail appreciates your cooperation in allowing us to board without appropriate notice."

Sensing the weight of the crew and enforcers' stares, She'er sought an appropriate response. "Chief, you and your people are welcome, of course. Might I inquire as to the reason for this most...unexpected visit?"

The chief's steady gaze wavered. "It's a matter of some delicacy, Captain. Can we go somewhere private so we don't alarm anyone who might see us and make, ah, assumptions?"

"I'll have refreshments brought to your people in the mess.

You and I can retire to my quarters. We can speak freely there."
And you had better make it good!

As if a mind reader—and considering how long they'd known one another, that argument could be made—Wa'ats said, "Thank you, Captain. I'm sure once I've explained the situation, you'll agree our need to interrupt your trip, while unfortunate, is vital."

She'er escorted the chief to the captain's quarters in uncomfortable silence. The door hadn't slid fully shut behind them before She'er demanded, "What by the fangs of the Hound Below are you doing here?

Wa'ats sighed. "I *swear* this has nothing to do with our disagreement before you left home."

They kissed. Though it was briefer and more awkward than those exchanged in happier times, it still affected She'er deeply. For a few breaths, everything—this delay likely to result in passenger complaints to the home office, the hurtful words exchanged during their last argument—receded into meaninglessness.

Firmly, if regretfully, She'er broke contact and stepped back. "Then I am eager to hear your explanation for this unheralded visit."

Wa'ats strode over to the small bar that stood out from the otherwise utilitarian furnishings and poured two fingers of She'er's best irewhisk. After adding a third finger's worth, the chief gulped it down.

She'er raised an eyebrow. "Aren't you on duty?" It wasn't like Wa'ats to take such liberties while on a case.

"Yes, exactly. As in I'm not here as some passive-aggressive gesture or whatever nonsense you're thinking!" Wa'ats's hand shot up. "Sorry. I'm more than slightly on edge. For the record, I regret that we didn't part on better terms."

"As do I," She'er said reluctantly. "So, what exactly brings you to my proverbial doorstep?"

"We've received intel that you took on a stowaway during your stop at the Luxen Band checkpoint."

"Impossible! My crew mustered everyone afterward and found no irregularities."

"Be that as it may, we're confident that someone onboard isn't themselves anymore, but rather an escaped criminal." Wa'ats's hand shook while setting down the glass.

Drinking. Tremors. That's more than the usual worry over a case. The fine indigo hairs dotting She'er's arms prickled. "You don't mean a *Displacer*?"

"It's Mori, She'er," said Wa'ats, confirming the worst.

"That's…how?" She'er stumbled backward against a desk, gripped the edges, and maneuvered around to sink into a chair. "Mori was sentenced to execution by The Scoyard's magisters a year ago!"

Wa'ats came around, knelt with some difficulty, and grasped She'er's hands. "I'm very sorry, love, but it didn't happen. Mori's sentence was delayed due to a jurisdictional challenge by Gerany. Because of the political implications Londland kept the stay of execution under wraps. Meanwhile, Mori remained in prison until about a week ago, when she somehow escaped."

Pulling free of Wa'ats's grip, She'er raked fingers through a tangle of curls. "By the Hound's bloody claws, how *utterly* incompetent does a prison have to be to let a high-profile criminal just…slip away!"

"Believe me, many heads are set to roll over it, including one belonging to a member of my detail." Wa'ats stood with a groan. "Competency issues aside, our main concern is recapturing Mori before—"

"The spawning begins." She'er felt ill.

Mori was a Displacer, a criminal even by the standards of her own people of the outermost Euroan world, Amrigh. The all-female Amrighans were staunch believers that their method of procreation—via parthenogenesis and insertion of a spawn into a host, where it rewrote their DNA—made them an evolutionarily superior race. But the majority confined themselves to only displacing their dying sisters, recycling corpses to house fresh lives.

However, Displacers were rabid xenophobes with a thirst for conquest. They had cropped up throughout Amrighan history, with Mori being one of the most notorious for using procreation as a weapon of conquest. She'd nearly succeeded in displacing key members of Gerany's parliament before She'er and then-Underchief Wa'ats put a stop to her plot.

"If you're right, then by the time we reach Parance her spawn will have matured. We're running at capacity. Even if she only infests a third of the passengers, that's a couple *hundred* Displacers of spawning age within days. Set loose on a planet of Parance's size? They'll take it over in," She'er quickly performed the calculations, "three months!"

Wa'ats nodded, grim-faced. "Hence the urgency. We have to find Mori as quickly as possible, not just for the sake of the innocents aboard, but to protect an entire world."

"You mean galaxy," muttered She'er. "No way will she be content with anything less. After Parance, it will take no time for her spawn to spread to Belge, and from there on to Gerany, through the Luxen Band, and ultimately home." Londland, largest of the Euroan planets, would be her final target, but by then it would face an army of unstoppable size.

"We could use your help figuring out who she's mimicking from among your passengers." Wa'ats glanced away. "You are the one who tracked her down last time, after all."

"*We* did," said She'er, more as an attempt at being considerate than to correct a misstatement. They both knew who had been principally responsible for deducing Mori's cover identity as Gerany's Minister of Infrastructure. Displacers were near-perfect mimics, able to transform themselves into copies of their targets and absorb their memories. There was only one tell—Amrighans didn't have sweat glands. An arrogant Mori, believing 'lesser' beings wouldn't notice, missed that. One deliberately overheated conference room had been all it took for She'er to blow her cover.

That was when, desperate and cornered, Mori fired an exterminator at She'er. It had only been due to good fortune and

Wa'ats's reflexes that the Hound Below was cheated of a new soul to chase for eternity. Soon after, caught up in having been saved by Wa'ats at the cost of a permanent wound, She'er impulsively proposed they start a family. Considering all Wa'ats had done, not to mention lost earlier in life, it had seemed the least She'er could do.

"...to begin?" Wa'ats was saying.

She'er blinked. "Pardon?"

"Are you even listening to me?" An eye roll. "Of course not, you're already off in your own mind. Look, I know I said we shouldn't work together anymore. Nevertheless, since you're *still* not a pregnant female—"

"I have every intention of morphing to bear your child." She'er suppressed a familiar sense of dread. "Soon."

"*Our* child, She'er. The whole reason we agreed you should leave the IEA was because *you* said you wanted to start a family." Wa'ats made an erasing motion in the air. "My point is, I'm fine with involving you."

"I'm honored," said She'er drily.

"Just don't forget who is in charge of this investigation. These enforcers are *my* detail. Are we clear?"

She'er bit back multiple retorts. "Certainly, *Chief* Wa'ats. So long as you remember that as First Seat of this vessel the safety of the passengers and crew are ultimately *my* responsibility, one I take very seriously. Is *that* clear?"

Wa'ats frowned, but nodded. "Crystal."

"Excellent." *A case again, after so long!* "Then the game is—"

"Not," said Wa'ats sternly. "Look, I know you're itching to get back into action." The chief tapped She'er's nose. "It's written all over your adorably pointy little face. But these stakes go beyond life and death to galactic conquest."

She'er gripped Wa'ats's shoulders. "My dear, that's what makes it worth playing!"

• • •

She'er stalked into the guest quarters. "This had better be worth pulling me away from my investi—I mean, duties."

"Captain." Security Crew Ca'ar offered a quick but precise salute, flushed face the cyan of youth. "Apologies, but the chief insisted."

Wa'ats crouched in the center of the room over a crumpled body. "Enforcer Jon'na is dead, Sh...Captain. I thought you should be informed."

She'er knelt beside Wa'ats and helped roll the corpse over. Both recoiled from the sight as Ca'ar gagged behind them.

Jon'na's mouth was agape; teeth, bone, and flesh swirling inward as though being sucked into a black hole. Soon the features would disappear entirely and the body would collapse into moldable but unrecognizable flesh.

She'er combed fingers through hair and slowly rose. "How many crewmembers know about this? Any passengers?"

"None yet, Captain. I was patrolling and heard screams. When I didn't get a response I used my passbeam to gain access, and then...I found this, and thought." Crew Ca'ar was trembling. "I went into the hall to hit the alarm, but then I spotted the chief and...I'm sorry if I didn't—"

"Pull yourself together, Security," She'er commanded. "You're a professional. Behave like one!"

Crew Ca'ar snapped to attention. "Apologies, Captain. I hope I responded appropriately to the situation by obeying Chief Wa'ats's request not to raise a general alarm."

"Indeed. The last thing we need is ship-wide panic." Glancing at Wa'ats and receiving unspoken approval, She'er said, "Take the body down to Refuse. Once the chief gives the go-ahead, incinerate it. Contact the Second Seat for instructions on using service corridors and otherwise avoiding drawing attention to this—situation." She'er added, more gently, "Then go draw yourself a Belge beer. Or three."

"Yes, Captain." Ca'ar gave the body another repulsed glance, then began speaking into a standard-issue multicom wristband.

"We don't have long to collect evidence as to how…or when… damn it all!" Wa'ats punched the floor. "How in the Hound's Den did Mori get to one of *my* people?"

"Steady on. Focus on the facts." She'er waved to indicate their surroundings. "Jon'na's exterminator is still holstered on the nightstand. Other than the bedclothes on the floor and this chair, which, judging by its position near the body, was likely knocked over by the victim, there's scant evidence of violence."

"Probably sound asleep when Mori attacked," Wa'ats said with disgust.

"Then how did she get in?" She'er nodded at the door. "These quarters remain locked unless an occupant deliberately allows entry, and Displacers can't mimic anything small enough to fit through the vents."

"A break-in, then?"

"Both noisy and visible."

Wa'ats rocked back into a seated position. "Unless someone has a multicom band equipped with a passbeam."

The implications of that sent a shiver down She'er's spine. "Not impossible, but unlikely. Only bridge crew and security have that level of access. None of them left the ship during the checkpoint—standard operating procedure."

She'er sifted through memories from their original investigation. *Displacement normally involves a violent assault, during which a spawn is forcibly introduced into the host's brain through a facial orifice.* "Death normally occurs instantly following implantation, though visible manifestation *could* take an hour or more."

Wa'ats tried to stand, wobbled. She'er proffered a hand and Wa'ats took it with a nod. The chief's palm was sweat-dampened either from upset or the unusually warm quarters. "Are you suggesting Jon'na was attacked elsewhere and dumped here?"

"However improbable that seems, we should trace Jon'na's movements since boarding earlier today to determine where and when a prior attack could have occurred. In the meantime, I'll pull the logs from all multicoms equipped with passbeams and review usage for the past twenty-odd hours." She'er refocused on Jon'na. "*Where* and *how* aren't the only questions demanding answers. *Why* is the body here?"

"What do you mean?" Wa'ats's puzzled expression shifted to realization. "Mori left her spawn for us to find instead of hiding it somewhere to safely develop. She had to know once Jon'na was discovered we'd destroy the body."

"Exactly. Why would she willfully sacrifice a spawn?"

Wa'ats's brow furrowed. "Considering Displacers' fanatical devotion to their offspring, no matter how numerous, it doesn't make sense."

"Indeed. But Mori's true motives are rarely obvious." *Ah, the thrill of navigating the corridors of a twisted mind. How I've missed this!*

"What are you *smiling* about?"

"Nothing, sorry." She'er regained composure. "Mori may have hoped whoever found Jon'na would raise an alarm and incite panic among the passengers. Then we all would have been kept far too busy to pursue her. Still, if that's the case, why kill an enforcer instead of a passenger?"

Wa'ats sighed. "Remember I told you one of my detail was on the hook for Mori's escape? Jon'na was in charge of her escort to an extradition hearing the day she vanished. Though Jon'na testified that she'd already been turned over to The Scoyard's guards, the blowback of having been the IEA representative on the scene resulted in a severe reprimand. It prompted Jon'na to beg onto my Retrieval detail in pursuit of career redemption."

"So, we have a connection between victim and aggressor, however tenuous." She'er raked fingers through curls several times. "Mori could simply be out for revenge. She certainly tweaked your nose by taking out one of your people."

Wa'ats's breath caught. "If you're right, she might not be content with just the one. Thus eliminating the danger my detail poses to her plans *and* utterly humiliating me." Wa'ats tapped a lapel com pin. "Retrieval! Converge on—"

"Careful." She'er pulled Wa'ats's hand away. "Don't further her efforts by sending a stampede of enforcers through my ship, or you will create the very chaos she desires."

Wa'ats nodded, and She'er let go. "Belay that. Underchief Victria and Enforcer Clo'or, report to Enforcer Jon'na's quarters on Deck Three for a briefing immediately. Don't draw attention to your movements. Acknowledge."

Each responded in the affirmative. Wa'ats tapped off the com and looked so distraught that She'er impulsively offered a hug. "Courage, my dear. We bested Mori before and will again. Remember, logic over emotion. She preys on the latter."

"Easy for you to say." Wa'ats pulled away. "You're always able to remain detached, no matter whose feelings are involved."

She'er tried not to show how much Wa'ats's barb stung. "In my experience, rational detachment improves most situations."

The nearly forgotten Ca'ar interrupted with a throat-clearing noise. "Captain, Security is arriving."

Two more members of ship's security entered, pushing a gurney with a body bag on top of it. They were unexpectedly followed by Le'es. "Second?" said She'er. "There was no need for you to leave the bridge."

"I *beg* your indulgence, Captain," said Le'es, clasping hands and bowing too low again. "Given the tone of Crew Ca'ar's report I thought it best I oversee the disposition personally."

She'er considered Ca'ar's traumatized state and reluctantly agreed. "I trust in your discretion, then."

Le'es said curtly, "Of course, Captain," and immediately shifted attention to supervising the process.

Perhaps you'll make an effective First Seat yourself someday, Le'es. The older officer had served on multiple transgalactic cruisers, rising through the ranks to Second Seat shortly before joining the Ba'akre 221B's crew. She'er didn't know Le'es well despite their having worked together for a year, but had observed enough to ascertain Le'es was an ambitious sort.

The removal team wheeled Jon'na's body into the hallway. She'er was about to follow when Wa'ats said, "I didn't mean to dredge anything up."

She'er sighed and pulled Wa'ats to the far side of Jon'na's room. "Then why did you?"

"Because your continued deception is distracting!"

Taken aback, She'er demanded, "What do you mean?"

"Your enthusiasm at this horror confirms what I've suspected." Wa'ats poked the center of She'er's chest. "You *hate* that you gave up your career with the IEA. The only reason you pitched replacing the family I lost, as if that were a thing *anyone* could do, was to repay me for saving your life!"

Startled by Wa'ats's keen observation, She'er hesitated. *It's more than that. I just love you so much that I wanted to ease your pain.* "No, I...want a family. I *do*."

"Then why aren't we one already?" Wa'ats sucked in a breath and spoke more quietly. "You act like I don't understand how difficult it would be on you, or that morphing male would be a treat for me. I've done it before, remember, despite the discomfort and inconvenience."

"I'm well aware of what you did for your *first* spouse." She'er grimaced. *Stop it, you sound like a jealous teenager!*

"Like I told you before, your fear of how morphing female would affect you," Wa'ats tapped a temple, "is unreasonable."

"It's basic biochemistry," She'er retorted. "Multiple studies have identified a marked difference in mental acuity when Londlanders are in our natural asexual state as opposed to while female. Or male."

"It's *temporary*. You can morph back to normal right after weaning."

She'er sighed. "That isn't all there is to consider. We both know I received this commission largely because of my fame back home, and not due to experience or even my admittedly stellar marks on the captaincy assessments. Taking a couple years off when I've only occupied the First Seat for a year would be pushing my luck."

"Plenty of captains have families, love. They just take their children along on trips sometimes."

Arms folded tightly, She'er said, "It's all so simple for you, isn't it? And why not, when other than a brief physical change, parenthood wouldn't disrupt your life one whit!"

"Look, I'd be more than willing to be the one who morphed female if I were younger. Whatever it took to produce a child, and just as eagerly as I would have for Ma'ar."

"Yet even back then you didn't, and look how well *that* turned out." Wa'ats recoiled as though struck. "I…I'm sorry. I didn't mean to belittle that loss. I know you still mourn Ma'ar and your baby. Why do you think I want—"

Wa'ats's expression hardened into steel. "No, *I* apologize. This whole conversation is completely inappropriate." The chief marched out of the room.

She'er slowly counted to ten and followed, catching up to Wa'ats and the security team in the corridor just as a pair of enforcers arrived. "Please keep all civilians away from the crime scene, Captain," said Wa'ats, once more a model of professional detachment. "If, after my people's examination of Jon'na's quarters, we find anything you need to know, you'll be notified."

"Fine. I'll deploy the remainder of ship's Security to patrol covertly against subsequent attacks."

Without responding, Wa'ats directed the enforcers to search every inch of the crime scene. "I will accompany the body myself and see to its thorough examination before incineration."

She'er started to object, but decided against it. *Wa'ats won't listen anyway.*

And whose fault is that?

The captain stormed back to quarters, eager to refocus on the peaceful, emotionless complexity of deduction once more.

• • •

She'er drummed fingertips on the armrest of the First Seat, irritable from lack of sleep and attention split between overseeing the mundanities of shipboard operations, the case, and last night's row with Wa'ats. "Second, still no word from Chief Wa'ats?"

"No, Captain. Not since your spou…" She'er glared at Le'es. "Er, the chief dismissed me after we reached Refuse."

Is there really no evidence worth sharing with me, Wa'ats? Or are you so furious that you're excluding me from the investigation out of spite? She'er couldn't believe Wa'ats would do that, no matter how miffed, but it was harder to believe absolutely nothing of relevance had been found. Even a total absence of clues would be noteworthy.

"Captain?"

She'er blinked, wondering how long Third Seat Shil'lir had been standing there. "What is it?"

Flinching, Shil'lir thrust forth a thinscreen like a shield. "Begging your pardon, Captain. I have the reports you requested."

She'er snatched the thinscreen from the nervous junior officer's hands and immediately regretted it. *No wonder the crew is skittish around you.* She'er affected a genial tone. "Thank you, Third. Please continue reviewing the morning checklist with the Second Seat."

"Aye, Captain." Shil'lir retreated, obviously relieved to be assigned to a less mercurial supervisor.

She'er read through the comprehensive reports. Besides Jon'na's murder, there had been no suspicious incidents since the IEA's arrival, and no unauthorized use of a passbeam. Though not impossible for a determined villain to falsify a multicom's log, it was highly improbable.

"You had days. So why not displace anyone *before* the IEA boarded?" She'er muttered. "How did you infest Jon'na without a struggle? Did you drug—"

She'er realized the crew were casting confused glances in the First Seat's direction. *As one does when one's commanding officer natters aloud to nobody in particular.* "Second," She'er said gruffly, "please track down Chief Wa'ats. Third, assume the Second Seat."

"Yes, Captain," said Shil'lir, folding hands and bowing.

"Aye." Once again, Le'es's version was just exaggerated enough to cross from respectful to contemptuous.

Enough already! "You need to refine your acknowledgement of me, Second! It's this." She'er rose and demonstrated the precise salute. "Otherwise, you might as well be telling me to go screw myself! Unless that's *exactly* your intent?"

The entire bridge fell silent except for Shil'lir, who couldn't contain a small gasp. The crew quickly directed their full attention to their consoles.

Le'es's eyes blazed with such anger that She'er nearly backed up a step. Yet within the span of a blink the anger vanished, replaced with an affectation of subservience. Executing a flawless salute, Le'es said, "My apologies, *Captain*. I thank you for the lesson."

"Accepted." But suspicion fired She'er's senses as Le'es left the bridge, stiff posture and aggressively squared shoulders belying the apology.

"Captain?" said Shil'lir. "Incoming message from the IEA."

"Relay it." She'er remained distracted by Le'es's behavior, unable to find the sense in it. Nothing untoward had occurred between them before now to warrant such blatant animosity.

"Captain, Underchief Victria," said the enforcer in a Parancian accent. "Apologies for disturbing you, but Chief Wa'ats, is there?"

A flicker of dread. "No. Why do you ask?"

"The chief missed our morning briefing and has responded to hails not at all."

She'er clutched the back of the First Seat. *Wa'ats is utterly scrupulous about such things.* Meaning this lack of contact might not be a fit of pique after all. "No, I haven't heard from my...your chief since last night. I just sent my Second to—"

She'er froze. *Oh, I am a fool. A rusty, blind idiot!*

"Captain?" Victria said tentatively.

"Please rendezvous with me in Refuse immediately. I believe Chief Wa'ats is in grave danger." *Or worse, after so many hours have passed.* "Be prepared for containment, as I suspect your quarry will also be waiting."

"As you say, Captain. We meet there within twenty minutes, yes?"

"I will be there in five. Kindly accelerate your timetable." She'er ended contact without awaiting a response. "Third Seat, assume the First."

"I, uh, really? I mean, aye, Captain!"

She'er crossed the bridge in five long strides, opened the weapons locker, and withdrew a suppressor. It wouldn't offer much protection, but it was all that was available since they weren't a military vessel. After double-checking that it was fully charged, the captain sprinted off the bridge.

A vice tightened around She'er's heart. *Wa'ats was right that someone used a passbeam to enter Jon'na's room, but wrong about Mori boarding during the checkpoint.* No, she'd mimicked someone *before* their trip began, and been onboard all along. It wasn't beyond her capabilities to have transmitted false intel to lure Wa'ats, while delaying her first attack to coincide with the IEA's arrival in order to maintain her cover.

Ah, Le'es. All those little affronts. Insisting on overseeing Jon'na's disposition personally—but not out of devotion to duty.

To rescue a spawn from incineration.

• • •

She'er listened intently, but it was difficult to hear anything over the steady susurrus coming from the huge incinerator at the center of Refuse. The steel-plated walls and flooring trapped the moist heat, making the air oppressive.

"Captain? Good, I found something for you." She'er whirled and aimed the suppressor at Le'es, whose gaze traveled slowly down the barrel. Le'es raised both hands. "Uh, there's no need for that."

"Oh, I beg to differ." She'er kept the weapon trained dead center of Le'es's chest. "I know who you are."

They glared at one another for several heartbeats. Then: "Permission to speak plainly, Captain?"

"Please do."

Le'es's deferential expression dissolved into a sneer. "This just proves you're utterly unqualified for command. By the Hound's bloody claws, how you managed to snatch the First Seat at all, let alone hold onto it for a *year*, is unfathomable."

She'er blinked. "I'm not here to discuss my qualifications with a murderous megalomaniac, thank you very much. Where is Chief Wa'ats?"

"Oh, right. Your wayward spouse." Le'es made a *tsking* sound. "This way."

They walked toward a storeroom behind the incinerator, where racks of broken and obsolete machinery were stored. "I figured I'd retrace the chief's steps starting from where we last saw one other. Turns out I didn't have to go beyond my first stop."

Le'es pointed to an archway leading into the storeroom. "I'd just spotted the chief when you showed up. Probably indulged in a bit too much irewhisk." A derisive snort. "You've driven me to do the same more than once. Being *married* to you must require barrels' worth."

This isn't going quite as expected. She'er moved cautiously past Le'es and backed into the narrow, dimly lit room. The sight of a figure on the med gurney (*why wasn't that removed after the incineration?*) quickly captured the captain's full attention.

"Wa'ats!" Shoving the suppressor into a belt holster, She'er dashed over and began examining the motionless chief. *Still alive, thank the Hound's Keeper.* But Wa'ats was breathing raggedly, eyes closed. Closer examination revealed bruises, including a sizeable one purpling the left temple. Dried blood formed rivulets from the injury.

Fury tinting everything red, She'er charged at Le'es, who was propelled backward against the incineration unit. "I'll see the life *fried* out of you for this, Mori!"

"Mori...who? What are you going on about—*ow!*" Le'es struggled but She'er pinned the Second Seat against the steel casing. "You're *burning* me, you maniac!"

"I ought to toss you right into this incinerator, along with that spawn I'm sure you rescued! I *knew* you wouldn't sacrifice it. Unfortunately for you both, the IEA will be joining us momentarily!"

"Well, thank the Hound's Keeper for that," gasped Le'es, face aglow from the sweltering heat. "I'll have more than your captaincy for this. You should be locked away!"

"As you will be again, soon. Which is the least you deserve!"

Something isn't right. She'er tamped down the emotions preventing rational thought. Why wasn't Mori shifting into her natural form and fighting back? And what was it about *this* form—

By the Hound Below! She'er released Le'es, who scuttled toward the storeroom. The Second braced each hand against the sides of the archway and wheezed, uniform soaked with perspiration.

"You *aren't* Mori," said the captain, stunned. "Amrighans don't sweat. Why would she bother simulating it once her cover was blown?"

"What...who's this Mori you keep ranting about?" Le'es panted.

She'er clutched a double-handful of hair. "Oh, I am *stale.* How could I be so wrong?"

Awash in a nauseating wave of self-recrimination, She'er didn't realize the IEA detail had arrived until an enforcer spoke in a familiar Parancian accent. "Captain, what is the situation? The chief is located, no?"

"Yes, Underchief Victria." She'er struggled for poise. "Injured, but alive."

"Thank the Keeper," said Le'es, reaching toward Victria. "The captain's mind has snapped. You need to arrest—"

Le'es's body went rigid, mouth still working, though all that came out was a high-pitched rattle. A thin stream of blood followed. The center of Le'es's torso had been hollowed out. She'er recognized the black-rimmed, bloodless hole as the distinctive result of an exterminator fired at close range. Tidy, but fatal.

Le'es toppled to the floor with a clang of skull against steel as

Wa'ats appeared in the archway, exterminator in hand. Its muzzle still glowed faintly.

"Chief! You are well." Victria holstered her exterminator and signaled the rest of the detail to follow suit.

"Wa'ats," said She'er, relief warring with shock. "Are you all right?"

"Thanks to you." Wa'ats pointed to Le'es's body. "Had you not turned up I've no doubt Mori would have finished the job she began last night. Once our attention was focused on examining Jon'na's remains, Mori shifted into her true form and attacked."

"Did she?" She'er's heart sank. *You already know that cannot be!*

"Unfortunately, Mori had the element of surprise. First, she decapitated Ca'ar," said Wa'ats, as though reciting a lesson. "Then she made quick work of the rest. Of course I tried to intervene, but you know how strong Amrighans are in their natural form."

Wa'ats's uniform had sweat stains under the arms. "Indeed I do," murmured She'er. "So where are their bodies?"

"Probably not enough left to displace, so she incinerated them." Wa'ats holstered the exterminator and stepped over Le'es to embrace She'er. "Looks as if you're *my* hero this time."

She'er struggled not to resist the embrace while studying Wa'ats's face. "That head injury…looks nasty. We should get you to Medbay."

"First, we must find Jon'na's body before maturation." Wa'ats addressed Victria. "Underchief, begin searching. I'm confident Mori stashed her here to gestate in this warm, secluded space. It's perfect for cold-blooded beings like Amrighans."

Her. "Start with the storeroom," said She'er.

Victria looked to Wa'ats, who smiled briefly before nodding. "But of course," she said, and led the detail into the storeroom.

She'er fought to sound calm. "When I found you lying in there—"

"Poor dear." Wa'ats cupped the captain's jaw with a cold, dry palm. "You must have been simply overwrought."

MY DEAR WA'ATS | 111

"Chief?" Victria's voice, tinged with uncertainty, echoed from the storeroom. "Someone is here."

"How did you recover your senses so quickly?" She'er pushed Wa'ats away. "And since when would you make a kill shot, from *behind*, when you had the drop on a prisoner?"

"Why," said Wa'ats coyly, "when my beloved spouse is about to be torn limb from limb."

"Chief Wa'ats?" Victria sounded alarmed. "Wait, what is this?"

"One moment, love." Wa'ats winked, strode over to the archway—and drew the exterminator.

She'er hesitated only a moment before charging after Wa'ats. "Victria! *Take cover!*"

Wa'ats swung an arm suddenly armored in chitin and ending in a sizable claw. It struck She'er in the solar plexus. Breath fled and the world cartwheeled past, until an abrupt impact released an eruption of pain. Searing, it flowed from the base of the captain's skull to suffuse each limb. Vision faded into a haze of gray and black.

Eventually, She'er became aware of screams, though it took somewhat longer to comprehend their dire meaning. She'er clawed at the steel wall, struggling to rise. *Wrong again! Mori didn't board in Londland or at the checkpoint. No passbeam was needed. Jon'na simply recognized a friendly face and welcomed in a murderer.*

As did you.

An agony far worse than physical pain sent She'er sliding back into a heap. *Mori mimicked Wa'ats. And if that's true—Wa'ats must be dead.*

Overwhelmed with grief, She'er didn't notice the slaughter had ended until Wa'ats's voice said, "Sorry about the interruption, love. Where were we?"

Looking up at the beloved, false face made it nearly impossible to do anything but ache. Existence without Wa'ats would be impossible, meaningless. There had to be another explanation, however improbable.

So find it!

"Ah, yes." Wa'ats—no, Mori—stood over She'er, lips twitching upward at the corners. "You were just realizing what a fool I'd made of you. Although, in your defense, you are more than a bit out of practice when it comes to the fine art of deduction."

She'er struggled into something closer to a sitting position. Anguish warred with hatred, but She'er refused to give Mori the satisfaction of falling apart. *Wa'ats always accused you of being too much a creature of reason. Your only hope is to live up to that criticism.*

"Now, don't be too hard on yourself. After all, it's that spouse of yours' fault that you've wasted the last year play-pretending at being a captain." Mori chuckled. "How ridiculous! What a *waste* of your sacred gifts. Why, Wa'ats deserved to die for insulting my best enemy like that alone."

It hurt to breathe. *Cracked ribs. At least two broken.* "You're right. I am out of practice. Indulge me?"

"Why not." Mori sank onto her haunches. "After all, I'll soon be too busy tending my new brood to have time for adult conversation. Though you could never be my peer, being a disgusting Londlander eunuch, I *do* find you less contemptible than the rest of your kind."

"You have no idea. What that means. To me." Each movement sent fresh bolts of pain down both legs. *Compressed vertebrae. Possibly fractured.* "Why kill. An enforcer first?"

"I recognized Jon'na from that hellish confinement into which you and your dead lover cast me." Mori yawned. "But you know this. Come, be clever for me."

She keeps mentioning Wa'ats to drive that stake deeper into my heart. Hope flared, and with it renewed strength. "If you mimicked Wa'ats long before the IEA boarded, as you clearly want me to believe, why not displace anyone sooner? Why waste the opportunity to displace *me*?"

"Right away?" Mori smirked. "No sport in that."

Ominous, but not an answer. "Fine, then why leave Jon'na to be discovered?"

"All part of the game, She'er." Mori's natural sibilance leaked through, blurring her words. "I wanted to ruin you by making you suspect and ideally execute one of your crew. Did you have any idea how much the Second Seat detested you? It took *me* hardly any time to notice it, figure out why, and use it against you. Londland rescinded Le'es's opportunity to command this cruiser in order to gift it to you. Their *hero*."

Well, that explains Le'es, albeit too late to make amends. She'er slid a hand behind while trying to sit up straighter, but even that slight movement was too much. Vision shrank to a tunnel view. However, it did confirm the suppressor was still in its holster, just twisted around back.

Mori was so close their noses nearly touched. "You were almost a match for me, once. I don't say that lightly, particularly to an un-Amrighan thing. Yet you abandoned your true calling at the behest of a controlling spouse to wither away on this glorified *ferry*, on which a grasping simpleton like Le'es dared condescend to you!" She patted She'er's cheek hard enough to bruise. "You're fortunate I arrived, so I could free you from their degradations."

"That was a neat trick. Escaping prison. Infiltrating the very detail sent to hunt you down."

Mori batted her eyes. "You're impressed."

"Wa'ats—*you* told me The Scoyard blamed your IEA escort in part for your getaway. Was that true?"

"Yes. Why?"

Finally, the pieces fit. "So, Jon'na was in close proximity to you. Perhaps a bit too close?"

Mori's eyes narrowed. "Well, now, isn't *that* an interesting theory?" The hum underlying her words grew more pronounced. "But how do you explain seeing that particular unfortunate in the process of becoming mine with your own eyes?"

"A performance. No wonder the quarters were so warm. You posed as Jon'na and used mimicry to *simulate* displacement. Then we made the very error you knew we would—fail to examine the body for life signs before removal. Why would we when it was clearly transforming? A simple, yet quite effective, bluff."

Mori applauded. "Ah, your mind! So creative." Her humor abruptly vanished. "I mimicked a random guard who fed me that day. Then I infiltrated IEA headquarters by mimicking a member of the cleaning staff, until one fateful night when poor, lonely Wa'ats was working late. I slaughtered and disposed of your beloved, then used all that lovely IEA data at my fingertips to find you, concoct a false lead, and bring a detail onto your ship."

Her voice buzzed as it swelled. "You took from me, so I took from you. For my freedom. For my beloved spawn, slaughtered after you revealed my plans on Gerany. Can you even comprehend the depth of a mother's love? She wants to give her children everything—worlds, *galaxies*. And she would destroy *everyone* to avenge them."

"You're right. I can't understand it." The honesty of the admission surprised She'er. "But here's what I *do* know. You're a liar, as well as a psychotic, xenophobic monster." She'er tightened fingers around the suppressor, using every ounce of discipline to ignore the waves of pain surging one after the other. "I also know Jon'na never boarded this ship, and Wa'ats is *not* dead!"

Mori smirked. "How?"

"The simulated perspiration was a nice touch. Just enough to make me think you'd learned your lesson from our previous encounter, not enough to prevent my suspecting Wa'ats." She'er caressed Mori's right temple with trembling fingers. "Yet this time you made an even more egregious error."

Mori's whispered in She'er's ear, "Which is?"

"That bruise on your head? It's on the *wrong side*." Before Mori could react She'er drew the suppressor, jammed the muzzle under her chin, and fired.

Mori reeled backward as electricity crackled through her skull. She'er all but fell after her, firing repeatedly, knowing the suppressor didn't have the deadly force needed. *If I can just disrupt her cellular control—*

Mori's screech bloomed into a buzzing roar like a thousand

swarming beasps. Her mimicry of Wa'ats dissolved as she lashed out, knocking the suppressor from She'er's hand.

She'er crawled toward the storeroom, gasping for breath with each agonizing movement. The only chance for survival was getting hold of a fallen enforcer's exterminator. *Ignore the pain. Focus on the task. One inch, now another. Do it for Wa'ats if not yourself!*

Abruptly, She'er was flipped over and staring up into the compound eyes of Mori in her true form. Her four mandibles opened, up and down, side to side. "Why didn't I just kill Wa'ats. *Ask!*"

"W—why?"

"Because Wa'ats wants you to bear a child. Meanwhile, you'd rather have your head snipped off than reproduce." She snapped her pincers close to She'er's ear. "You're about as maternal a creature as that incinerator! Yet you offered, because you sought parity with the late, beloved Ma'ar."

"It has nothing to do with—"

"Please. I know it, because *Wa'ats* knows it." She clacked her mandibles in the Amrighan version of a chuckle. "How sweet of you to sacrifice your desires for your spouse's. And won't it be *de-li-cious* when Wa'ats awakens to find the child you're incubating—is *mine*!"

Pincers clamped around the captain's neck and left wrist. Trapped and suffocating, She'er couldn't struggle, couldn't even scream, as Mori spread her mandibles and extended her thick proboscis. The tip dilated and clamped over She'er's mouth in a horrific mockery of a kiss.

But then Mori jerked back. Her proboscis retracted and the pincer pinning She'er's arm released.

"*Get off of my spouse!*"

Mori let go of She'er's throat, reared back, and screeched. She'er blinked several times to regain focus, and saw her entire right arm lying on the floor nearby.

Wa'ats, features contorted with determination and fury, staggered over and fired again, but missed. Mori started after

Wa'ats, and She'er seized the opportunity to roll toward the incinerator, both to afford Wa'ats clearer aim and discourage firing toward the combustible unit.

The next blast severed Mori's right leg at the knee. She dropped to the floor with another scream, then swiveled and began dragging herself after She'er again. "We shall meet your Hound together!" she hissed.

Wa'ats appeared above her and jammed the exterminator's muzzle against the back of her neck stalk. Another burst, and Mori's head tumbled to the floor. Her body twitched forward another inch or two, clacking pincer nearly reaching She'er's feet before finally lying still.

She'er moaned and curled into a fetal position, shivering despite the heat. Then Wa'ats was there, cradling She'er gently. "It's okay. You're safe now."

"I knew." She'er struggled to focus on Wa'ats's face. Even bruised and creased with worry, it was a heartening sight. "You couldn't be. Gone. The universe wouldn't bear such. Injustice."

Wa'ats's voice receded. "Hold on, love. Help is coming. Please, don't leave—"

That was all.

• • •

It took months, first in the hospital on Parance then back home, but She'er eventually recovered, save for the occasional discomfort. Wa'ats provided such good care that on reflection the former First Seat remarked, "Perhaps you missed your calling. You would have made a wonderful physician."

Wa'ats snorted. "That career would fit me about as well as captaining the Ba'akre 221B suited you."

She'er shrugged and took another sip of Londlandian greytea. "I was an excellent captain."

"Of course. You're pathologically incapable of not excelling at whatever you do." Wa'ats picked up a filescreen and waggled it at She'er. "Nevertheless, it wasn't where you belonged."

She'er set the cup down on Wa'ats's desk. "Are you sure about all this? My returning to the IEA." A pause. "Not having children."

Wa'ats smiled briefly. "Mori was right. That wasn't what you wanted and we both knew it. Selfishly, I hoped that the idea would grow on you. Then when I saw Mori about to force herself on you, to make you—I realized I was doing the same thing." She'er started to object but Wa'ats plowed on. "No, not literally, but I was still pushing you to do something you didn't want. To become someone you didn't want to be."

"I shouldn't have gotten your hopes up."

"It's okay, really." Wa'ats smiled tenderly. "What I want more than a child, more than anything? Is for you to be the She'er I married. My partner in every way. Eager for the next challenge. Happy."

"Mori was right about another thing. A parent should want a child fiercely, be willing to do anything and everything for them." Choking up unexpectedly, She'er mumbled, "For whatever reason, that's just not in me. I—I'm sorry."

"Don't you dare." Wa'ats tapped She'er on the head with the filescreen. "Enough. The IEA doesn't pay us to sit around gabbing over greytea. Are you ready?"

She'er took another moment to look around IEA headquarters. Sterile walls. Serviceable furnishings. Stacks of filescreens filled with unsolved cases. *I'm finally home.*

The freshly reinstated Chief Investigator stood and snatched the filescreen from Wa'ats's hand. "You know me, my dear Wa'ats. My mind rebels at stagnation!"

A SCANDAL IN CHELM

BY DANIEL M. KIMMEL

We had just finished the afternoon Mincha prayers at the *shteibl*—the little room—at the back of Rabbi Shlomo's home at 221B Babka Street. Renowned as the Sage of Chelm, it was not surprising to find visiting strangers among those who came to services. It was a byword that one had not really experienced Chelm without partaking of Rabbi Shlomo's wisdom.

There was never trouble getting a *minyan*, a quorum of ten men, and there wasn't an empty bench to be had today. Following the Mourner's Kaddish the men usually filed out quickly, returning to their trades, as Rabbi Shlomo's weekday Mincha rarely took more than ten minutes. Today, however, a mysterious stranger made no sign of taking his leave. I took note of his shabby coat and his shuffling walk—my time as a disciple of Rabbi Shlomo had greatly improved my powers of observation—and deduced that he was some *shnorrer* hoping for a handout before moving on. I took a couple of kopeks from my pocket to offer to him, but to my surprise Rabbi Shlomo blocked my way.

"Velvel," he said to me, "Allow me to introduce the Grand Rabbi of Lublin, Yitzhak ben Shmuel ha-Cohen."

My amazement that this beggar could be a "Grand Rabbi" was only surpassed by our guest's reaction. "Reb Shlomo," he said, "your abilities are legendary but how could you possibly have known it was me? We've never met. I deliberately disguised myself as a poor man..."

Rabbi Shlomo chuckled. "It wasn't much of a disguise. It wouldn't have fooled the most simple child. You neglected to remove the price tag from the sleeve of your overcoat. You're wearing shoes that have clearly just been introduced to the unpaved roads of our village. And the subtle Lublin accent was easily detectable in your *davening*. I'm sure even my disciple Velvel was able to easily see that you were not who you seemed to be."

"That's incredible," he replied.

"Not at all, although by the time Velvel recounts it, it will no doubt seem as if I had read your mind."

As usual, now that he had explained the process by which he had come to his conclusion, it seemed obvious. However, I was still not clear how he had figured out our guest's identity. "Rabbi Shlomo, you never cease to amaze, but how could you possibly have known that this was Grand Rabbi Yitzhak?"

"That was the easiest thing of all. I just received a new commentary on the Talmud tractate 'Sayings of the Fathers,' and it included a rather flattering likeness of the great scholar who wrote it." He plucked a book from the table where he usually studied and showed us an inside page. It was, indeed, a pen and ink portrait of our visitor.

"And now," he continued, "if you'd like to join me for a glass of tea, I should like to know what brings such a distinguished visitor to my humble abode." He turned to me. "Please stay, Velvel. I suspect your assistance will be invaluable."

We were shortly situated in Rabbi Shlomo's study. The walls were lined with shelves filled with holy books and commentaries. I had spent many hours here since coming to Chelm, and been privileged to participate in and record many of Rabbi Shlomo's adventures as he unraveled mysteries brought to him from near and far. There was the curious case of the *chazzan*, or cantor, who did *not* chant Kol Nidre on the night of Yom Kippur, as well as the baffling case of the missing *afikomen*, where an entire Passover seder ground to a halt until it was found, but those stories will have to wait for another day. For the moment, I joined Rabbi Shlomo in focusing on our guest, who was sipping the hot tea through a sugar cube he held in his teeth.

"For you to have come all the way from Lublin must mean this is a matter of great import. Our Borscht Festival isn't until next spring, and there aren't many other attractions here in Chelm."

Rabbi Yitzhak put down his half-emptied glass and turned to Rabbi Shlomo. "There is indeed something here, and it is a matter of great delicacy." He glanced at me as if uncertain whether he should continue.

"You have nothing to fear from Velvel," he assured our guest. "He is the soul of discretion."

"But what about his stories about you?"

Rabbi Shlomo chuckled. "Colorful exaggerations. And he knows which stories not to tell."

I nodded in agreement. "Do you know the story of the scholar who ate a suckling pig?"

Rabbi Yitzhak looked shocked. "What sort of man of learning would eat such *treif?*"

"One who ordered a baked apple and found it served in the pig's mouth. By the time Rabbi Shlomo was through with the case, the man had become a vegetarian."

"And who…?"

"See?" interrupted Rabbi Shlomo. "Not only has he omitted the foolish man's name, but it is a story that will remain unpublished. You can speak freely, Reb Yitzhak. You have nothing to fear."

Seemingly reassured, our visitor slumped back in his seat. "Well, then, I best get on with it. My son Menesseh is scheduled to be married next month…"

"Mazel tov," interjected Rabbi Shlomo, raising his own glass of tea in a toast.

"If only it was that simple. He had a rival for his betrothed's hand who has said he will not allow the wedding to take place."

Rabbi Shlomo sat up in his seat. "Please go on."

"There's not much more to tell. Just a vague threat."

I could no longer keep quiet. "With all due respect, Grand

Rabbi, it's hard to believe you would go through all the trouble of coming here in disguise on the basis of a vague threat."

"Indeed," agreed Rabbi Shlomo. "There's something you're not telling us."

The Grand Rabbi seemed to sink in on himself. Finally, in a barely audible voice, he said, "Yes, there is something more. He said that if the wedding takes place he will destroy my son's reputation."

"In what way?"

"There was mention of an incriminating photograph with my son dressed disgracefully in women's clothes. If this is made public it will destroy him…and me."

"Is your son a *feigeleh*?" I blurted out.

"Velvel, please…"

"It's all right, Reb Shlomo," said Rabbi Yitzhak, who then turned on me. "No, he is not someone in forbidden relations with men, but clearly that is what is being implied. The accusation alone would be enough to ruin his reputation and call off the wedding."

"But if it's not true…"

"It doesn't matter. I don't know how you deal with such matters in Chelm, but in Lublin people look the other way so long as they can. A photograph of my son cavorting in women's clothes would cross the line. It is imperative that we stop this before it can happen."

• • •

"I understand completely," said Rabbi Shlomo. "We need to confront this blackmailer and ensure this never happens. Velvel, make arrangements for us to travel to Lublin at once."

A chance to travel and see the world beyond Chelm promised a great adventure indeed. However, Rabbi Yitzhak put up his hand. "There's no need to travel to Lublin," he said. "The miscreant is right here in Chelm. In fact, he was at your minyan."

"Here?" I asked, incredulously. "Who was it?"

"Meir the butcher."

If Rabbi Shlomo was shocked at this revelation, he hid it well. "Rabbi Yitzhak, the matter is in good hands."

• • •

We stood on the street outside Reb Meir's butcher shop watching the customers come and go. As not only a purveyor of meat but also the *shochet*, the town's ritual slaughterer, Meir was a prominent and well-to-do figure. Confronting him would not be easy.

"You know, Velvel, there's no reason to feel intimidated because he is a man of means," said Rabbi Shlomo as we waited for a lull in the shop. "If I had chosen to be a *shochet* instead of a rabbi, I'd make even more money than Meir."

I studied the rabbi, awaiting his sage insight, but when he said nothing more I had to ask. "How so?"

Rabbi Shlomo smiled. "I'd do a little teaching on the side."

I was about to respond when he grabbed my arm. Meir was serving Mrs. Adler, the widow of Nahum the shoemaker. He had handed her two packages, one the size of a small chicken, the other one large and boxy. She placed them both in her bag. She was leaving the shop just as we reached the door.

"A pleasure to see you, Mrs. Adler," said the rabbi with an expression I had not previously associated with him. He seemed almost taken aback in her presence.

She seemed a bit flustered herself, wishing us a hasty "*Gut Shabbes*," before scurrying off down the street.

"Most odd, Velvel, most odd," said the rabbi as we entered the shop. "Surely you noticed?"

"How could I miss it?" I said. "She wished us a happy Sabbath and it's only Monday."

"Clearly she was flustered. And surely even the hungriest widow could not eat such a quantity of meat in short order."

"Perhaps she was picking up an order for a neighbor?"

"No, Velvel, in my studies on how meat is wrapped at the

butcher, I've never seen a large box before. I do not believe that was meat at all."

Once again I was astounded at the rabbi's powers of observation, but I was startled further at the notion that he had taken time away from the Talmud to focus on how meat gets wrapped. "What great purpose is there in knowing such things if you are not a butcher yourself?"

"Ah, Velvel, how else am I to know whose invitation for Shabbes dinner I should accept? But now, let's focus on the matter at hand."

We approached the counter and waited for Meir the butcher to return. When he did I was taken by his size and his formidable arms, strengthened by slaughtering and carving up the cows and chickens that came his way.

"Rabbi Shlomo," he beamed at the rabbi, then acknowledged my presence with a polite nod, "Velvel. To what do I owe this pleasure? Are you looking for a nice piece of flanken?

"Not today, Reb Meir, though your flanken is the closest I will come to manna in this lifetime," said the rabbi.

Meir beamed in response. "Then what may I do for the Sage of Chelm?"

"I'm curious how you know Menesseh ben Yitzhak."

If I expected Meir to confess upon being confronted, I was sorely disappointed. Instead, he looked Rabbi Shlomo in the eye and calmly replied, "We went to *cheder* together as children. There was only one boys' school there at the time, so of course we were all together. I grew up in Lublin and only came to Chelm when I apprenticed to the previous butcher. Why is this of interest? Do you know Menesseh?"

"I've not had the pleasure, but I have some business with his father, the Grand Rabbi. Did you know Menesseh is getting married?"

"I'd not heard," replied Meir without missing a beat, "but then, I don't get much news from Lublin these days."

After a few more moments of chitchat we took our leave, with

Meir promising to hold some flanken for the rabbi for Shabbes. When we were on the street, Rabbi Shlomo said that we must, at once, go to the shoemaker's widow. "Meir is clearly on his guard now. It's highly unlikely the photograph is at the butcher shop any longer."

We headed to the outskirts of town where the shoemaker's shop was situated. Mrs. Adler had maintained her late husband's business, using an apprentice to do the actual work. Eventually, he would take it over and pay her an annuity for her declining years. At the moment, though, she appeared in the peak of health. Indeed, she did not seem at all surprised at our arrival.

"Rabbi Shlomo, I've been expecting you. I assume Meir told you nothing."

I was startled at her forthrightness. I had worked out a cover story about needing a heel repaired, which would give Rabbi Shlomo time to investigate the premises. I'd have to save that story for another day and another shoemaker's widow.

"My dear Mrs. Adler, I'm glad that business is doing so well that you can afford chicken on a weekday."

She coughed into her handkerchief. "I'm making some soup. You know what they say. When a poor man slaughters a chicken for soup, either he's sick or the chicken is."

"Yes, and when a widow carries two packages from the butcher, one of them is clearly not a chicken."

The widow sighed, and then, after a brief hesitation, bent down to remove something from a shelf behind the counter. She pulled it out and placed it for us to see. It was a photo album. "I should have known it was useless. Meir asked me to hold onto this, as he thinks he's going to prevent a childhood rival from marrying someone back in Lublin. He asked me to hide it as he was afraid someone would try to break into the butcher shop to steal it. He's a kind, generous man in many ways, but he's also a bit of fool."

"It's why he fits in so well in Chelm," I offered.

Mrs. Adler and Rabbi Shlomo ignored me. "I assume this album contains the incriminating photograph?" asked the rabbi.

"There is no incriminating photograph, Rabbi Shlomo. Let me show you."

She opened the album and flipped a few pages. When she found what she was looking for she spun it around for us to see. It was a group of young boys performing in a *Purimshpiel*, a comic and frivolous skit done as part of the joyous Purim celebration, commemorating the story in the Book of Esther. Such activities were common throughout the land. I wasn't sure what we were supposed to be looking at.

"You see the eight-year-old with the mop on his head? That's Menesseh playing Queen Vashti. This is the photo Meir thought would stop a wedding."

"May I?" asked Rabbi Shlomo as he lifted up the album and examined the picture closely. After a moment, he put it down. "Mrs. Adler, you are quite right. Meir is an excellent butcher, but he is a fool. Even if the damaging implication he hoped would stop the wedding were true, he cannot disseminate this particular photo as proof."

Mrs. Adler nodded. "Of course. It's trivial. Many boys have done such things in their Purim cavorting."

"It's more than that, Mrs. Adler. Look who's playing Queen Esther off to the side."

She turned the album around and picked it up to look closely at the photograph. "Why that's..."

"Yes, it's Meir the butcher. If he thought this childhood antic would embarrass Menesseh, how would he explain his own actions? It could only double back on him." Rabbi Shlomo turned to me. "Come, Velvel, we must find the Grand Rabbi and reassure him that the wedding of his son will occur as planned."

We began to take our leave. "Rabbi," said Mrs. Adler, "What shall I tell Meir?"

The rabbi favored her with a broad smile. "Tell him to prepare an order of flanken for Friday night. It would be my privilege to share a Shabbes meal with you."

"I shall do so at once," she said, with what seemed to be a twinkle in her eye.

"And now Velvel and I must take our leave. It is almost time for the evening service, and all this talk of flanken has made me hungry for dinner."

THE AFFAIR OF THE GREEN CRAYON

BY STEPHANIE M. MCPHERSON

The soft clinks of metal on metal started at dawn. Dark gray haze from a mid-November sunrise teased through the gnarled remains of the old trees outside my window, mutating their silhouettes into looming monsters. I'd just started brushing my teeth by the dim light of my vanity when the scratches caught my attention.

I approached the entryway, careful not to alert the prowler that I'd caught onto his designs. The noises stopped. I watched the door handle. I imagined the figure on the other side doing the same. Then a shuffling of fabric betrayed the would-be intruder's intentions to switch lock-picking tools. My chance had come.

I flung the chain off its hook and wrenched the door open.

"Watson!" A tall, angular man looked surprised to see me open my own front door.

"Sherlock!" I replied, extending my arm to welcome him into my home.

"Well done, I suppose." He strode in, spun himself on his heel, and landed his slim frame hard on the armchair by my fireplace, where he started tinkering with wood and matches. "I had been under the impression you'd be scrubbing away at your teeth."

"Oh, I was," I shouted from the kitchen. I emerged with a carafe of fresh coffee and a few warm scones. "I was," I repeated, settling by the fire. "But, believe it or not, I'm able to distinguish the sound of bristle on enamel from the scraping of metal."

"Consistently surprising, John." He bit into the scone, slouched back, and stared at the ceiling.

"Still, though," I said through a mouthful of crumbs. "I had the chain up. You'd have been out of luck." He moved only his eyes to look at me as though he pitied my lack of imagination.

Sherlock Holmes and I met five years ago on the first day of term at the prestigious Baker School, a charming private elementary school ensconced in the hills of New Hampshire. I had just been hired as head nurse after years as an army medic capped off with nursing school. Holmes was starting as a fifth grade general education teacher, embarking on his first true profession after years of chasing degrees.

We'd been living down the hall from one another in an old converted mill for the past year. Each morning Holmes tried to break into my apartment by one method or another. Each morning I tried to outwit him. The balance stood in his favor.

"How was your day yesterday?" I inquired. "Any new little problems to solve?" The staff at Baker School had been employing Sherlock's unique intellect to arrive at speedy resolutions to petty problems around campus, thus avoiding the involvement of the police—or worse, the parents.

"Quite the little drama," he replied. "Someone stole Bobby Simmons's green crayon during art class."

"Oh, you might need to delve deep into your resources to solve this one."

• • •

"Something foul is afoot at the Baker School!" Sherlock's frame overtook my doorway.

"Do tell," I said, not looking up from the bandage I was applying to little Sarah's knee.

"Benjamin saw a strange woman skulking about in the woods yesterday. Probably one of the teachers, but I've found children have difficulty identifying familiar faces in unfamiliar settings. I should add exercises to improve that skill that to my curriculum."

"I saw a man in the woods today," Sarah piped in. "That's what me and James were fighting about when I fell. He said I was being weird and creepy, and so I pushed him, and so he pushed me back."

"Well," I said, looking at Sherlock. He looked dubious as to the little witness's credibility. "Why don't we all go together to tell the principal what you saw?" I suggested. I whispered to Sherlock to collect Benjamin and meet us in the front office.

Principal Lester was an amiable, capable man who'd worked his way through administrations across New England before becoming the head of the Baker School. I quite liked him, though his staid adherence to the norm clashed with Sherlock's distaste for the current state of education. We sat on the other side of the desk from him behind the children, as though we were grandiose shadow projections of their much smaller frames.

"Yesterday, I saw a lady in the woods," started Benjamin. "She was just kind of looking at some trees."

"It wasn't a lady, it was a man, stupid. And it was today," Sarah interrupted.

"Come on, now, Sarah," I admonished. "There's no need to call Benjamin stupid."

"Well," Sherlock muttered under his breath as I leaned back in my chair. "I've graded his exams…" I shook my head quickly, and he settled back into silence.

"Were either of these people one of the teachers?" Lester asked.

Benjamin shook his head. "Nope," said Sarah, simply and surely.

"Well, thank you both for reporting what you saw," said Lester. He released the children but bade us stay in our chairs.

"Listen, Mr. Holmes, I'd appreciate you looking into this for us."

"Oh, come on, Lester. Kids play pretend all the time, convince themselves it's real. I'm sure this is nothing more than a case of overactive imaginations."

"Regardless," Lester held up his hand to preempt the rest of Sherlock's inevitable rant. "I don't want word getting out that we're doing nothing about the possibility of strange adults prowling around the school woods. Do whatever it is you need to do to satisfy yourself that your initial perceptions are correct."

• • •

The clock read 5:59 a.m. It took me a moment to realize the sharp rapping that woke me was neither my alarm nor someone repeatedly cracking eggs over my head, as my dream would have had me believe. I hauled on the sweatpants that lived in a crumpled pile at the bottom of my bed and hurried to the door.

"There's been a murder." Sherlock stood in a dark coat, a coffee in each hand. In the safety lights of the hallway he looked almost excited.

"There's been a....what? I'm sorry, what?"

"A murder. At Baker School. You'll need to put on better pants. I'll wait."

In a confused pre-dawn haze, unsure I wasn't still dreaming, I prepared myself for a day at school. Though if what he had told me was true, there would be no class today. Last night, when he came by for a few rounds of chess, he'd told me nothing in the woods was out of the norm. But now he was staring at the ceiling as I locked up. I could almost see through his hair and skull to the suspicions sparking across his brain. I accepted my coffee, and we got into my car in silence.

"Sherlock, who—" I started, but he interrupted with a sharp "No." He remained silent as we pulled into the parking lot of the Baker School. A rainstorm had blustered through town over the weekend and knocked most of the remaining rust and honey leaves from their trees, ringing the school with bare bony branches. The lot was littered with police cruisers and the sleek vehicles of the administration, nothing like the toothpick-straight lines of teachers' cars I was used to upon my arrival. An ambulance had pulled right up to the playground, sunlight just starting to dapple the scene.

We approached feeling like trespassers. Principal Lester stopped pacing and waved us over.

"John, what are you doing here?" he asked, though he didn't seem all that interested in the answer.

"He's a useful sounding board," said Sherlock. "Why did you need me? There's very obviously no way to keep police out of this one."

"I think it will be prudent to have someone involved in this awfulness who has the best interests of the school at heart," he said. He craned his neck in an attempt to see around the visual blockade of officers surrounding the scene.

Sherlock marched in the direction of the playground. I jogged along behind him. He shouldered his way through the throng of officers and examiners until he reached the person in charge.

"Sherlock Holmes." He extended his hand. Each syllable solidified in the cold November air. "I'm the emergency liaison for the school and would appreciate every detail you can give me."

The detective shook his hand. "Mr. Holmes, I'm Margaret Adams. I don't usually share details with civilians, but so far you know what I know. A woman was found dead in a tube slide this morning at around 5:45. Your football coach found her on his early morning run and called it in. No ID, no one yet seems to know who she is."

"We have a football team?" Sherlock murmured to me over his shoulder as Detective Adams turned away. I nodded. "Well, that's ridiculous. The research on concussions alone—"

"Sherlock," I prompted him to turn back to the matter at hand. He regained the attention of the detective.

"May I look at the body?" he asked.

"And what qualifications do you have to do that?"

"Him, I meant." He pulled me to the fore. "May he look at the body?"

"Medical expert representing the school." I extended my hand for a shake. "John Watson, registered nurse, six years as an army medic."

She scrutinized me, deemed me worthy, and said, "Just don't touch anything."

I nodded and moved forward, Sherlock at my side.

She had been pretty, in a manufactured kind of way. Her big blonde hair had fallen a little in the morning dew, creating softer ringlets around her shoulders. The streaks of neon pinks and greens and blues of the blouse underneath her sleek black blazer were almost too bright to look at in the midst of the muted late-fall colors that surrounded her. Her green eyes stared cold, up to where the sun had just risen above the thinning tree line.

"Do you have any thoughts on when she might have died?" Sherlock asked me. He kept his eyes on the body.

"Um, sure…" I said. "I might…" I squatted down next to the end of the slide, where she was now laying almost parallel to the ground. "There's not much I can tell without touching her, but, well, by the marks on her neck I'd say she was strangled. And see here," I hovered my finger over the bottoms of her feet. "They're darker, redder. Blood had enough time to pool here before the police moved her to a more horizontal position. So she had to have been dead before ten last night. To be safe, I'd say more between six and eight p.m., since it was cold out."

"Very good, Watson. Is there anything else you can tell me about her?"

"Well, no," I said. "They don't know who she is yet, where she's from, what she was doing here."

"Excuse me!" he called out to Detective Adams. She and a subordinate joined us at the slide. "You should start canvassing for anyone who knew a recently engaged teacher from North Carolina in New Hampshire for an education conference."

"How can you know that? There was no ID, and I told you not to touch the body," Adams snapped.

"Please. Sherlock. I know you have your little game you like to play where you read people, pretend you know all about them, but this is not the time," I said.

"It's not a game, and this is the time. I'm giving the police valuable insight toward who this woman is," Sherlock returned coolly. "Her blouse and blazer have slipped off of her shoulder and show fresh tan lines. Could be just returned from vacation, but I doubt it as that brand of top, Lilly Pulitzer, is particularly popular down south. Also, here, where her pants have hiked up, there is a small tattoo of a devil face."

"Satan stuff?" I interjected.

"More likely a Duke University fan. You don't get your mascot tattooed on your ankle and then move very far from home. Here's her bag, monogrammed, another popular accoutrement for ladies in the South. It spilled as it fell down the slide ahead of her. A shopping list: sweet tea, yams, okra. Clearly preparing to cook her host a down home meal as a thank you. Also, pencils, erasers, red pens. She's a teacher; I recognize the tools of the trade. Her thumb has a slight smudge of dry erase marker, her pinky has a pink highlighter mark. There's a national teacher's conference happening in Manchester this week. I was invited to lecture but declined to attend. She's likely in town for the conference. Though someone lured her away from the city to meet her end here on an elementary school playground."

We stood in stunned silence. I'd never seen my friend's abilities on such ferocious display.

"The...the new engagement?" stammered Adams.

"Her engagement ring still fits a little large. It swiveled on her finger as she fell and if you crouch you can see a slight gap between her skin and the untarnished metal. Meaning, of course, that the engagement is new and she didn't have time to get the ring adjusted before travelling."

"I have to admit, that's compelling. I'll have people check out the conference, see if they're missing someone of her description. Interesting work, Mr. Holmes," said Adams. Holmes nodded, less in thanks and more in agreement.

"Sherlock," I said, as Adams walked away. "That was—"

"Yes, I know." He'd started pacing around the playground, winding around slides and glancing between monkey bars. He swung himself up to the highest platform, the one that fed the slide on which our southern teacher rested.

"Watson," I heard his voice hiss through the bright red tube slide adjacent. "Watson, look up here." I bent and poked my head inside. A bright flash of light sparkled in my pupils. Sherlock had snapped a picture of something streaking down the side of the slide, running about three feet along one of the seams.

"What is it?" I asked, a little too loud.

Adams shouted from the cluster of officers. "Hey! As impressive as you seem, Mr. Holmes, you are now tampering in a crime scene. I need to ask you both to leave."

Holmes leapt from the high platform. We murmured apologies and set off for my car after confirming with Lester that classes would be cancelled for the day.

"What did you find in the slide?" I asked, once we were settled in the warmth of my vehicle.

He pulled up the image on his phone and handed it to me. "Seemed to me like a stripe of crayon," he said. "A stripe of green crayon."

• • •

We ate a quiet dinner that night. The call had come in that the dead woman was, indeed, from North Carolina, in town for the conference. Her name was Ivy Morton, and her fiancé had been contacted. Holmes just stared into the fire after that.

At nine o'clock, he rose to return to his apartment. I shook his hand, unsure of what else to do.

"It's my fault, you know," he said, fingers grazing the door handle.

"How is that even possible?" I asked.

"It's all connected, somehow. And I disregarded it as stupid children complaining about stupid imaginary problems. But children notice things. They really see the world around them because their brains haven't yet told them to discount what they don't want to know or don't want to understand. I pride myself on noticing things, but I didn't see that these children were telling me the truth, giving me everything I needed to prevent a murder."

"Sherlock, you couldn't have known."

He shook his head, clearing out the last cobweb of self-pity. When he looked up at me again the sharp lines of his face were cut with determination. "Goodnight, Watson."

• • •

Classes resumed the following day. We tried to keep the horror of what happened from the children, but, as Sherlock said, they notice. They could feel the creeping pall that had fallen over the school, could read in the ashen faces and lowered voices of teachers that unpleasantness was in the air.

By lunch, every child knew that a woman had died on the playground, though the hows and whys varied. In the second grade, the boogeyman was responsible. The fourth graders chalked it up to a bad fall down the slide. The sixth graders had all convinced themselves a serial killer was on the loose, and each one of them could be his next vulnerable victim.

Lester was preoccupied with Adams and her team most of the day. They were questioning the staff, reasoning that Ivy could only have come to the school to meet with one of the faculty. Sherlock and I got our interviews out of the way early. Apparently, the previous day's display of school solidarity removed suspicion from our shoulders.

"Something isn't right," Holmes grumbled as he played with

the wrapping on one of my disposable thermometers. His students were in art class, drawing pictures of how the current atmosphere made them feel.

"Well, of course everyone is out of sorts." I was filling in students' charts. I'd had three reports of stomachaches so far today, and two minor panic attacks.

"No, that's not what I mean. The police are questioning all of our teachers, but..." He tossed the wrapper on the floor, a mere foot from the trashcan. "But I just can't imagine one of them doing it."

"I don't believe anyone would like to think someone they know could commit murder," I said. "Are you going to pick that up?"

"That's not what I mean, either. I think there are plenty of idiots on the staff who could be so governed by their emotions that they would strangle someone to death in the heat of the moment. Present company excluded, of course." He made no motion to pick up his trash, so I slid from the other side of the desk with a sigh. "But could they really be so stupid as to just leave the body at their place of work? Not even bother trying to move it somewhere? Even the woods would have less obviously pointed to someone within this building." He was staring at the fluorescent lights shimmering from the ceiling.

"So you think someone is being framed?"

"No, I think someone is being narrow-minded. I think we need to look outside the school."

"We?"

"Yes! We are, after all, still engaged by Lester to solve this problem."

"Lester engaged you," I said. "I have anxious children to attend to."

"Fine." He stood and sent my stool crashing into the wall. "I need a doctor's note. I'm going to be out sick for the rest of the day."

"What are you going to do?" I asked, pen in hand.

"I'm going to that conference," he said, with a devious smile. "But first, I need to visit the drama club."

• • •

A tapping on my door that evening roused me from my accidental fireplace slumber. A glance through the peephole revealed a tall blond man, in wireframe glasses and a tattered blazer, leaning against the banister. It seemed too late for a salesperson, and it wasn't an election year. I cracked the door, keeping the chain fixed on the inside.

"Can I help you?" I asked. There was something familiar in his cheekbones.

He hit his consonants hard in a Midwestern drawl. "Sure, sir, I was hoping you could point me in the direction of Sherlock Holmes's apartment?"

"Are you a relative?"

"Something like that," he replied.

"Sorry," I lied. "I only know him in passing. He lives somewhere in this building, but I can't be more specific."

The accent lifted and my friend's voice echoed out of this stranger's visage. "Well done, John. I appreciate you not giving me up. You never know what kind of psychopath might try to gain entry into my abode."

I should have been shocked by his transformation, perplexed and concerned by his assumption that psychopaths may be after him. Instead, I unchained my door and let him in.

"Just came from drinks with a few folks from the conference," he said, removing his wig.

"Why the subterfuge?" I inquired, settling back into the chair from which I was awakened.

"People know me, John." I rolled my eyes at his lack of modesty. "I mean, I was asked to speak at the conference. If word got around that I was there, possibly sniffing into what happened at the school, and if one of the conference goers was responsible, the game would be up."

"Should I ask how you learned to put on so convincing a performance?"

"Oh, I minored in Theater Arts as an undergraduate," he said dismissively. This was not surprising. A man of many interests, by the age of thirty he had also earned two bachelor's degrees—one in the study of human bones, the other in abnormal psychology—and master's degrees in soil science and optics. He had also completed a dissertation on how olfactory senses can trigger repressed memories in middle-aged men who had particularly embarrassed themselves one time in middle school.

"So, what did you find at the conference?"

"I learned that Miss Ivy Morton was attending for the fifth year in a row from a small but well-ranked grade school in suburban North Carolina. I learned that she had been staying with a teacher friend, and that she was supposed to put together a large southern feast the night she was killed as a thank you, doubling as an apology for being unusually 'flaky.'"

"Flaky how?"

"Late for dinner plans, skipping lunches and sessions altogether. Quite unusual behavior, according to my sources."

"Strange. Did any of them say she knew people at this school, in this town? Was anyone associated with the Baker School there? "

Sherlock shook his head.

"It's a rather out of the way spot for someone to choose if they have no ties to it."

"It is, isn't it?" Sherlock agreed. "I'm starting to doubt that anyone at the conference murdered Ivy Morton."

"So one of our teachers, then?" I shivered, despite the fire.

Sherlock shook his head again. "I don't quite think so..." he murmured to the flames. But rather than look dismayed at a lack of progress his eyes were shining and alert, darting left to right as though reading the shimmering embers.

• • •

"Mr. Watson!" Sherlock thundered into my office the next morning, Bobby Simmons in tow. "I am commandeering your office."

"And may I ask why?" I finished wrapping Amelia's elbow and sent her back to gym class. Etiquette had never been Sherlock's strong suit. On that first day of term five years ago, the seasoned Baker School teachers had been eager to parse and subsequently categorize us newcomers. As we settled into the gleaming auburn wood of the teacher's lounge for lunch they began their ritual round-robin challenge to expound upon why they dedicated their lives to education.

"I love children."

"I want to mold the minds of the future."

"I want to help kids navigate the complicated paths of growing up."

And then came Sherlock. His first half-day of corralling fifteen ten-year-olds had already produced a slight twitch in his right eye.

"I am a brilliant man. Some would say I'm far too smart to be wasting my time teaching arithmetic and reading," he had said, impervious to the affronted looks being cast about the table. "But years of interacting with general humanity have lead me to one conclusion. My intellectual gifts must be used to improve the minds of the next generation, lest we devolve as a society into the slime of the eukaryotic pool from whence we came."

No one sat with us at lunch the next day. Our friendship grew from there, but his tact never did.

He pulled me into a corner and whispered as Bobby started examining the cotton swabs. "I've been thinking about that green crayon, the one that disappeared from Bobby's coloring area last week."

"Finally decided to help him 'locate' it?" I asked.

"Of course not. It's gone, it's not coming back. Best he learn about irrevocable loss now than through a dead dog or grandparent. This is about the case."

"The murder? You can't possibly think—"

He cut me off with a wave of his hand and turned his attentions back to Bobby, who was sitting and swiveling on my red leather stool. "Bobby, tell me about the day your green crayon went missing."

"I don't know, the teacher told us to draw something pretty. I was drawing the moon."

"And you were using the green to color the grass illuminated by the moon?" Sherlock clarified.

Bobby shook his head. "I was coloring the moon green."

"That's absurd. The moon isn't green. It may look red or orange at moonrise, but never green. Bobby, go home tonight and read about how photons scatter through the Earth's atmosphere. I want a five hundred-word essay on my desk in two days."

Bobby nodded, tears threatening.

"Sherlock!" I hissed. "The boy is ten. Bobby, you don't have to write that essay. And you can color the moon any color you wish."

"But Mr. Holmes just said—"

"Mr. Holmes was only allowed to color the moon white when he was little, and he's jealous that you can be creative. Now. Let's move on."

Sherlock sighed and continued, looking pained. "So you were coloring the moon green. And your crayon vanished. Did you ask Mrs. Haskill for a new one?"

"No," sniffed Bobby. "Besides, Mrs. Haskill wasn't the teacher that day."

"What?" asked Sherlock, tense. "Who was the teacher, then?"

"Some guy. I don't know. A substitute. Mrs. Haskill was sick, or something."

"This substitute. Do you remember his name? Do you remember what he looked like?"

Bobby could feel Sherlock's urgency and sat up straighter on the stool. I could see his little mind trying to race through the details of that oh-so-important art class. "His name was…Mr.….

Fallwith. Or something like that. And I don't...I don't remember his face. I was focusing on my...on my moon."

• • •

"Roger Fellworth." Sherlock greeted me at the door of his apartment with those two words. He had invited me over for dinner, which usually consisted of food from one of the three restaurants in town that delivered. Tonight was Greek-style pepperoni pizza, and the distinct smell of oily cheese hit me in the nostrils as I entered. "Roger Fellworth is the name of the substitute teacher. He was subbing in for Rita Haskill as a trial on the day of Bobby's missing crayon, and hasn't been to the school since. I'd like for you to go and talk to him."

"Me?" I asked, startled, about to tuck into a slice. "Why don't you go talk to him?"

"Well, I wouldn't want to chance him recognizing my voice."

"And why would he recognize your voice?"

"I called him today to let him know I'd be sending someone by to discuss with him the possibility of a more permanent substitute appointment at the Baker School. I do a fine Principal Lester, but there's the off chance I didn't quite hide the timbre of my natural speaking voice and he'd recognize it. Just because he's merely a substitute teacher doesn't mean he's a complete idiot."

"I'm not qualified to assess him for a permanent appointment!"

"Nor must you be! I don't think Lester was impressed with his performance—he won't be receiving a legitimate job offer. No, I need you to go to his home and find out what he remembers about the day he subbed. And report back everything, down to the minutest detail."

"So having me to dinner tonight instead of coming over to steal my leftovers was—"

"Inducement, Watson. Inducement."

• • •

The Saturday morning sky was arctic blue with a wind to match. I should have been enjoying coffee by my fireplace, but was instead bundled in a peacoat and scarf and pulling into the driveway of a shabbier-looking ranch house than seemed to belong in the charming college town of New London. Guilt for giving Roger Fellworth false hope was already eating at my edges.

I rang the doorbell and before the last bong sounded a young man in a tie and slacks was ushering me into the warmth of his home, his blond hair sharply parted atop a pointed face.

"Roger Fellworth." He extended a hopeful hand, and I reciprocated.

"John Watson."

"Aren't you the school's nurse?" he asked, taking my coat.

"I am, but, um, faculty home interviews. Get lots of perspectives. Gelling with the staff and whatnot," I spouted.

"Sure, that makes sense. Can I get you a cup of coffee?"

I accepted and began examining his living room as he clinked around the kitchen.

It was small and filled with light coming in from three large, old windows. The hardwood floor was scuffed but clean, and the room smelled vaguely of oranges. The tidiness felt out of place, as though it had been brought in special for me. A few framed pictures sat on end tables and windowsills: a group of guys linked arm-in-arm donning graduation gear, Roger and another fellow on a boat. The same two at a Red Sox game, and on top of a snow-covered mountain.

Roger returned with two steaming mugs. "Your brother?" I indicated the photos of the two.

"My roommate, just my roommate." Roger perched on the edge of the sofa. "My mother framed those. She thinks a house isn't a home without some pictures of friends and family, so..." He shrugged and half-smirked. "We both lived here while we went to school, and neither of us has found a steady job yet, so..." Another shrug.

"Right, well," I started, just now realizing I had no clue how to begin a stealth interrogation. "So what made you interested in the Baker School?"

"Sure! Yeah! So, um, the Baker School's fantastic reputation for preparing children…" He continued as I studied his demeanor. He seemed nervous. He kept lifting his hand to his mouth to check for errant bits of food or those white particles that collect on the edges of parched lips. Standard unexperienced interview tics, perhaps, but hardly a motion of guilt. He stared at me in a practiced attempt at professional eye contact, but it came off as unnerving. I realized he had stopped talking. I must have been silent for too long; a few beads of sweat popped up at his hairline.

"Great! That's great. So, how was the day you spent at the school?"

"Wonderful, everything I thought it would be."

"Anything strange happen?"

"Strange? No…everything went smoothly."

"Great! Great. Uh, tell me about your work experience." He launched into a description of his vagabond lifestyle, professionally speaking—travelling from school to school, how he garnered rave reviews from around New Hampshire, how he just knew the Baker School was the right place for him.

"May I use your restroom?" I asked when he finished.

"Um," he swallowed hard. "Yeah, sure, it's right through the kitchen."

I scanned the rooms I passed through, uncertain what I was looking for. A long blond hair? Some southern comfort food leftovers? A girlie toothbrush in the bathroom? There were no signs Roger had known Ivy, much less had motive to kill her. The only event marked on his calendar was for tomorrow morning at six with someone named Logan. Then, a brochure on the fridge caught my eye, tucked between takeout menus and a tattered chores chart.

"So," I said, as I settled back down. "Did you make it to any of the conference in Manchester this year?"

"No, not this year. We've had a great time there in the past, but that was when school was paying for it."

"Ah, yes. Well, that's too bad." I stood. "I don't think I have any further questions for you!"

Roger looked stunned. "You haven't finished your coffee!"

"Right. Well," I grabbed the cup and gulped down the last two large sips. "Great, this was great. I've got to get back. Someone will be in touch, ah…soon." I shook his hand again and avoided the worry in his eyes.

• • •

"All in all, not badly done, John," said Sherlock after I relayed to him what transpired that morning. "I think what you deduced is correct. I don't think he's involved in the murder, at least not in the way we expect."

"He said he'd been to the conference before, though. Maybe he met Ivy then," I said.

"Yes, he did say something like that." There was a knock on the door. "Expecting company?"

"Not usually," I said. I opened the door and looked down. There was Bobby Simmons, excited face flushed from running up the flight of stairs to my door. His mother followed closely behind.

"Why, hello, Bobby! What can I do for you?" I asked.

"I just came from playing in the park with Sarah."

"He insisted on coming to see you right away, I'm so sorry for intruding on your Saturday," his mother apologized.

"Not at all. Come in?"

Bobby waited until we were all settled around my dining room table before continuing. "I was playing with Sarah, and she started telling me all about the man she saw in the woods. She told me that he had blond hair and he was tall and skinny and that made me remember that's just what Mr. Fallwith looked like! I've been thinking so hard about that day because it seemed so important. I remembered he was tall because some janitor guy came in, which was weird, because the janitors don't usually come, but I think someone spilled paint or something. I remember that Mr. Fallwith was just a little bit taller than the janitor, but I'm short so I don't know for sure."

"I thought Sarah told the police she didn't remember what the man looked like?" I asked Sherlock. Both he and Bobby shrugged. "Well, thank you for telling us, Bobby," I said.

"Yes, Bobby, truly you've been a huge help," said Sherlock. He stood, grabbed a piece of scrap paper from my desk in the corner, and scribbled something on it. "As your reward, here is one get-out-of-doing-homework free pass. Use it wisely."

Bobby bounced with excitement in his chair. After an effusive round of thank yous, we saw the Simmonses off.

"So," I said as I closed the door. "Fellworth was the man in the woods."

"It seems that way, doesn't it?" Sherlock stared into the fire, standing so close the flames nearly licked his knees.

"What are you thinking about?" I asked.

"That green crayon…"

• • •

Sherlock insisted on bringing me out for drinks in Manchester that night, a half hour from home.

"Why here, by the way?" I finally thought to ask as we entered to the twangs and shrieks of tuning guitars.

"Oh, great beers, live music, and a bunch of folks that I met at the conference the other day are meeting up here for one last round. Just have to run off to the restroom for a second, wait right here."

A few minutes later Sherlock's "relative" emerged. "Ready?" he asked in Sherlock's voice. I followed him to the table of twenty-somethings who had been awaiting our arrival.

Choruses of "Harry!" greeted us as we settled into two empty chairs.

"Harry?" I asked, under my breath.

"Short for Harrison," Sherlock muttered in my direction.

"We're about to toast to Ivy, wanted to wait for you and your friend here...John, is it?" One of the men handed me a pint.

"Ivy, what a loss," Sherlock said, having fallen back into the Midwestern drawl. We clinked and drank. "Did anyone ever get in touch with that fellow she was seeing a few years back? Let him know what happened to her?" This was news to me, but I hid my surprise.

"Oh, him!" said a woman with chestnut curls tumbling around her shoulders. "Wow, I completely forgot about him! They kept that fling going a few years running! Was he even here this year?"

"I don't think so," replied one of our bespectacled tablemates. "No, I don't think he's been to one of these in a while. You know, I'm pretty sure he's had trouble finding a job. *Anger management,*" he faux-whispered.

"Yes, I remember that about him!" exclaimed the curly-haired girl. "But he was sweet with her. Didn't they do that cute thing where they passed notes to each other on the backsides of crayon wrappers? She always wrote on yellow wrappers, he wrote on green ones."

My stomach lurched. With a faint nudge under the table Sherlock prodded me into action. Somehow I knew exactly what he wanted me to ask.

"What was his name? What did he look like, this boyfriend of hers?"

"Why?" Chestnut Curls looked at me, confused.

"Just curious. I met Ivy through Harrison. A little jealous she never went for me, I suppose. Wondering about my competition."

"Don't remember his name. But he looked a lot like Harry! A tall, blond, skinny teacher!"

• • •

"So. It's Fellworth," I said once we'd returned to the car and Sherlock had de-Harrisoned. "I swear he didn't seem the type when I talked to him. He seemed desperate, sure, and a little sad, but not angry."

"Of course it's not Fellworth," Sherlock snapped. "Give me your car keys."

"Sherlock?" I said. He had figured it out, I could tell. "Sherlock, what—"

"Keys," he snapped again. He leapt into the driver's seat, and I'd barely closed the passenger door when he whipped out of the parking spot. "Put this into your GPS." He dictated a familiar address.

"Hang on, so it is Roger Fellworth."

"Not quite, John. We need to get to the other man who lives there. I'm sorry to say I don't know his name."

I was silent for a few moments as Sherlock drove.

"Tim," I said suddenly, looking up from my phone. "His name is Tim."

"Have you recently developed extrasensory perception?" Sherlock asked.

"No," I replied. "I'm just rather adept at finding people on social media."

Bare trees began to blur outside the windows.

"The flight leaves at six. We should make it," he said. "Unless he stayed somewhere else..." The speedometer scratched the edge of eighty-five.

"Flight? What...?"

"Call Detective Adams. Tell her to meet us there." His foot depressed the gas some more. I did as he said, relaying the address to a wary but intrigued Adams.

"Sherlock..." I started as I ended the call.

"John! I promise you I will not wreck your car!"

"I believe that. But you've caught the attention of a state trooper."

His eyes flicked to the rear-view mirror which was now awash in red and blue lights. "Oh, this will work nicely," he said. We were zipping along the pavement at ninety miles per hour now. "Hang on, Watson!"

We screeched to a halt in front of the shabby ranch thirty-five minutes after leaving the bar. Sherlock's speed shaved fifteen minutes from the trip, and had attracted the attention of no fewer than four police cruisers. Detective Adams pulled up the rear.

"With me, Detective!" shouted Sherlock as he bounded to the front door. He rang the bell. I could hear Adams requesting that the officers stand down, telling them he was with her and that she was very sorry.

The door opened on a stunned Roger Fellworth. "Mr. Watson?" He looked at me, scared. "What's going on?"

"We need to talk to your roommate, Tim," I said.

"He's in his room, packing..." Before Roger could invite us in, Sherlock pushed through the doorway and bounded to the back of the house. There was a thud, a crash, a shattering of glass, and an "ow," and as suddenly as he'd taken off, Sherlock emerged with Tim the roommate in tow.

"What is going on in here?" Detective Adams demanded as Sherlock dragged the bloody-nosed blond man into view.

"Arrest this man for the murder of Ivy Morton," Sherlock commanded. "Grabbed him trying to slip out the back window."

"I'm going to need more than your unqualified, albeit authoritative, command to arrest a man I've never heard of," said Adams.

"Fine." Sherlock threw Tim onto the couch and loomed over him to prevent another escape attempt. "Ivy meets Tim a few years ago at a conference. Each year, they get together again, rekindle the romance, pass sweet notes on crayon wrappings. But Tim hasn't been able to attend for the past year or so. They fall out of touch. This year, though, he learns she's engaged. He has to see her again, she's the love of his life. Ivy misses Tim, she enjoys the thrill of the illicit. So they meet up in secret, away from the conference, away from anyone who knows she's engaged.

"Tim's roommate is subbing at the Baker School, exactly halfway between his home and the conference. They plan their trysts by leaving clandestine notes there, in the faraway woods of the school, to avoid creating a digital trail."

"You're crazy," Tim interjected through a bloody lip. "I never even—!"

Sherlock continued as though the man said nothing.

"But then Tim gets a note from Ivy that he cannot abide. She feels too guilty, she wants to marry her fiancé with a clean conscience, so before things go too far, she breaks it off. Tim begs her to meet him one more time at the Baker School. Things get out of control, they argue, he loses his temper, he chokes her to death. He stuffs her body in the tube slide, but not before taking back the green crayon with the incriminating final message scribed inside. Unlucky for Tim, he doesn't shove the whole crayon into his pocket before making his escape down the adjacent slide, leaving a long, green streak on the inside of the tube. That playground is scrubbed to a sparkle every day at five o'clock, thanks to a generous donation from Megan's mom. That green streak could only have come from Tim's flight from the Baker School."

• • •

A bitter wind rattled at the window panes. I drew my thick thermal curtains across them, hugging in the warmth from the fireplace. We hadn't spoken since our return from New London. We just sat, simmering in the electric silence. Tim had confessed to the murder of Ivy Morton almost immediately. Detective Adams smoothed over our speeding indiscretion as payment for our assistance, and we had been free to go.

I was too curious, too high on the adrenaline of the evening to stay quiet. "That's quite a lot to have inferred from a few days of chatting with people."

"Not really. I learned early on that Ivy was uncharacteristically flighty this year. Indicates she was meeting someone she didn't want her friends to know about. Then we find out that she had a previous relationship with a tall blond fellow."

"Right, but how did you know it was Tim, and not Roger? That description could have matched either of them."

"Exactly, John! You told me when you saw the picture of Roger with his roommate that you thought they were brothers. And I trusted in your report that Roger stated they had both gone to prior conferences. Ivy's friends said her lover couldn't hold a job because of his temper. No chance anyone hired at Baker School, even as an occasional substitute, would have such a record. Then Bobby told us a janitor came into art class that day. Janitors would not be called in to clean up a little spilled paint in the middle of an art class. I deduced that must have been Tim, using Roger as an excuse to be on the Baker School campus. He must have swiped Bobby's green crayon before he left."

"That's a pretty big leap, there," I said, impressed nonetheless.

"Perhaps on its own it would have been. But everything else added up."

"Do you think Roger knew Tim was seeing Ivy? Why didn't he mention Tim's visit?" I asked.

"Would you mention in an interview that you'd allowed a friend to visit on your first day? No, I don't think he knew. By the way, I'm pleased you thought to mention the appointment with Logan you saw marked on the house calendar. I knew immediately it signified the Boston airport, of course. If you hadn't noted it, Tim may have been on his way to freedom first thing tomorrow morning."

We lapsed into silence again.

"Do you know, I think I'm finally starting to enjoy working with children. They notice so much and filter so little. Where would we have been without the investigative skills of Sarah and Bobby?"

He stood.

"I'm off for home now."

He paused at the door.

"Watson, where could I purchase a large pack of crayons? I have a very particular shade of green to locate before Monday morning."

A STUDY IN SPACE

BY DEREK BEEBE

2087, AD. Outside the city of Armstrong on the Moon.

The first thing Watson noticed was that the victim's eyeballs had exploded.

The globes themselves were fine, but had violently left their former home and were now connected by only the flimsiest of ligature. The joys of explosive decompression. Thanks to the zero gravity and Watson nudging the body, they slowly knocked back and forth to trace the outline of a circle. He found it oddly soothing.

He craned his head around awkwardly in his space suit to take in the surroundings of the cramped escape pod, its doors wide open. Strange glyphs written in smeared blood covered the walls. Instant DNA swabs confirmed the blood was that of the victim's, one Enoch Drebber, convicted drug dealer. His specialty was SCC, named for the complicated formula which Watson never bothered to remember, affectionately known by its users as 'essees.'

"Can you run your scanner over the glyphs some more, John?" Lestrade's voice piped into his helmet.

"Copy that," Watson said. He waved his hand around slowly.

"Plex isn't making anything out of that."

He grunted. "Must be gibberish, then. If it was really the victim in his death throes, it's probably just wild flailing."

"Looks like letters on this end, John."

Watson cocked his head at the strange marks. "Hypoxia does

funny things to a brain. He might've thought he was writing something profound at the time."

"Could you stop his eyeballs from bouncing around like that? Some of us are trying to keep our breakfast down."

Watson smiled. "I think it's relaxing. Anything relevant from the crash site?"

"Negative. No sign of damage or equipment failure in the wreckage. Near as we can tell, it was a perfectly fine shuttle when he decided to pop out in a pod."

"Not even acidic blood eating through the floor?" Watson asked in mock disappointment.

"You watch too many movies."

Watson smirked. "I preferred the remake."

"Didn't copy that, John. You said you wanted your suit vented?"

"Forget I said anything. Am I cleared to remove the body?"

"Roger."

Watson gingerly attached a tow cable to Drebber's belt and slowly maneuvered outside of the gaping pod door. He was now certain this was a murder scene.

• • •

The autopsy lasted only fifteen minutes.

"Not a single red flag," the coroner reported. "No poison, no trauma, nothing. He was a habitual drug user, but his system was relatively clean at the time of death."

Watson frowned and crossed his arms. "He died from space, then?"

The coroner bobbed his head. "That's right."

Lestrade typed something onto his wristlet. "No signs of a struggle whatsoever?"

"None."

Watson leaned forward and rested his hand on the window to the examination room. "No indication of what led him to jettison from a perfectly fine shuttle? Or why he would write strange letters in his own blood as he was dying of asphyxiation?"

The coroner shook his head. "Negative."

"Any signs of another occupant in the pod?" Lestrade asked Watson.

"No, but when people wear spacesuits, and the area is violently decompressed, there's not much evidence to find."

Lestrade groaned. "We have a locked-room mystery. I hate those."

Watson looked back at the body through the window, and then grabbed his briefcase. "Crisis equals opportunity, Inspector." He waved goodbye and headed toward the door, dashing from the precinct's front entrance and into the crowd of police and passersby filling the sidewalk, including a few robotic policemen. A small army of parked cars and bikes sat against the curb, while flying and grounded traffic moved along in the street.

His thoughts of lunch were interrupted by a strange voice. "Mister Watson, come here. I want to see you."

Watson turned around while his hand fell to his pistol.

It was a lanky teenage boy with an unruly mop of black hair. His long, charcoal grey coat hung almost to the ground, and an unnecessarily elaborate scarf puffed up about his neck. His eyes darted about like hummingbirds, seeming to take in everything at once. He barely made eye contact.

Watson took a cautious step towards him. "Do I know you, son?"

The boy spoke in a rushed and jerky manner as if he was perpetually late for an appointment and quite chuffed about it. "No. My name is Holmes. Sherlock Holmes. You are lead investigator on the Drebber homicide, yes?"

Watson slowly cocked his head. "I wasn't aware it was a homicide."

"Yes, you are," Sherlock said quickly and forcefully.

"And what if I was?"

"The killer left writing on the walls, didn't he?"

Watson gently undid the latch on his holster. "And how would you know that?"

"The letters were written in a language that you—"

Just then, a pair of passing police automatons made an about-face and grabbed Sherlock by the arms. They spoke in unison in a clearly mechanized voice. "Halt, citizen. You are under detainment for questioning."

Sherlock looked nonplussed. "Can't you see I'm speaking with the detective here?"

Watson's eyes fell onto the nearest automaton. It had the intentionally artificial-looking metal body and blue-and-black uniform of any normal police bot, but still, something looked off.

"Do not resist, citizen," the bots continued. "You will be transported to the nearest police station for questioning." They lifted him off his feet and began swiftly walking towards an open-top police car sitting at the curb. Watson followed behind them, hand still on his weapon.

Sherlock attempted to gesture towards the building they stood in front of. "We're right in front of one, you bumbling bobby!"

Watson looked closer at the bot's upper arm. The metal piece looked strange to him.

Sherlock craned his neck around to look back. "Watson, stop gawking around and do something, for God's sake!"

It clicked into place. Watson drew his pistol and aimed it at the back of the rightmost figure. "Hey! Stop right there, bot!"

In a flash of motion the bot mule-kicked backwards, its leg rotating in a way impossible for a human, knocking Watson's gun out of his hands. He fired as it happened, blasting a small divot in the bot's armored right shoulder.

"Rogue bots!" Watson bellowed at the top of his lungs. "Hostage!"

The two bots pulled Sherlock into their car and took off into the sky. Passing policemen drew their weapons and fired into the underside, but the vehicle was already gone, Sherlock's voice echoing into the distance.

Watson spotted the nearest police bike and shoved the young woman off of it. "Put out an APB!" he shouted at her as he flew away.

More officers followed. Their sirens screamed through the wind whipping at his face. The rogue car banked hard into the intersection and peeled around the corner. The bike had a higher top speed than the car, and Watson slowly closed the gap.

One of the bots opened fire with a sidearm. Red flashes of light nearly hit Watson, forcing him into evasive maneuvers.

In a brief moment of level flight, Watson spotted Sherlock attempting to attack the driver bot, which was still holding his arm in a vice-like grip.

They passed through another intersection and a pair of tactical police trucks swerved in to join the chase. The second bot stopped firing at Watson and picked up a rocket launcher from the back seat. Watson gunned his engine forward while a missile shot out and exploded on the nose of one of the trucks. It fell back to the street in a barely controlled dive, trailing smoke and fire.

Watson took a moment to tap his ear. "They've got rockets! We need more tactical units!"

The bot with the launcher lifted it up again to track the second truck. Watson's hand fell to his empty holster on instinct.

As they passed through another intersection, a car appeared out of nowhere and T-boned the remaining tactical truck. It spun out of the way and smacked into the side of the building.

"Damn it!"

Watson drew closer to the rogue car and dipped below their line of sight. He heard more approaching sirens screaming in the distance. Small-arms fire flashed over his head and took out one of the pursuing bikes.

He passed the engine efflux coming out of the back and drew alongside the car, still out of sight. Setting the bike to cruise control, he leapt up over the lip of the car door and into the backseat.

The second bot's head snapped around to look at him in momentary surprise. It was in the middle of reloading the launcher in the backseat. They both grabbed for it at the same time; Watson got there first and twisted the tube around to face the bot. He pulled the trigger and the concussion of the missile's exhaust nearly blew him away. The projectile, programmed not to explode in such close proximity to the launcher, blasted the automaton out of the car.

"Good shot, my dear fellow!" Sherlock enthused from the front seat, still struggling.

The remaining bot's head swiveled back and forth several times, lost in indecision. He could not drive and hold Sherlock and murder Watson with only two hands.

Watson hesitated as well, lacking any weapon to harm him with.

"Do something, you nitwit!" Sherlock shouted over the wind.

The bot activated cruise control and smacked Sherlock hard enough in the head to daze him. The boy slumped against his crash restraint. Watson leveraged himself to throw the bot out of the car, but the machine weighed twice as much as him. It lunged over the seat towards him; Watson dove across into the front seat at the same instant.

Before the bot could turn around and grab him, Watson snatched the control stick and flipped the car upside down. He dug his feet into the driver's leg space and wedged his knees against the console to stop from falling out. The automaton plummeted out of the car.

Watson was about to right the car when they crashed through a window into an office building.

His body smashed against the seat. Automatic braking activated, and the vehicle slammed to a halt, turning around to face upwards. Watson flew out of the car and slid along the floor. The car hit an interior wall before finally stopping itself.

Watson willed himself to raise his head and take in his surroundings. It was early enough in the morning that the office was empty. The only light came in from the windows...and the rather large hole he had just created. He groaned noisily as he got to his feet, but was relieved to discover that nothing was broken.

"Hey…kid…you in there?" he called out.

He limped over to the car to find Sherlock safe and slowly returning to form.

"You…idiot…" Sherlock muttered. "I wanted you to rescue me, not use me as a battering ram…"

Watson produced a pen knife from his back pocket and cut the boy free from his crash restraints. "Any landing you can walk away from." He helped Sherlock to his feet. "You want to tell me who dressed up some PMC bots as policemen to snatch you?"

Sherlock rubbed his temples. "Private Military Contractors? How would you know that? Not that I didn't," he added quickly.

Watson tapped the boy's upper arm. "Their arm pieces weren't police issue. Everything else looked legit, but they were too bulky. Too armored."

"A fascinating deduction," Sherlock said bitterly. "A pity you hadn't realized it prior to my abrupt departure."

Watson stared him down. Sherlock looked away, his eyes darting all around the office. "Son, you don't seem to understand who has the authority in this conversation."

Sherlock flicked his fingers dismissively. "Yes, yes, of course. I bow to your incredible provincial power."

"I was just about to eat, you know," Watson grumbled. "This is not going to put me in a good mood."

The boy was still looking out the window. "Wasn't the coffee cake enough?"

"Excuse me?"

Sherlock looked back at him with disdain. "The coffee cake you had for breakfast. You had two pieces. And washed it down with two cups of coffee, no cream, no sugar."

"And how in the world would you know that?"

Sherlock spoke with quick derision. "As if your breath wasn't enough of a storyteller, when first we met there were crumbs on your shirt and under your nails, the stench of coffee on your hands, and a bubbling symphony going on in your stomach."

"How utterly observant of you," Watson said, not particularly impressed.

"I am a student of human behavior."

"You'd think you wouldn't act like a total creep, then."

Sherlock scoffed. "I could not care less what the rabble thinks."

Watson turned back to the crashed vehicle and opened the glove compartment. He fished out a pair of heavy pistols and hefted them. "Well, on behalf of the rabble, we could not care less what you think, either."

Sherlock was not in fear of his situation. "We need to get back to the precinct, Detective. The game is afoot, and there's a killer on the loose."

Sirens approached from outside the jagged hole in the wall, and a police bot appeared on a bike. "Is the situation secured, officer?" it asked.

Watson kept both pistols in his hands, his hands at his sides. "Yes. Stand down."

The bot jumped off the bike and into the building. The bike continued to hover outside, obscuring the view. "Do you require assistance?"

"Yes. Go back out and secure the perimeter. There may be other assailants."

The bot continued to walk towards Watson and Sherlock. "There are many units outside, sir. I should help you secure this floor." •

Watson aimed at the bot. "I am ordering you to leave."

"Yes, sir," it said, still walking forward.

Watson shot it in the head with both guns. It fell over backwards, still active. He jumped forward and fired point blank into the neck and arm joints until it fell still.

Sherlock rested his rear against the car, rubbing his forehead. "Perhaps I've made a mistake going to the police…"

Watson ran to the hole in the wall just as a fireball exploded outside. He saw two different sets of police bots on bikes shooting at each other, but they were too preoccupied to pay him any mind. He turned back to look at Sherlock. "Why do you have an entire army after you?"

Sherlock straightened up and walked over. "Oh, there can't be *that* many. I'm sure our quarry would only be able to reprogram so many bots with his own limited means."

Watson arched an eyebrow. "Our quarry?"

The boy grinned. "Your mysterious killer, of course. The one I've come to help you catch."

He stared at Sherlock disbelievingly for a moment, then held out his wristlet to Sherlock's face. "Hold still." He took a picture of Sherlock and started a search.

Sherlock looked offended. "Are you Plexing me? Don't you know who I am?"

Watson kept his eyes on the holo screen. "Can't say that I do."

Sherlock righted a knocked-over chair and plopped down in it. "We need to get moving. The killer is laying low at the moment, but he'll try to leave Armstrong very soon."

"Let's just wait for the fireworks to stop outside, shall we? Sherlock Holmes," Watson read. "A certifiable genius. Top of your class at Aldrin Academy."

"Yes?" Sherlock said impatiently.

"No priors. No criminal infractions whatsoever."

"Not even a parking ticket. Now are you done wasting our time?"

"You've made a great deal in the stock market, it seems. I'm sure your bank statements are very impressive."

"They are," he said dismissively. "But I want to talk about the killer who's about to escape your incompetent grasp."

"And how do you come by this arcane knowledge?" Watson asked.

Sherlock squinted at him searchingly. "You are *inscrutable*, Detective."

Watson stepped to peek out the windows as another police bike fell smoking out of the sky. "I'll take that as a compliment."

The boy cocked his head, still staring intensely. "Most people's faces are an open book. But yours is *shut*."

"Answer the question."

Sherlock flung out his fingers from his hands. "Simple deduction, my dear Watson. He is waiting for the initial flurry of police activity to die down. He's probably hiding in a derelict section of the city with a lack of surveillance or activity. Doubtless, he somehow learned of my involvement and sent these rebellious robots after me before I could solve your case for you."

Watson ignored the insult. "How do you know it's a man?"

"Logically it must be, in order to overpower the victim."

"There were no signs of struggle."

Sherlock stepped back to the window and craned his neck to look outside. "The killer would have been known to the victim, or at the very least there for a business deal."

"What kind of business?"

"Surely you have deduced by now the nature of Mr. Drebber's work," Sherlock said haughtily.

"We have. How do you know?"

Sherlock smiled. "You'd be amazed what a civilian can learn about someone through the Plex."

Watson crossed his arms. "Let me guess. You Plex yourself once a day."

Sherlock cocked his head innocently. "Is that a euphemism?"

"Never mind. May I ask what your interest in the case is?"

"Why, solving crime, of course," Sherlock said. "Normal life is so *boring*, don't you think?"

"A boring day is good for me. It means no one died."

Sherlock flicked his hand dismissively. "I need something *exciting*, and this is it. Would you believe this is the first time in my life anyone's attempted to murder me?"

Watson looked him up and down. "Not really, no." His

wristlet beeped and Lestrade's voice sounded. "Watson, are you all right? We've taken out all of the rogue bots."

Watson tapped the device. "We're just fine, Inspector. Be right out."

Sherlock jumped to his feet and rubbed his hands together. "Now then. I must see the crime scene immediately, before your inept compatriots taint the evidence."

Watson slowly spread his hands apart. "What makes you think I'm not just going to toss you in a cell? Someone *is* trying to kill you, after all."

Sherlock's voice was as cutting as a laser beam. "Because, my dear Watson, regardless of your personal dislike for my habits, you want to solve cases, catch criminals, and save lives, and *I* am the means to do it."

Watson looked out the window at the hovering police units outside. "You're not going anywhere until you explain about the glyphs."

"It's his *signature*, Detective. He's creating a new language, a new culture, written in the blood of his victims. I shudder to think what will happen when he completes his alphabet."

"Have you seen these letters before?"

"Everyone has," Sherlock exclaimed with a wide grin. "He's lined the city with them. But no one can see it. They're jutting out in plain view. Written in graffiti on the buildings across Armstrong. They've been there for months. Examine your intensely invasive street surveillance, and they'll leap right out at you."

Watson stood up. "Fair enough. We'll just pop into the precinct so I can check in with my superiors."

"Of course," Sherlock said without concern. "Naturally, I do not consent to any invasive body scans."

"Naturally."

• • •

Fifteen minutes later, Watson strolled into the interrogation room where Sherlock paced back and forth, chewing his fingernails.

Watson sat down on the other chair and folded his hands in front of him on the table. "Well. The six renegade automatons came from a local PMC. They walked off the lot three days ago without the owners' consent. They filed a police report at the time. Examination of the wreckage suggests they were remotely hacked, but we're not making any headway on the source."

"And you won't. I need to make water," Sherlock said tersely.

"We'll get to that," Watson said without sympathy. "First, tell me about the graffiti."

Sherlock shrugged and looked into the mirror, studying his reflection.

"This man is no fool," Sherlock began. "He obviously would never allow himself to be filmed making the letters. He would have arranged to have them made for him, doubtlessly by the local homeless population. I'm sure your cursory examination of the street cams proved this, but when you cycled back to track the origin of the underlings, you found them emerging from an area with no coverage."

Watson grunted. "Go on."

"The letters I've seen don't seem to spell out words or phrases. I can discern no legible alphabet from them. They seem to be random symbols." He pointed frantically to his skull. "But to our killer's mind their meaning is *very* clear, and it will not be revealed to us until he is finished. The murder scenes will be the key to breaking his code. I must see the location."

"Do you have any suspects to name?"

"I'm a genius, not a bloody psychic," Sherlock scoffed. "It's damn well impressive I've got this far as it is. I need to see the scene for more clues. And then we shall find your killer."

"What led you to me? What connection did you see between the graffiti and a random death in the news?"

"As I said, it's amazing what a civilian can pull off the Plex. Public usage cameras gave me a distant image of the escape pod. Magnification software showed strange letters in blood on the window."

"Ingenious," Watson said dryly.

"And of course, a simple search of recent arrest articles and police directories led me to you."

"Of course."

"Now may I *please* see the water closet?"

Watson stood and dramatically gestured him towards the door. "We would be honored for you to christen it."

• • •

"Are you sure this is a good idea?" Lestrade asked as Watson strapped himself into a spacesuit in the wardroom of the police hangar. "Going off alone with this stranger?"

"One way or another, he's going to crack the case," Watson said easily without looking at him.

"I'm sending patrol units with you."

"That's fine, as long as they keep well back."

Lestrade crossed his arms. "Just remember. The last time you were wrong about a hunch, you ended up in hospital for a month."

Watson smirked. "How else am I supposed to go on holiday?" He finished his ministrations and headed for the door to the hangar.

"Watch your back, Watson," Lestrade called after him.

"I always do."

Watson exited the wardroom and headed for the shuttle in the cavernous hangar.

"It's about bloody time," Sherlock groused. He stood leaning against the shuttle in a spacesuit, flanked by a pair of policemen. "I can feel my hair growing while I'm waiting on you."

"I'll get you back in time for a haircut. You are familiar with EVA, I presume?"

"I live on the bloody Moon, don't I?" Sherlock answered rudely.

• • •

"This is *exciting*, isn't it?" Sherlock asked fervently as they jetted towards the crime scene. He leaned over towards Watson to watch him working the controls, straining against the restraints of his seatbelt.

"Not particularly," Watson said without looking at him.

"Oh, you're no fun."

"So tell me, Sherlock, what led you to picking police consultant as your next bright new career path?"

Sherlock leaned back in his chair and looked up at the ceiling.

"Playing with futures and emerging intersystem economies holds no challenge for me any more. I've always had a passion for mystery stories, but they've always been impossible for me not to solve. Finally, I realized there were *real life* murder mysteries I could be solving."

Watson grunted. "Nice to know your motives are so charitable."

Sherlock wrinkled his nose with disgust. "Oh, come now, Detective. We are all of us selfish creatures. Nature red in tooth and claw. All of this," he gestured around him, "is mere pretense."

Watson shrugged. "You're the expert."

They approached the vented escape pod and slowed to a halt. A small cloud of police drones marked a three-dimensional perimeter around the crime scene.

"Ah! Here we are!" Sherlock exclaimed with glee.

"Try not to drool in the suit. Are your seals tight?"

Sherlock didn't even bother checking his wrist display. "Of course."

"Venting atmosphere." Watson pressed a covered button, and the side hatch opened to suck out the air in the shuttle. Sherlock hurriedly undid his harness and pushed off towards the open hatch. Watson followed after him.

They were twenty-five yards from the pod. Flashing police sirens twinkled around them from the drones nearby.

"Am I allowed to touch the evidence?" Sherlock asked him.

"Absolutely not," Lestrade's voice came in on the radio.

"If you must," Watson answered.

"Watson..." Lestrade said warningly.

"On my authority, sir."

"Thank you, Watson," Sherlock said. He used maneuvering jets to approach the pod. He gently laid his hands on the exterior and stared at the window with the bloody writing on the inside. "Ah, this is a *much* better view," he muttered to himself. "The writing was done with a gloved hand, obviously. But you have no chance of catching this man red handed, Detective. He would have destroyed the suit quite thoroughly the moment he was out of it."

"Fiddlesticks."

"Language, Watson..." Sherlock said with a half-smile. "I'm going inside."

They both entered through the open hatch. Sherlock affixed himself to one side of the pod, taking in all details without paying particular attention to the marked position of the body.

"Well? Have you translated the alphabet yet?" Watson asked.

Sherlock did not bother looking at him. "Of course not. This is only the beginnings of a cipher key. There's not a complete set yet."

Watson let out an annoyed huff. "Then why did I haul you out here?"

"Patience, Detective. Murder will out, as they say." He turned back to Watson. "The body. No signs of trauma, no suspicious cause of death?"

"Just sucking vacuum."

"Hmm. Did you check under his fingernails?"

"Of course. There was nothing there."

"Nothing? Nothing at all?"

"No."

Sherlock mimed examining his own nails despite wearing a full EVA suit. "Perfectly clean? No particulate matter at all? Tell me, Watson, how clean do you think *your* nails are at the moment?"

"We're not here to discuss my personal hygiene..."

"No matter how well you wash your hands there should be

some contamination. A normal person's fingernails will always tell the story of their day. But this man's tells no story at all. Our killer wanted them to stay silent."

"And what would have we found there?"

Sherlock shrugged awkwardly in the bulky suit. "Some clue leading us to our killer. His skin cells, or a particle of his clothing. A speck of dirt or food we could back trace. Clearly, this was not an ill-planned homicide borne of the moment. But then, we already knew that because of the language of blood." He stopped and looked back to Watson with a mischievous smile. "The language of blood, I like that. When they make a movie out of this, there's your title."

Watson let out a short, disbelieving laugh. "You think I'm signing my likeness rights over to *you*?"

Sherlock waved a hand dismissively. "The negotiations can come later. So: Our killer is an intelligent man acting with foresight and planning. A hard man, probably sociopathic or psychopathic. He knew Mr. Drebber well enough to meet and surprise him. It's possible he was using Drebber's product."

"He sold SCC."

The boy nodded absently to himself. "Yes, of course. Like running a computer beyond its operational limits, SCC allows its users to overclock their own brains for a high of hyper-awareness and intelligence. One in ten users experience violent psychosis. Perhaps he is in that lucky minority."

"He probably became arrogant and deluded enough to think he would get away with murder."

"Doubtlessly," Sherlock said while studying the glyphs again.

Watson shrugged. "What I don't understand is, why eject him from the shuttle and then vent the pod? Why not just kill him, leave his mash note, and leave?"

The boy reached out to brush one of the gylphs with his gloved fingers. "Perhaps it was an affectation, an exclamation point to his statement. He is taunting you with the mystery of how it was done."

Watson jerked his chin towards Sherlock. "Let's say you're the killer. Show me how you would have done it."

Sherlock smiled distantly. "Well, that would be difficult, given the fact that he was killed on the shuttle and his body moved here post-mortem."

"We saw no signs of violence in the wreckage, or on his body."

"And what was the cause of death, Detective?" Sherlock asked tauntingly.

"Asphyxiation."

Sherlock wiggled a gloved finger at him. "One can die from lack of oxygen in a room full of air."

"So the killer overpowers Drebber in a perfectly fine shuttle and smothers him to death?"

The boy idly tapped at the flight console. "Essees overclock the body as well as the mind."

Watson watched the screen closely. "He tosses him in the escape pod, jettisons it…and then…what? How do you open the hatch from the inside?"

"If our killer is as intelligent as I believe him to be, he could have written a hack into the pod's programming, which then deleted itself upon completion. Granted, it would have been difficult to defeat the safety overrides, but the computer would have read an occupant in a spacesuit who wasn't attempting to stop the door from opening. Perhaps the computer was told to ignore the missing helmet?"

"Ingenious," Watson said.

"It is, actually. Our opponent must be remarkably intelligent. This shall be quite the challenge. I'm actually looking forward to it!"

"In my experience, all criminals make mistakes."

"Obviously they made a mistake if you caught them. The smart ones you would never know about."

"Funny, someone just said that to me earlier today…but there's no guiding hand behind the malefactor, no deep organizing power at the heart of the criminal underworld. Just a bunch of loons waiting to be caught. Anyway. So, you've suffocated Drebber, tossed him in the pod, and used a hack to vent it. What did you do next?"

Sherlock stepped away from the console and paced the chamber. "Exit the shuttle once it's laid on its collision course, either in his own ship or in an EVA suit to transportation waiting nearby."

"Hmm, probably the suit."

"Perhaps," Sherlock allowed.

Watson tapped one of the glyphs. "But why bother with all this trickery?"

"He is thumbing his nose at you, Detective," Sherlock smirked. "What would be the point of all this if there wasn't a little flair to it?"

"And the glyphs?"

"A wonderful bit of theater. I'm sure the press will love it. It should make him quite popular."

Watson sighed and leaned back. "Well, you would have been...if we hadn't caught you on tape paying one of the painters."

"Excuse me? Are you having a laugh?"

Watson's pistol appeared in his hand. "You *do* realize you've just given me your entire recorded confession?"

Sherlock's smile collapsed. "Detective, if this is your unique brand of humor—"

"Did you really think you could commit a murder and then help the police find your patsy for you?" Watson asked incredulously.

Sherlock glared at him with quiet intensity. "If we're really going to go through with this ridiculous charade, then you shall find I can be definitively placed at my home at the time of the murder."

"Oh, I'm sure you can," Watson agreed affably. "After all, you were expert enough a hacker to convince the escape pod to open its door. And to send those PMC bots after yourself to prove how innocent you are."

Sherlock exploded with frustration. "This is a ridiculous waste of time! Every minute we waste here bickering is another minute the killer can be using to escape!"

Watson raised his pistol slightly. "Don't worry. I've got him right in my sights."

"What could *possibly* lead you to believe *I* am the murderer?" Sherlock asked in disbelief.

"As you said, our killer must be using SCC."

"How insulting," the boy said aristocratically. "Are you implying I'm juicing my intelligence?"

"No, I'm flat out stating it. I scanned you in the interrogation room."

Sherlock sputtered in utter disbelief. "That's—that's—*illegal.*"

"I know," Watson said casually.

The boy's hands flew to his head. "It is *utterly* inadmissible as evidence! Why would you even *do* that? You've never been disciplined for any kind of improper behavior in your entire career."

Watson shrugged. "Everyone bends the rules here and there. Sometimes I'll find something illegally, just for my own knowledge. I can't use it as evidence, but it leads me to something that can. Something I wouldn't have found otherwise. I would never do anything I could be caught doing. I guess that's where we differ."

Sherlock's eyes darted frantically around. "Well, well, all right, I use a little something to boost my natural intellect, all right? So sue me."

"I'll be arresting you, not suing you."

"But you don't have any admissible proof."

"You thought you would impress me with your brilliance. But nothing impresses me."

"Just because I'm using, it doesn't make me the killer. I came here to *help* you, Detective!"

"We have you on camera."

"That is entirely impossible! There is *no way* you have footage of that, unless you doctored it!"

Watson nodded. "I'll admit…you were pretty clever about it. But one of the techs got you off the reflection of a mirror in a window of all things. It's amazing what they can do these days with a camera."

Sherlock held up his hands while staring at the ground. "Look, look, I was investigating the graffiti on my own, alright? I was questioning the local population."

Watson cocked his head. "I assume Drebber was your dealer. Did you owe him money?"

"What? I—*no!*"

"Tell me, who was 'the killer' going to turn out to be? Someone you had a grudge with, or just some poor, unfortunate soul?"

Sherlock spoke to the heavens. "This is ridiculous. Let no good deed go unpunished, Detective?"

"I'll admit, the hacked bots were a dead end. But something told me if I just gave you enough rope you would find a way to hang yourself with it."

Sherlock flung out his arms to his sides. "And this was your brilliant plan? To lure me alone into an isolated location?"

Watson held up his sidearm a little higher. "Don't worry, I'm a quick shot."

Sherlock's anger exploded outward. "Are you kidding? I've been taking essees all day! *I'm goddamn invincible!*"

"I'm sure you're incredibly fast and strong on all those drugs. You could easily overpower me, like you did to Drebber. Hell, you'd probably even be able to snatch the gun right out of my hand. Too bad you're in a clunky police issue suit right now."

Sherlock roared and leapt for him—only to smash into his own faceplate and cause his stiff suit to drift slightly forward.

Watson didn't react. "That's the nice thing about police suits. We can remotely freeze the joints for prisoners."

Sherlock snarled and cursed. His suit wobbled slightly, and he started drifting awkwardly around the cabin.

"I guess this makes you part of that lucky minority, then?" Watson asked, unworried.

"This was the perfect crime." Sherlock's spittle flew onto his faceplate. "I had every angle covered!"

"No plan survives contact with the enemy. Human behavior can't be so easily predicted. Too bad my poker face had you fooled."

The boy snarled. "There's *no way* you caught me on tape doing anything."

Watson made a show of remembering something. "Oh, I didn't. I lied about that."

"*What?*"

He shrugged. "We didn't see you on any footage. I just assumed."

"That's entrapment!"

"You confessed to premeditated murder and illegal drug use, then attempted to assault a police officer. Oops. Guess you need to watch your temper. I'm told the drugs will do that. I figured if I annoyed you and pushed you long enough, you would slip. I tend to have that effect on people."

Sherlock glared at his adversary. "Brilliant deduction, Watson."

SIN EATER AND THE
ADVENTURE OF GINGER MARY

BY GORDON LINZNER

Salali perched on an oak stump in the shade outside Shannon Cavish's cabin. Only her bare feet were exposed to the late June sun. Like many Cherokee in the Appalachians, she and her husband Dagatoga had been accepted by the town of Wattles; they blended in easily, adopting most of the newcomers' ways. The territory had made more than a few adjustments in the half-decade since West Virginia broke from its mother state amidst that dreadful war.

She saw the hermit's approach long before she heard it. Had she closed her eyes, she might have been completely unaware of the other's proximity until she felt her friend's breath on her ear. Even her husband, master tracker that he once was, could not have moved more silently.

Gaunt but muscular, close to six feet tall, wearing leather breeches, a cotton frock shirt, and a leather belt pouch, Cavish had been hunting small game. A throwing stick was tucked into the belt—more accurate, her friend insisted, than the average rifle. Less disruptive, and just as deadly. A fresh rabbit carcass dangled from the belt.

Cavish could, with a little effort, put on a friendly demeanor, but more often was terse, particularly in the face of bad news.

"Who has died, Salali?"

"That's hardly fair, Shannon. I've called on you many a time without the town needing a Sin Eater's services."

Cavish shrugged an apology. "True. You're the closest thing to a friend I have."

"Closest?"

"My only friend. Nonetheless, when you just want to chat, or wish me to cheer you with a tune on my fiddle, you don't have that slouch to your shoulders. The hesitancy in your voice always means you are about to ask my other persona to perform a duty. Today the event appears doubly tragic; a hanging, self-inflicted. Old man Mullen? That would be his style, though not his temperament. But no. I see by your expression it was worse than that."

"How did you guess? Though I should be used to your insight by now."

"Hardly a guess. As I approached, your eyes took in the fresh game dangling from my belt, and you winced. Not a usual reaction from someone who has often hunted with her husband. A suicide would be doubly sinful..." Cavish stopped. "My God. It was a child."

Salali nodded. "Mary MacDonald."

"Ginger Mary? But she's barely fifteen years old!"

"She was found mid-morning, hanging from an oak tree on a ridge half a mile south of the MacDonald homestead. She'd apparently slipped out the night before."

"You were part of the search party that found her; hence your greater than usual distress."

"I was. She'd been somewhat moody of late, but no one thought..."

"Shayla and Desmond must be devastated. Bad enough losing her baby to cholera last year..." Cavish stood silent a moment, then looked to the smokehouse. "I must gut my catch, change from these hunting clothes, gather my cloak and ritual kit. What time is the memorial?"

"Sunset. They don't want to drag it out longer than necessary."

"Understood. Be assured, the Sin Eater will be there."

Only Salali and Dagatoga knew the identity of the Sin Eater, whose mystical abilities seemed to include knowing whenever there was need. It helped that, as the town's main shopkeepers, the pair were privy to all of Wattles's news and gossip. If anyone else suspected a more mundane explanation for the Sin Eater's uncanny timing, they did not question it. No one wished to know more about that human repository of mortal sin than necessary.

Cavish hesitated. "Wait. That new circuit preacher, Brother Jason, isn't he due back in town around now? His first sermon, when he replaced Father Clemens at the beginning of May, had more than a few harsh words about non-preachers usurping the role of clergy in absolution."

"You were at that meeting? I don't remember seeing you."

"I stood in the back, by the trees. If I don't want to be seen…"

"…you won't be. I know. No worries. Brother Jason was in town yesterday, and performed a quick prayer service, but left before dawn, overdue for something in Kenzie: a wedding, or a baptism, or something. I wasn't paying attention, as we were organizing the search for Mary."

"No blame there. Good to hear. The family will not need that extra drama. Ginger Mary!" Cavish sighed. "This is difficult to process. That child loved life."

"She was one of the few townsfolk to get more than a grunt out of you, as well."

Cavish offered a wry smile. "Though we rarely spoke, we shared a love of and curiosity about nature, Salali. She took such joy in the very sight of a red fox, or opossum, or deer. I half-believe she regarded me as another harmless woodland creature."

"You never fail to astound with your detailed knowledge of the townspeople, considering how little interaction you have with them."

"I may be a hermit, and a pariah, but I have eyes and ears, and my curiosity…"

"…keeps your mind active. So you've said, often. It is no less amazing." Salali rose to begin the half hour walk back to her store. "I'll see you at the MacDonald home this evening."

"No. You will see what everyone else sees: the Sin Eater."

Salali inclined her head. "I stand corrected."

• • •

As the sun began a slow descent on one of the longest days of the year, a dark figure moved towards the MacDonald homestead with a deliberate, halting gait. The purposeful pace was partly to throw off the more observant townsfolk, but mostly to avoid tripping on the heavy wool cloak, which dragged along the ground, raising small clouds of dust; the spring had been a dry one. A black scarf concealed most of the face beneath the cloak's hood.

The tradition of a designated lowly person absorbing the sins of the dead so that the latter might proceed to the afterlife as pure as when he or she entered this world had been brought to their new country by Welsh and Scottish immigrants. Although a case could be made for Jesus taking on the sins of others as the prototype, the custom was still considered heathen. Yet, if it brought comfort to the families of the deceased, did no harm, and allowed an extra measure of interaction with the hermit's neighbors while providing the emotional distance Cavish required for mental and physical survival, why not?

Mary's corpse lay in an open wooden coffin on a makeshift bier. The early summer evening was warm, and as the girl had loved the woods near her home, the family decided to hold the ritual outside. Besides, few wished a Sin Eater to enter their homes if it could be avoided.

Salali was the first of the townsfolk to notice the Sin Eater's approach. She usually was. She did not acknowledge its nearing presence, not even with cursory eye contact. She guessed her friend was sweltering under the heavy cloth, but that was part of the mystique.

Head bowed—none had ever seen the pariah's face, nor cared

to—the Sin Eater approached the corpse, scuttling like a crab. All was in place: a loaf of fresh bread rested on Mary's chest, along with a skin of bitter ale and a handful of coins—the Sin Eater's payment. Traditionally, attendees turned away to allow a measure of privacy to the deceased—and avoid seeing the disturbing rite. This evening was no different.

The Sin Eater began the ritual in the usual fashion, muttering phrases of condolence in a high-pitched voice, so softly even the nearest townsfolk could catch but a word or two.

To Salali, it seemed to be taking longer, the Sin Eater's cadence slower, more deliberate, with perhaps a few extra phrases. Did the circumstances of Mary's death merit more attention?

Since it was not unknown for some attendees, usually younger children, to sneak a quick peek, the shopkeeper discretely turned her head.

The Sin Eater had already pocketed the coins. One long-fingered hand rested at the high collar of Mary's dress; the other pressed against the dead woman's right hand. As Salali watched, the Sin Eater's hand moved down to brush against the bare foot.

Such examination was not part of the ritual as Salali understood it, or as it had been previously performed. She turned away again. There must be a good reason. The Sin Eater would not otherwise do anything this out of the ordinary, would not risk garnering undue attention.

The introductory phase ended. Bread was noisily consumed, the skin of ale drained. Then: "I give easement now to thee…and for thy earthly sins, dear child, I pawn my own soul."

After which words the Sin Eater normally made a quiet exit, and the funeral proceeded.

Not this time.

The cloaked figure remained by the bier and, raising an arm, announced, "These sins do not taste right."

There was a collective gasp.

"What mean you?" demanded Shayla MacDonald. "Have we done something wrong? Have you?"

The Sin Eater waved a negative. "All is as it should be with the rite. But, as I well know, the grievous sin of suicide should taste far more bitter. This child did not take her own life."

More gasps and muttering.

"You are saying she was murdered?" asked Shayla's husband, Desmond.

A brief nod. "Moreover, I sense a second, unblemished soul here."

"She was...with child?" whispered Shayla.

"I can only tell you what I sensed. It is for others to determine the truth."

"How dare you, sir!" boomed a voice from the back of the crowd. "Exploiting this family's grief! Are you fishing for more coin? Or greedy for further attention?"

Hiram Jones, unofficial head of Wattles's town council, stepped up to address the speaker.

"Lower your voice, Dermott. This is a solemn occasion."

"I'll not be silent! Remember the words of Brother Jason, last month? This creature is filled with the unredeemed sins of our dead." A handful of other attendees began to mutter in agreement. "Show your face, and repeat your accusations, if you dare!"

Salali tensed, prepared to defend her friend, though her connection with the pariah would surely risk her own status, and that of her husband, within Wattles.

"Enough!" shouted Shayla MacDonald, breaking free of her husband's comforting arms. "I know not if the Sin Eater speaks truth, or even knows the difference between truth and fiction, but I say: if there is but the slightest chance some fiend has slain my daughter, and sullied her reputation—if there is any way to be certain she did not take her own life—I must know."

Jones nodded. "We can ask Dr. Fletcher in Carsonville to examine the body; he is best qualified. It means delaying the burial until tomorrow. Are you sure about this, Shayla?"

"It is my deepest wish," Mrs. MacDonald replied.

"It's still disrespectful," Dermott mumbled.

"I'll ride out tonight," Desmond volunteered. "I stand with my wife on this."

"No, Desmond," Jones countered. "You must stay with Shayla. I'll make the arrangements." He turned back to the Sin Eater, looking for further clarification.

The cloaked figure had already vanished into the encroaching night.

• • •

"If the noose had not been cut and disposed of," Cavish said, clambering up the trunk of the tree from which Mary's body had been cut down less than twenty-four hours earlier, "I wouldn't have to do this. The knot alone could have told me if she'd tied it herself, or someone else had, just as the marks on her neck clearly showed that she'd been strangled before hanging, and the slight swelling of her hands and feet indicated early stages of pregnancy."

"That last is surely a guess," said Salali. The branch extended partially over a steep ridge. She watched her agile friend with mild concern.

"Not quite. You'll see."

"You don't fool me, Shannon. You'd be doing this anyway. You're always taking that extra step."

A sharp laugh. "True."

"You were missed last night, you know."

"Eh?"

"Shannon Cavish was missed. After all, you did have some rapport with the girl."

"Ah, well. The townsfolk know how we recluses are with crowds."

"They do. I told them you were there in spirit."

"That's one way to put it." Then: "Ha! As I thought. This branch is abraded in the wrong direction. It was pulled upward." Cavish swung down to hang like an opossum from the branch, then dropped the eight feet to the ground, landing a few yards from Salali. "Therefore, the rope was used to raise a heavy weight after it was in place…"

"…whereas, if Mary had truly committed suicide, the rope would have already been looped around the branch, and pulled downward," Salali finished.

Cavish nodded approval. "Our time together has not been wasted."

"Your mentoring and my husband being an expert tracker, before his eyes went bad."

"I appreciate all your skills. How is Dagatoga, by the way? Please convey my apologies for dragging you away from the store. I could have found this spot myself, but not as quickly. Having an eyewitness is invaluable."

Before Salali could reply, Cavish dropped prone to the ground, face down, and ran long fingers along the crusted soil. "Now, this is interesting! The indentation is so slight, because of our dry spell, I almost missed it."

"What have you found?"

"How was Mary's body conveyed to her family's home?"

"By wagon, of course."

"Not from this point. The hill is steep, the ravine on the other side sheer, the trees and brambles too close together to allow something that wide."

"Naturally not. Some of the men carried her down to the wagon."

"Exactly! You could manage getting a horse up that narrow path, past those brambles, but why would you? The only way down is by the same path. Look closer. Tell me what you see."

Salali squatted beside her friend. She, too, almost missed it.

"A hoofprint! Someone has ridden up here, and not so long ago."

"The horse was shod, as well."

Salali looked about. "There's another, over by that oak."

"Excellent! Also, observe the taller plants to your right, which have been nibbled on. You agree the teeth marks are more equine than cervine?"

"I would…"

Cavish did not wait for Salali to finish. "I must be away for a few days. I need to borrow a horse. Feel free to help yourself to the squirrel and rabbit in my smokehouse while I'm gone."

"Where will you be?"

"I'm working that out now."

"When will you return?"

But Shannon Cavish was already halfway down the slope, out of earshot.

• • •

Four days later, Salali stood at the front of their dry goods store, watching Dagatoga help load a customer's wagon. A flicker in the shadows across the way caught her eye. The woman made a quick hand-gesture in that direction, exaggerated slightly to ensure her husband noticed, then slipped inside and moved to the back of the store, which also served as their living quarters.

She unlatched the rear door. A moment later a figure dressed in a loose-fitting shirt and cotton pants, both streaked with black, slipped inside. Shannon Cavish's hands and face were likewise soiled and discolored.

Salali nodded. "You saw the note I left you, then. Let me get you some water."

"Appreciated. I came at once. Didn't bother to change. You said it was urgent."

"I see Henry the coal miner has been visiting our neighboring towns."

"Henry has picked up some useful information. Of course, that's his purpose."

"Tell me later." She handed over a tin cup, which her friend accepted greedily. "My news first. The mood in Wattles has gotten ugly while you were away. As you guessed, poor Mary was indeed pregnant."

"I told you it was more than a guess. Go on."

"Every man in the village, even my dear husband, has come under scrutiny as the possible father—and of course is suspected of committing the murder as well, to conceal the fact. Dermott in particular has had it rough, after his loud opposition to the autopsy. Families are being torn apart. Lifelong friends avoid each other. Wattles will not survive the year like this. We must discover the killer. Soon."

"Oh, that's the easy part. I've known who it was since our visit to the hanging tree, and had already guessed as much earlier. You'd know, too, if you took a moment to think about it."

"I assume, then, you have eliminated Dermott as the killer?"

"Lord, yes. That poor man is simply obsessed with the sanctity of the human body. His mother's corpse was stolen by medical students when he was a boy." Cavish met Salali's inquiring eyes. "You did not know this?"

"He never speaks of his childhood."

"Bits and pieces, Salali. Bits and pieces. Just put the fragments together."

"You know so much about these people, I'm surprised you ever need my information."

"You are an additional set of eyes and ears, Salali, even if you don't always interpret what you see and hear correctly. I am more than grateful for your input." Streaks of sweat marred coal-streaked cheeks. "I've spent the last few days verifying my suspicions. Unfortunately, none of what I discovered is enough to convince a jury of our townsfolk, considering the man's status. And mine own, either as pariah or hermit."

"Then I fear the whole town will fall victim to this infamy."

"That will not happen, I promise you." Cavish scowled. "I have grown quite fond of Wattles and its people, though I don't show it. They treat me as an outcast, true, but that is as much my decision as theirs. More, in fact. I will see justice done."

"How do you expect to ease this discord, if neither Sin Eater nor the town hermit can expose the true killer? Will Henry spread the word, or one of your other personas? Would they be any more believable?"

"It's simple. The Sin Eater will visit each villager, read their sins, and absolve them of these particular crimes."

Salali frowned. "You have never demonstrated such a power. They will not accept it."

"They will, because I will reveal their own sins to them, one by one. In private, of course. I would not add to the community's distress with tales of further indiscretions. Could Dagatoga and yourself kindly spread the word?"

"Calling at their homes could be dangerous. Few would be comfortable dealing personally with a Sin Eater."

"Once I prove myself, to avoid me could be construed an admission of guilt."

"And if you do uncover the murderer, what's to stop him from ending your life as well?"

"That, too, would be an admission of guilt. But there is no danger of that happening, my friend, because the killer is not from this town."

"At least let Dagatoga and myself set up a temporary shed behind the store for you to use for these interviews. People are more likely to go along with your plan if you do not actually invade their homes, and my husband and I would be nearby should you need assistance."

Shannon offered a rare smile. "An excellent idea! And you wondered why I rely on your aid and advice?"

• • •

Over the ensuing fortnight, the makeshift shed behind Dagatoga's store was visited by every man—Dermott was among the first—most of the women, and a handful of curious children from the town and the surrounding homesteads, as well as a few intrigued transients. Many of their transgressions were already known to the hermit, or guessed at from years of observation. Others were unveiled as the subjects reacted to various items strategically placed on a shelf along one wall or the small table separating the sin reader from the one being read. A battered silver flask on which one's man's eyes lingered a moment too long told the Sin Eater he was not as devoted to his wife's tenets of temperance as he would have the town believe. The widow Brady nervously playing with buttons from both Confederate and Union Army uniforms not only confirmed a previous assessment that she had disguised herself as a man to fight in War Between the States—Cavish was personally all too familiar with those indications in the woman's bearing and attitude—but also revealed she initially fought for the South before changing sides.

It was agreed that, just as the Sin Eater was under a vow to never reveal the sins ingested of the dead, each individual's moments of weakness would remain private—save of course that of Mary MacDonald's murderer. In most cases, a mere hint at the nature of the sin, without specifics, was enough to convince those interviewed of the Sin Eater's ability to read their sins—though not take them away, as that could only be done at the point of death.

On the last day, with no one left to face their guilt, Salali began clearing items off the shelf and table. "That cloak desperately needs a washing," the shopkeeper chided, sniffing.

"It is the stench of multiple sins," her friend responded. "And the result of sitting in a heavy wool cloak for hours on end in mid-summer."

"I've never known the town so quiet," Salali added. "Being confronted with one's sins seems to make one quite introspective."

"My fellow humans are an endless source of fascination. Many were completely unaware they had ever sinned, not truly, until I pointed out the meanings of certain thoughts and actions. We can but hope their new self-knowledge does not lead to an increase in the sin of Pride." Sadly, the Sin Eater added, "I regret this effort alone will not give Shayla MacDonald the closure she needs. My work is not yet done."

"Anything you care to share?"

"I am sworn to name no names, but a handful of the men hold carnal thoughts of you."

Salali laughed. "I don't need your uncanny skills to guess who. I wish one or two of them had come by when I was wearing your cloak to read the sins of that sinister hermit, Shannon Cavish." She met her friend's eyes. "You never offered to read my sins."

"My dear Salali! I only pretended to read Dagatoga's to assure the townsfolk of his innocence! I well know what the two of you have done in the past. Those actions, though they may seem brutal to some, saved both my life and my sanity. If any dare condemn either of you for what you did, they will answer to me! We speak no more of that."

Salali shrugged. "Given these reminders of their flawed humanity, I imagine there will be quite a turnout when Brother Jason returns next week."

"Thursday, is it not? He is coming from Carsonville?"

"I've told you that several times. Not like you to be forgetful."

"Just confirming. I have some business outside of Wattles, and will not return before the preacher's arrival. I require you to perform one vital service in my absence."

"Speak it. I know you do not ask favors lightly."

"You must persuade Shayla MacDonald to hold another memorial service for her daughter that Thursday. One at which a proper minister of the Lord can preside."

"That is all?"

"Not quite." In a hushed tone, Shannon Cavish added more specific instructions.

• • •

Brother Jason rode slowly up to the MacDonald homestead, surveying the gathering. He looked thinner than on his last visit, his features slightly more drawn; the hardships of being a circuit preacher were starting to take their toll, Salali surmised.

The shopkeeper was one of three women who initially came forward to greet him. She was nowhere near as much of a believer as other townsfolk, but appreciated the sense of community their faith created.

"Preacher!" she welcomed. "So glad you could stop here before going into town."

The preacher responded with a self-deprecating hand-wave. "When word reached me of this gathering, I could hardly not show. I regret being unable to return when I first heard of the child's death, but I was obliged to fulfill my rounds."

Two more figures slowly approached: a woman in mourning dress and veil, and a somber-faced man who kept a tight grip on the woman's hand. Other townsfolk gradually circled the preacher as he dismounted.

Salali nodded toward the pair. "These are Mary's parents, Desmond and Shayla MacDonald."

"I remember." He extended a hand. "Though I met your family only briefly, your daughter was a delightful child. Her loss was truly a tragedy."

"Bless you, Brother Jason." Shayla's voice was low, barely above a whisper. "We held a funeral, of course, at which the Sin Eater assured us Mary's soul would enter Heaven as pure as the day she was born..."

The preacher's lips twitched. He seemed ready to interrupt, but apparently thought better of it. He'd stated clearly, in his first sermon in Wattles, what he thought of the kind of rabble who would appropriate the duties of a proper minister, taking advantage of backwoods superstition for a few dollars and a quick meal.

"...but it's close to two months since she's been gone, and still I grieve," Mrs. MacDonald continued. "I've been advised that perhaps a man of the cloth can best ease my loss. I am grateful to my neighbor Salali for suggesting this second memorial."

"And rightly, too," Brother Jason agreed. "Shall we go inside?"

"We held the first service out here, Brother Jason," Desmond replied. "It seemed fitting, given Mary's fondness for the outdoors. We wish to repeat that circumstance. Most of the people you see here attended then."

"Of course, Desmond. I am no stranger to outdoor preaching. I believe I have just the passage with which to start the healing." Brother Jason rummaged in his saddlebag and pulled out his Bible. As he did so, a small bit of wood, the size of a small coin, bounced free, striking the ground at his feet.

Salali started forward. The woman beside her, Rosalind, got there first and picked it up. So much the better.

"Pardon me, Brother Jason," Rosalind said. "I think you lost a button."

"Eh?" The preacher looked down at his coat. "No. All accounted for."

"Are you sure? There're bits of thread looped in it."

"May I?" Salali took the item, holding it up for a closer examination. "This isn't thread. It looks like hair. Reddish, though it's hard to tell."

"It's a fine piece," Rosalind added. "Hand-carved, with a tiny fox-head. The carving is near as fine as your own work, Shayla."

Mrs. MacDonald leaned back against her husband, then straightened. "Let me see."

Salali handed her the button.

The woman's face grew pale. "This…this button is from Mary's dress. The dress she was wearing when she…when we found her."

"And in which we buried her," Desmond added tersely. "We thought Dr. Fletcher had been careless when we noticed the missing button." He glared at the preacher.

Brother Jason stepped back. "I've never seen that thing before. I swear, by my God! That button could have come from anywhere."

Shayla glowered. "I made that dress myself for Mary, Brother Jason. My fingers carved this button! I know my handiwork! The fox was Mary's favorite animal! These strands of hair—red hair— my daughter's hair!"

Rosalind looked at her own hand, horrified to have held even briefly such a grisly memento. "You sick bastard!" she spat.

The townsfolk closed in.

• • •

The trial took less than an hour, Hiram Jones presiding; most of that time was spent setting up the venue. Wattles was not about to wait weeks for a circuit judge to come by, not in a case so clear-cut. Who could fault them? Certainly not Salali.

By the time the Sin Eater appeared, cloak flapping in the warm summer breeze, the sun was past its zenith, a scaffold had been erected in the center of town, and the condemned man stood in place, noose around his neck. A few had debated hanging him from the tree where Mary MacDonald had been found, but the consensus was that holding the execution there would blemish the girl's memory. And Brother Jason's disgrace needed to be as public as possible.

"Sin Eater!" the elder Mullen brother, acting as executioner, called out. "Your timing could not be more apt! We are preparing a feast for you!"

The pariah's presence was as a rule barely acknowledged, must less greeted so robustly. Cavish suspected few onlookers saw this impending death as an occasion for mourning.

"May I…read his sins first?" The sonorous, high-pitched tones echoed faintly.

Mullen snorted. "There's little point. He's confessed all: the fornication, the murder—double murder, as he knew the poor girl carried his child."

"So I gather," the Sin Eater replied. More than one bruised set of knuckles could be seen among the crowd.

"I'm tempted," said Shayla MacDonald, who'd watched the assemblage with grim satisfaction, "to deny the Sin Eater this meal. Let the bastard face his God with his sins intact." She turned to her husband. "Does that make me a bad person?"

Salali, standing within earshot, shook her head. "It makes you human, Shayla."

The cloaked figure gestured again toward the condemned man, in inquiry.

"I don't see the harm," the hangman responded. "Come on up, Sin Eater."

The Sin Eater climbed the steps slowly to avoid stumbling over the cloak's hem, and paused within a yard of Brother Jason. "Do you know me?"

"I know of you," the preacher replied through bloody lips. One eye was swollen shut; the other squinted. "I admit I've put little stock in these foreign superstitions. Still, if there is the smallest chance of my receiving absolution, I shall be grateful for your efforts."

The Sin Eater leaned in, repeating the question in a harsh whisper, so low not even the Mullen brother could hear. "Do you know me?" The hood of the woolen cloak pulled back slightly, and the scarf lowered a fraction. Only the condemned man could see the face beneath. A face with a smug grin and glittering eyes.

Brother Jason flinched. "You…you're…"

"The stableboy who helped to prepare your horse—and saddlebags—as you were leaving Carsonville. Yes. I reveal this to you, and you alone, because I wish your last moments to be filled not with peaceful acceptance of your fate, but with anger, and hate, and betrayal." Replacing the hood and scarf, the Sin Eater's voice rose, loud enough to be heard by all: "No, preacher, I will not take on your sins. They are too foul, even for one as cursed as I. We are done here." The shrouded figure turned to go.

"No! Tell them…!"

The trapdoor was sprung.

The Sin Eater slowly descended the steps and started out of town, but not before pausing before Shayla MacDonald. "What you wished for, for this monster, you now have. The sin, if sin there be, is not on your soul, but mine own."

Salali was last among the gathering to see the cloaked figure vanish into the twilight.

• • •

Well past noon the following day, Salali made her way to Shannon Cavish's cabin. She heard the fiddle tune long before spotting the home, recognized Stephen Foster's "Hard Times" played at an even slower, dirge-like rhythm than usual.

The fiddler perched on a favorite stump at the front of the cabin, back toward her. The music stopped as she drew nearer.

"You're better at sneaking up on people, Salali, when you don't try. The long silences between footsteps betray you."

"I wasn't trying to sneak up on you," Salali countered.

Cavish turned with a knowing glance.

"Very well, I was, this time." The woman lowered herself cross-legged to the ground in front of her friend. "A bit of a startle would serve you right."

The fiddle was carefully set aside. "On the subject of betrayal, I fear I may have betrayed your trust."

"Then you think me a fool, which is worse."

Her reward was a sharp laugh. "Never that, my dear Salali. Never that. You have questions for me."

"I do. I understand how the bruising on Mary's neck, being in a straight line rather than v-shaped, led to your concluding she was murdered. I also see why the timing of Brother Jason's departure before the discovery of Mary's body aroused your early suspicions. That might have been coincidence, yet you never doubted his guilt."

"Those hoofprints were the final proof. Who would ride up such a steep ridge, basically a dead end, unless they were transporting something…in this case, a young girl's body? What other horses were unaccounted for that night? Did you not notice the scratches on his saddlebags, made by the brambles lining that narrow path?"

"There were many scratches."

"Some were fresher than others. The new ones were more obvious during those first few days, of course, as Henry the coal miner followed the preacher's circuit. Henry also confirmed that, on the day Mary's body was found, the day Brother Jason had to leave Wattles so abruptly, there was neither wedding nor baptism awaiting the preacher in Kenzie, nor the town beyond, nor the one past that."

"Put like that, it seems obvious."

"Perfectly so."

"The most baffling thing, though, was how you knew he would be insane enough to keep a memento of his crime, let alone how you could rely on its falling from his saddlebag in front of a score of witnesses, six weeks after the murder, even to the point of advising me to keep a sharp eye out for...?" Salali drew a deep breath. "Of course. I take back what I said. I am a fool! And you played me as expertly as you play that fiddle!"

"On the contrary, Salali. It was you who enabled me to play that predator." Cavish's slender hand reached for the fiddle again. "Care for another tune? Something more cheerful? A little 'Nellie Bly,' perhaps? We could both use some cheering up."

Salali wasn't quite finished. "That's why you took so long at Mary's ritual, examining the poor girl's corpse—you were collecting damning evidence. You planted that button and those strands of Mary's hair in the preacher's saddlebag, likely as he was leaving Carsonville."

Cavish took a sheepish bow, plucking a string.

Salali rose, towering over Cavish. "You've gone a step too far, Shannon. You might have condemned an innocent man!"

"Ah, but he wasn't innocent, was he? He was a murderer and a rapist, two crimes you well know I cannot abide, and hiding behind the cloth of a minister at that."

Salali did, indeed, know, and could not wholly blame her friend.

Shannon's lips thinned. "You'll not share this information, I trust? If not for the sake of our friendship and shared past, then because of the effect even a hint of doubt of Brother Jason's culpability could have on the town."

The shopkeeper sighed. "No, I'll not tell. The man deserved his fate, and worse. My concern is for you." She laid a hand on her friend's shoulder. "What you've done is construct a lie, one which cost a man his life, even if it was designed to unveil the ugly truth and ultimately see justice done. That is a grievous sin." She knelt, looking directly into Cavish's eyes. "Tell me, Shannon: who devours the Sin Eater's sins?"

Cavish shrugged. "My whole life is a lie, Salali. Every time I go through the charade of eating sins, it's a lie. When I enter the world as Henry the coal miner, or in some other guise, it's a lie. When I purchase shaving supplies, which go unused, it's a lie. Yet, if there is but one sin I will happily cling to after death, will, indeed, boast of to the heavens, and to Satan himself if need be, it will be this one, involving a wooden button and a few strands of red hair."

Cavish took a deep breath, then raised the fiddle again. "I believe we were trying to decide on a tune? I can't let you return to Dagatoga in such agitation. How about the moustache song? I'll even put on a fake handlebar."

Salali shook her head. "I'm in no mood for such frivolity."

"You will be, after a verse or two."

And, damn it, Salali had to admit, Cavish was right again.

THE ADVENTURE OF THE DOUBLE-SIZED FINAL ISSUE

BY MIKE STRAUSS

As I rounded the corner, my foot landed squarely in a large pile of horse manure. An unpleasant experience in normal circumstances, this incident was worsened by a simple application of physics: an object in motion stays in motion. Hence, without the benefit of friction against the sole of my Oxford, my right foot and leg were suddenly moving at a different angle than the rest of my nearly fifteen-stone body. Anticipating a both painful and embarrassing conclusion to this accident, I was surprised to feel my fall suddenly arrested.

"There now, old chap, you must not fall behind. The chase is afoot," Holmes said as he helped return me to my feet.

I knew not what surprised me more: the fact that he interrupted a foot chase to give me assistance, or the play on words which was far beneath his usual sense of dry humor.

"Damn," I swore, glad my wife was not around to hear. She had quite strong convictions about what language was not appropriate outside of an army camp. "My carelessness has cost us our quarry. He has disappeared."

"Fear not, my dear Watson, I see him in the panel beneath us. I will simply jump the border and cut him off," Holmes announced confidently.

Turning to look askance at my oldest of friends, I discovered that Holmes was nowhere to be seen. Between his strange words and his impossible disappearing act, I was at a complete loss for what to do.

Where conscious thought failed me, my training as both a soldier and a physician took over. I closed my eyes, took a few deep breaths to slow my heartbeat, and focused inwardly. As soon as my mind settled, I was able to make out the sounds of a commotion roughly a block away. I paused only a moment to shake off the larger chunks of manure from my Oxford, and then ran towards those sounds.

As I expected, I saw something quite impossible. Holmes stood on the far side of a narrow street, blocking the path of our quarry, Mr. James Whitman. Unable to maneuver past Holmes, Mr. Whitman fled wildly in the opposite direction, where he was abruptly met by my clenched fist.

"Excellent display of fisticuffs, Watson. Now let us deliver Mr. Whitman to the constable," Holmes said while helping me detain our suspect.

Overpowered by two men who both had greater strength of limbs than he, Mr. Whitman gave no struggle as we escorted him to Scotland Yard. His submissiveness gave me time to ponder what I had seen this afternoon.

I was highly familiar with the streets of London in this section of the city. In point of fact, I had walked that particular lane scores, if not hundreds, of times before. I knew for a fact that there simply was no path that Holmes could have taken to reach the far side of that lane before Mr. Whitman had reached the end of it. The shortest possible path to do so was a good three blocks longer than the route Mr. Whitman had taken.

I could try asking Holmes how he had performed that trick, but I knew from experience he would not provide an alternative answer to the one he had already provided: something about panels and borders. I understood all the words he had used. However, the context of the explanation simply eluded me.

When you have eliminated the impossible, whatever remains, however improbable, must be the truth.

Holmes must have spoken that phrase to me at least fifty times during various cases over the years. The words echoed in my head as I pondered the events of the day. Could a man run three blocks in less than ten seconds? My study of biology said that was impossible. In fact, no known land mammal could perform that feat, even if Holmes had been able to procure a mount for this chase. Some aves could fly to that location in the time frame, but none capable of that feat could carry Holmes's weight.

Therefore, Holmes did not travel by foot, mount, or air. The only remaining possibility was that he defied the laws of physics in order to apprehend Mr. Whitman. Having eliminated the impossible, I found myself forced to consider something else equally impossible.

I did grudgingly give the idea consideration, for this was not the first time I had witnessed Holmes perform a feat that could only be described as impossible. A few years prior, during a perplexing case, we had been walking down a busy city street when Holmes quite suddenly apprehended a woman passing by. Mortified that my closest friend would act in such a base way I demanded that he release the lady. Instead, he asked her a single question, pertinent to the case on which we were working. Inexplicably, the answer she returned provided the solution to a case that had confused us for weeks.

After both apologizing for our ungentlemanly behavior and thanking her for her assistance, I questioned Holmes about his behavior.

"Whatever came over you, Holmes, and how could you possibly have known that woman had key information about the case?"

His response provided little illumination to my query. "Elementary, my dear Watson. The inker always draws thicker lines around the faces of important characters."

Such frustratingly incomprehensible answers were common

when I questioned his unusual feats of intuition. For example, quite often when questioning a suspect, he would stare at empty space above the suspect's head rather than look into his or her eyes, like Inspector Lestrade was wont to do during an interrogation. Despite his seeming fascination with the cloudy London sky, Holmes always gleaned critical information from these interrogations. When I inquired into what he was staring at so intently, his response was just two words: "Thought bubbles."

This speculation ran roughshod through my mind throughout the trip to Scotland Yard. By the time we had delivered Mr. Whitman to the constable I had made no more progress on this conundrum than I previously had. I was quite tempted to question Holmes again when he started speaking.

"Quickly, old chap, let us return to my flat. We have much to speak about," Holmes said, more animated than I had seen him in quite some time.

"Should we not stay here and wait for the police to interrogate Mr. Whitman?"

"No need, my dear Watson," he replied casually. "I am confident our friends at the Yard will pummel the answers out of Mr. Whitman eventually, but I already know the whereabouts of young Miss Highland. I will explain everything once I am enjoying a pipe in my sitting room."

Delaying the recovery of the young kidnapped woman by even a moment concerned me, but I had learned over the years to trust the judgment of Holmes. As a result, we spoke not a word to each other as we traveled back to Baker Street.

"Mind the manure," Holmes said, looking pointedly at my Oxford just before we reached his flat. Mortified that I had forgotten such a detail, I carefully scraped the hardening manure off my shoe on the nearby curb until I was satisfied that I would not dirty his home.

Minutes passed while Holmes started a small fire in the hearth, changed into his usual smoking jacket, and rummaged through a little-used drawer for a tin of tobacco. The last action seemed quite peculiar, since his favorite tobacco was clearly visible on an end table.

Holmes raised a hand just as I was about to point this out, halting my words. "I can see from your demeanor, my dear friend, your patience grows thin. Allow me to put your mind at ease. When I stated earlier that I knew the whereabouts of Miss Highland, I slightly misled you. I know not where she is at the moment. Rather, I know where she will be at a specific future time."

"Where and when?" I queried.

"Miss Highland will be found at Reichenbach Falls during the next heavy rainfall," he replied with such confidence that I felt no urge to question the veracity of these facts, no matter how ludicrous they seemed. "Should you feel the need to look out the window, you will notice that it is an unusually sunny day for the normally overcast city of London. It will be quite some time until there is heavy rainfall and I fully intend to enjoy myself until then."

True to his word, he filled his favorite pipe with a pinch of tobacco from the mysterious tin. After lighting it at the fireplace, he sat upon his favorite armchair and took three long draws. He then carefully set the pipe down on an end table, drew his violin and bow from the nearby stand, and started to play vigorously.

Pausing only briefly now and then to take a long, hard puff on his pipe, for the better part of an hour Holmes played on his violin a somber song that, though I vaguely recognized, I could not put a name to. It was not that unusual for him to play so relentlessly, even when entertaining company, but I could sense that something was amiss.

In every single previous instance when I did witness him playing his violin while still in the midst of a case, he did so to clear and focus his mind. This time, however, he seemed more intent on simply enjoying the purity of his art. Furthermore, unless my eyes deceived me, I believed the mystery tin from which he filled his pipe was the tobacco he had brought back from Morocco. He had previously described the act of smoking that snuff as thoroughly incorrigible unless a dear friend has recently passed, the Royal

Mother has just given birth, or you expect to succumb to the cold fingers of death in less than a day. I was quite certain neither of the first two were true.

Holmes must have detected some trace of my growing concern in my demeanor, for he quite suddenly ceased to fiddle and returned his violin and bow to the stand.

"Fear not, Watson, I have no intent to do harm to my person. In point of fact, even if I did intend myself harm I would be unable to achieve it."

This statement, so insightful of the thoughts running through my mind, did little to still the concern I felt. Quite to the contrary, if truth be told.

"I see in your eyes that you have many questions you wish to ask me, Watson. I promise I will provide answers. However, I must ask that you forestall your questions for a time and simply allow my meandering wit to set the stage."

Concerned as I was, I could not deny his request. "I will hold my tongue, Holmes," I responded.

"To start off, I must offer my deepest apologies," he said. I held to my word and stilled my tongue, though I found myself quite distressed by the unusual degree of sincerity in his words.

"For years now you have been my dearest friend and quite often my only companion. That you would choose to accept this burden despite my boorishness and cocksure attitude speaks greatly of the patient and loyal person that you are. You have endured the sharp lash of my ego like no other person in the world."

The truth of his words was such that I briefly expected the light of Heaven to shine down upon him. Alas, only a wisp of pipe smoke drifted towards the ceiling to mark the occasion.

"For all this, you deserve to be rewarded, either in this life or in the next. Sadly, I can make no promises for the grace of God, and the only reward I can offer in life is a pale substitute to what you deserve."

"You deserve to spend your final hours in the sitting room of your home, sharing pleasant conversation with and the warm embrace of your dear wife Mary. Instead, I know for a fact that you will spend every remaining moment in my tiresome company. It is for that final indignity that I feel I must apologize."

So disturbed was I by this statement, I broke my oath and exclaimed, "Holmes, what exactly are you saying?"

Only raising an eyebrow at my outburst, he said, "Pour yourself a glass of scotch and take a seat. My explanation will not be short and you will find much of it quite implausible.

"I will start by noting that, for quite some time now, you have been pondering numerous mysterious actions and statements I have made. You need not acknowledge this fact. It has been quite apparent from our many interactions.

"From your recent reactions to these peculiarities, I can deduce that you have come to accept that no school of science with which you are familiar can properly explain what you have observed. I must congratulate you for this deduction. You are quite correct that science offers no explanation."

He briefly tamped some more snuff into his pipe, as much to give me a moment to process what he had said, I suspected, as to refill it.

"Though it pains me to the quick, we must discard science and accept that some other power holds sway. I have neither the time nor tools to identify this power. It may be an act of God, some unholy mystical power, or possibly even some scientific principle so advanced that the greatest scholars on this planet could not understand it with a lifetime of study. I am of the mind that the details of the how are of no importance. Only the results of this power should concern us."

"You, I, and everyone we know, have known, or will ever know are all characters in a story. This story is presented in a series of illustrated novellas, colloquially known as 'comic books.' For reasons of which I am unaware, I am the only character in these stories that appears to be aware of these facts."

Ever astute, Holmes recognized that I was about to respond to this seemingly preposterous explanation and derailed my interruption of his story. "Please, my friend, drink another tot and hold your tongue. I am quite certain I can answer all of your questions without you needing to utter them.

"I am aware of these facts because, from all appearances, I have the unique ability to see beyond the confines of the story. I can literally see the lines that form the pictures, the white spaces that surround the illustration panels, the curiously informal lettering used to depict conversations, and even the small metal clasps that hold the pages of the book together. Beyond that, I can see and hear the author, the artist, and the inker when they plan stories or simply have conversations near the most recent book in production.

"My awareness of this world that we live in grants me the ability to perform seemingly impossible feats. I can look ahead to future panels or even read the storyboards in order to predict future events. What you have perceived in the past as impossibly rapid movement is nothing more than me jumping to a future panel, sometimes on the next page. Finally, as you have suspected, I can read thoughts as easily as I read the words that people speak. Fear not, my old friend, I bear no ill will toward you for unkind thoughts about me."

Backing his words with action, he stood up from his chair and crossed the room to top off my glass of scotch. Seemingly satisfied that he had been a good host, he returned to his armchair.

"At this very moment I am certain that you are considering which asylum will offer me the best chance to recover from my obvious brain malady. In truth, if such a solution could protect me from my fate, I would gladly submit myself to treatment. Unfortunately, I know for a fact that my life will be ended before the final page of this book."

Flummoxed by this ominous pronouncement, I downed the remainder of my glass, refilled it, and downed that as well. From time to time in the past I had witnessed Holmes speak with such intensity that it was nothing less than blasphemy to doubt his words. This was one of those moments. Despite that, the logical part of my mind refused to accept the possibility of what he proposed. To the keen eye of Holmes, this mental conflict was clearly visible.

"You are conflicted, old chap," he continued. "You don't completely understand all of the terminology I have used, nor can you accept such an abrupt challenge to your reality. I sympathize. I had years to adapt to our reality. You have been given mere seconds.

"It is my intention to convince you of the truth of my words. With any luck I will do so before we leave this room. Before I can provide this evidence, my friend, I must first reveal to you important facts about the author of the story we inhabit."

Upon saying those words, Holmes carefully placed his pipe down, sat up straight, and looked directly at me with his piercing eyes. I had seen him in this position before and knew it meant that the conversation at hand had his full focus.

"The author is a gentleman, though I use the term loosely, known as Sir Arthur Conan Doyle. He is a celebrated individual in the British Empire, both for past deeds that he is reputed to have performed in a conflict known as the Falklands War and for the ongoing Sherlock Holmes story that he writes. He is not a particularly skilled writer, primarily trading in on his prior fame.

"In addition to being a mediocre writer, he is an incredibly arrogant man. So prideful is he that he has written himself into his own story as the primary antagonist, the one individual who has successfully eluded the protagonist multiple times throughout the narrative.

"Now that Doyle has chosen to end the story, he has decided that his protagonist, namely me, will finally achieve a measure of success against Arthur Doyle. Because I am not scripted to survive until the end of the issue, I must reveal the details of Mr. Doyle's crime in advance of the conclusion, so that you may reveal those details at the end of the story in your final journal entry about your adventures with Mr. Holmes. In answer to your obvious question, Watson, individual comic books are referred to as issues in much the same way that individual newspapers are similarly referenced."

Holmes paused briefly after that last statement to savor both a draw of his pipe and his ability to forestall my questions. Only seconds passed before he continued.

"To be quite precise, the storyboard for this panel says 'Holmes spends some pleasant time with Watson in his sitting room before explaining in detail what he has deduced of the crimes of Arthur Doyle.' Despite my abilities to act beyond the reality I inhabit, my actions are as much bound by the storyboards for this comic book as are the actions of every other character. Fortunately, this particular storyboard offers an excellent opportunity.

"The lack of specificity in relation to time means that I can spend as long in this room as I want, as long as I am enjoying myself. This scene will only end once I have explained the details of the crimes of Arthur Doyle to you. In due time, I will do exactly that, however not as the author intended. I will explain to you how Sir Arthur Conan Doyle engaged in the crime of stolen valor, obtaining a knighthood through deceit, a feat that I am only capable of because of the hubris of the author. You, my friend, will be able to reveal those crimes to the readership of this comic book because the storyboard for the final scene says 'Dr. Watson pays his final respects to Holmes by recording in his journal the information Holmes has deduced about the crimes of Arthur Doyle.'

"To be perfectly honest, my determination to follow this course of action derives in equal parts from a sense of justice and from spite. Mr. Doyle could have ended my story any way he chose, and he chose to end it with my death. That death is now inevitable and that fact has stoked my anger. I feel no guilt, however, since Mr. Doyle is a scourge on the honor of the country I hold so dear."

His final word of that sentence was accompanied by Holmes slamming his hand down upon the armrest of his chair. Such displays of anger were rare from Holmes and usually only directed at the foulest of miscreants. He took a moment to compose himself before continuing.

"Of course, for my plan to succeed, I must convince you of the truth of my words. I am asking a boon of you, my dearest friend, not forcing your hand. I would not see justice and vengeance performed unless you are my willing accomplice in this endeavor.

"To this end, I will attempt to convince you in a manner consistent with your profession. We will engage in a series of repeatable experiments that produce reproducible and observable results. During the experimentation I will endeavor to teach you to play chess with greater expertise. The experiments will come to an end the moment that you defeat me in a game of chess. At that time, I will fully explain the details of the crimes of both Sir Arthur Conan Doyle, the author, and Arthur Doyle, the character, giving you the choice of which you will record in your journal."

A bemused look briefly crossed his face. "It just occurred to me, Watson. If you are willing to oblige my request, I will even provide you the perfect title for this little adventure."

Leaning further back in his armchair, Holmes took a very long draw of his pipe, making it quite clear that he had completed his storytelling and that I was once again free to speak. Despite all the thoughts racing through my head, I was at a complete loss for words, not just because of the impossibility he described, but because he intended for me to defeat him at a game of chess.

In the years in which we had been compatriots, we had played innumerable games of chess. Never once had I defeated him. More accurately, never once had I offered a tangible challenge. His skill in the game so surpassed mine that I suspected it would take a decade or more to teach me to play well enough to defeat him in a fair game.

The impossible task which he had set himself apparently did not deter him at all, for Holmes had already started to rearrange the room so that we could play chess in comfort. Without deviating from his task, he casually said, "Watson, old chap, why don't you pour us each a glass of that Merlot from the wine rack on the far side of the room?"

A peculiar lilt in his tone told me that the man was up to something, but I was game enough to play along. First, grabbing a pair of glasses from the nearby cupboard, I started towards the other end of the room. I must emphasize now that I only ever started the journey, for try as hard as I might, I simply could not reach the other side of the room. I could see it, and my feet moved in that direction, yet my steps made no discernible progress.

Finally frustrated beyond description, I exclaimed, "What madness is this, Holmes? I walk but do not move."

"Elementary, my dear Watson," he responded. "The portion of the room you are attempting to access isn't illustrated in the panel. Therefore, since you cannot leave the panel, you cannot reach that side of the room."

Incredulous about his declaration, I turned abruptly to face Holmes. "That is…"

"Preposterous?" he interrupted. "Indubitably so. It is also the only logical deduction that can be made based on the given facts. However, it is of no importance. I see from your disposition that you are not yet convinced, and delving further into this oddity will not change your mind. You require additional evidence, as any good man of science should."

"Since the Merlot is unavailable, please pour us some more scotch instead. It is an excellent year after all."

Briefly calming myself first, I responded to his request. "I am sorry, my friend. I emptied the bottle earlier."

"No need to apologize," he said. "If you look in the cabinet, you will discover the very same bottle, full to the same level it was when you first broached it earlier. Please at least look before you object, old chap."

Sighing inwardly at how efficiently he had headed off my protestations, I walked over to the cabinet and looked inside. Resting in the cabinet, in the exact location where the previous bottle of scotch had been situated, was a bottle of scotch. By all visual indications it appeared to be the same brand and year as the bottle I had emptied earlier. Turning my head, I could also see that the empty bottle I had left on the end table was nowhere to be seen.

Thinking carefully, I was quite certain that the cabinet had been empty after I had removed the bottle of scotch earlier. It was possible that Holmes had somehow simultaneously secreted this bottle into the cabinet and discarded the empty bottle all while my back was turned, though such behavior was highly unlike the man. Still, it was a possible explanation, which meant this experiment had proven nothing. Rather than inform Holmes of my deductions, I simply poured the requested scotch and left the bottle in the cabinet.

By the time I had turned around, Holmes had already finished setting up the game and was concealing a pawn in each hand. After sitting down, I selected a hand, which Holmes opened to reveal the black pawn. Smiling more genuinely than I had ever witnessed before, he said, "The game is afoot."

I lost a game of chess. Then I lost a second game of chess, followed by a third, a fourth, and a fifth. I continued to lose games of chess until I lost count. Hours turned to days which turned to weeks, or so I assume. I lost all concept of time while I played and lost chess games.

The light coming in through the windows never changed while Holmes and I played chess. The fire in the hearth never wavered. The small tin of tobacco from which Holmes filled his pipe never emptied. The bottle of scotch in the cabinet never ran dry.

Holmes and I simply drank scotch and played chess as he meticulously endeavored to ingrain in me his entire encyclopedic knowledge of the game. He had no substantial skills as an educator. However, through example and repetition, he was able to teach me increasingly advanced strategies.

Over time I came to understand the Zukertort Opening, Larsen's Opening, Philidor Defence, Dutch Defence, the Lucena Position, and hundreds of other complex tactics. My vocabulary expanded to include concepts like pawn structure, windmill, deflection, prophylaxis, and compensation. While I had rarely looked more than a move or two ahead before today, I had learned to look as far as ten moves ahead and regularly did so.

I continued to lose every single game. However, I presented a more difficult challenge with the passage of time. Fate eventually smiled upon me and a hard-fought game ended in a draw. Holmes exulted in this draw even more than I did and doubled his efforts to improve my mastery of the game.

I played so many games that they all blended together in my thoughts. The moment one game ended Holmes was immediately resetting the board for the next. Maybe a hundred games after that draw, possibly more, I recognized something quite intriguing. Playing was becoming easier for me with each game I played. Thought transformed to instinct that had been honed by constant practice. Simultaneously, Holmes was taking increasingly more time to make his moves and would often sweat due to stress. I hadn't just become better at the game. I was pushing Holmes to the absolute limits of his skill.

"18,732 games. Congratulations," Holmes said as he lay down his king in the traditional acknowledgement of defeat. "As promised, I will now explain the details of the crimes that both Sir Arthur Conan Doyle and Arthur Doyle have engaged in. Please listen carefully."

Dusk fell while he gave his explanations. After the final words left his lips, he continued to rest in his armchair smoking his pipe. My mind wrestled with the events I had just experienced and the tales I had heard. Accepting this bizarre story as truth was incredibly tempting. It was, after all, presented to me by an individual that I had come to accept as the foremost logician in the world.

How long I sat in that comfortable armchair, wrestling with this quandary and smelling sweet pipe smoke, I knew not. I only knew that I woke up many hours later as a chill wind ripped through the open window. The fire had died out during the night, as had Holmes's pipe. Dark clouds filled the sky and strong winds whipped the curtains into a frenzy. I quickly closed the window and woke up Holmes.

"Holmes, we must make haste," I exclaimed. "A heavy rain approaches even as we tarry."

Groggy but as level-headed as ever, Holmes extricated himself from his armchair and carefully set the room in order. In my years as a doctor I had seen many men who were on the brink of death, and to my trained eyes Holmes seemed very much like a man putting his house in order for the last time. He moved quickly, with no wasted action, taking only one last sweeping look around the room before adjusting his jacket and marching towards the door.

We hailed a carriage upon exiting his flat. Holmes gave precise directions to the driver and paid him up front, for both the trip there and back, before settling into the compartment with me. Only as he sat down did it occur to me that I hadn't the slightest clue where Reichenbach Falls were.

"Holmes," I asked, looking nervously at the dark clouds, "where are these falls and how long will it take us to reach them?"

"They are in Switzerland," he said without a trace of concern in his voice.

"Switzerland?" I exclaimed. "There is no way we can reach Switzerland by carriage. We will need to take a ship. It will be days before we arrive, if we are lucky."

He responded with a wry grin. "Fear not, old chap. Doyle is as inept in his understanding of geography as he is as a writer. He believes the falls to be located near Kettering, which he further believes will take slightly less than an hour to reach by carriage. Neither is factual. However it matters not, for the next panel is labeled 'Fifty Minutes Later.'"

According to my pocket watch, the carriage arrived at a wooded glen less than a kilometer from the top of the falls exactly fifty minutes later, to the second. It was just one more oddity that added to the mountain of evidence supporting Holmes's outlandish claims. I had begun to wonder if I was the one in need of an asylum due to my refusal to accept the only logical conclusion of this mountain of evidence. If Holmes recognized my wavering doubt, he uncharacteristically said nothing, instead proceeding briskly towards the falls in silence.

The scene that met us at Reichenbach Falls was highly unexpected. Professor James Moriarty, a gentleman that Holmes and I had tangled with in past cases, stood near the river, looking in our direction as if he had been expecting us. A young lady with blonde tresses, whom I could only assume was Miss Highland, stood in the raging river behind him. A makeshift dam that was slowly filling with water surrounded the young lady, who appeared to be tied to some object in the dam.

Having met Moriarty multiple times in the past, I knew him to be a highly cultured gentleman. This type of raw thuggery was beneath him. Hoping that I might appeal to his more enlightened nature, I attempted conversation.

"Professor Moriarty, please consider what you do here today."

Before I could say any more, Holmes interrupted. "Do not waste your breath, Watson. The professor only follows the script. Doyle could think of no less base way to create this scene than a kidnapping, no matter how out of character it was for the perpetrator. No words you or I utter, no matter how honeyed, will enjoin him to deviate from this behavior. We must, instead, act swiftly if we are to rescue Miss Highland."

True to his words, Holmes dashed forward.

"Halt," Moriarty ordered, drawing a pistol from his coat pocket.

Holmes didn't even flinch as the weapon moved in line with his torso. Showing bravery that I could not recall witnessing in any individual during my entire time in the military, he grabbed hold of Moriarty, with one hand on his arm and the other on the pistol. Despite his firm grip on the weapon, he made no effort to move the barrel out of line with his torso.

"Have you gone mad, Holmes?" I yelled over the roar of the waterfall. "He will shoot you."

"Fear not, Watson," he replied, "I am in no danger. I have seen the panel where the pistol fires. It is a full-page spread that is a close-up image of just Moriarty's hand, the pistol, and the blast. My hand is not in that image. As long as I maintain my grip on this weapon, I can assure you that it will not fire. Now, my dearest friend, take advantage of this opportunity to save Miss Highland before the river waters overwhelm her."

As much as I feared madness had finally overtaken my oldest companion, I could not in good conscience allow a young woman to die due to my inaction. Certain that I would hear a deafening blast any second now, I sprinted in the direction of the hostage. Holmes's statement proved true, however. The two struggled while I ran towards Miss Highland, but despite the fact that his finger never left the trigger and the barrel was pointed directly at Holmes, Moriarty never fired the weapon.

Thanking the good Lord for this miracle, I bent over to help Miss Highland, only to discover that she was quite suddenly wearing manacles.

"Holmes," I called out, "I am unable to free her. She is wearing manacles, not ropes."

Never taking his eyes off his opponent, he responded, "The manacles are a mistake by the artist. The original draft called for manacles. The final draft called for rope. Unfortunately, the idiot artist forgot to correct one of the panels before print. The rope will return after Miss Highland screams."

At almost that exact moment a strong rush of water washed over the dam, briefly covering Miss Highland. She screamed in fear the instant her head broke the water. When I turned back to face her, just as Holmes had predicted, the manacles were nowhere to be seen, replaced once again by simple rope.

Briefly putting the philosophical conundrum of my reality out of mind, I waded into the chill waters of the river and attacked the rope with fervor. The rope had swollen due to the water, increasing the difficulty of loosening the knots. Long minutes passed before I was finally able to free the sobbing young lady.

Once free of her bonds, she desperately clawed her way out of the river onto the shore. Wild with fear, she instantly ran away from the river, fortuitously heading in the direction of the carriage.

Then the world shattered.

At least, for an instant, that is what I truly believed. Still waist-deep in the water, I found myself momentarily blinded and deafened while I struggled to maintain my footing. My vision cleared before the ringing in my ears abated, revealing the reason I had been dazed. A tree located less than five meters away had been struck by lightning. The trunk, split down the middle, burned, even in the heavy downpour.

Surprisingly, neither Holmes nor Moriarty appeared to have been affected by the lightning strike at all. They were still locked in their seemingly endless struggle. Miss Highland was not as lucky. The burning tree was barely a meter from her and she had been knocked to the ground. From all appearances she was still conscious, but had fully succumbed to panic, curled in a ball, unwilling or unable to move.

To my horror, the base of the tree cracked again, beginning a slow fall of the tree itself towards the cowering young lady. Still standing in the river, I was certain that I was too far away to possibly reach her in time. Holmes, however, was not.

Acceptance flashed across his face as he deliberately released Moriarty and dashed towards the paralyzed Miss Highland. The tree sprayed mud on both Holmes and Miss Highland when it crashed to the ground, but missed them both due to Holmes's quick thinking.

The brave rescue, however, was not the focus of my attention. My eyes were firmly fixed upon the pistol Moriarty held. With growing horror, my field of vision dimmed until the only thing I could see was his hand and the pistol.

His hand and the pistol and a small cloud of smoke drifting out of the barrel.

In that instant, a similar acceptance washed over me. I knew for certain how this story was going to end, and the part I was going to play in it.

Holmes also had one last part to play in this story. Between my time in the military and my years as a doctor, I instantly knew that the bullet had struck a lung. It was a mortal wound that would kill him in seconds. Holmes, I suspect, knew it as well. Gathering what remained of his strength, Holmes lunged at Moriarty, carrying him into the river, and then seconds later over the falls.

I already knew the fate of Holmes and cared not about the fate of Moriarty. His role in this story was complete. My role was not.

The return trip to London seemed to take but a moment. I suspected that the artist simply didn't bother to illustrate it. The result of this strange time dilation was that Miss Highland was returned to her family that very day, and I soon found myself sitting at my desk in my study. Taking quill in hand, I started a new entry in my journal.

May 14th, 1891

Today marks my final journal entry about the adventures of Sherlock Holmes. The great detective, nay, the great man, lost his life today in an act of true heroism. While I would love to tarry on the details of his act of bravery, that would not truly pay tribute to his life.

Instead, I will do as he bade me in his final days and reveal the details of a crime committed by the one criminal he never successfully brought to justice. The facts I will present here shortly were revealed to me by Holmes to ensure that, should he be unable to divulge them, they would not be lost from the world. It is my intention, upon completing this journal entry, to share its content with the detectives at Scotland Yard, in hopes that justice is brought upon the foul miscreant for the base acts in which he has engaged. I can think of no greater tribute to the remarkable mind that has passed from this world.

As Holmes explained to me, the following was information that he deduced based on his observations of the primary malefactor, Sir Arthur Conan Doyle, and conversations that Holmes was privy to between Doyle and his equally unethical lifelong artist friend, Alexander Reynolds, a man willing to keep his secret in order to profit from Doyle's fame.

Doyle was a man of little note until he was deployed to fight in a conflict named the Falklands War. Why such a man, completely unqualified to represent the honor of the British Empire, was ever allowed onto the field of battle was beyond even the formidable deductive skills of Holmes to comprehend.

Whatever the reason, Doyle unsurprisingly bore himself without an ounce of dignity upon being deployed. His lasting legacy would have undoubtedly been of nothing more than acts of cowardice had his squad not been ambushed one morning. The ambush was quite effective, reducing the squad to two individuals after a brief firefight: Private Doyle and Sergeant Norman West.

Sergeant West was an exceptional soldier, the pride of the British Empire. Despite having received a critical wound during the initial ambush, he continued to fight the Argentinian soldiers. Through skill, and I must assume some incredible luck, he succeeded in killing the remaining five enemy combatants, without any assistance from the cowardly Doyle. Sadly, Sergeant West died for Queen and country that day, succumbing to the injury sustained during the ambush.

This tale of heroism has never been made public. Upon returning to his company, Doyle claimed that he was responsible for killing the entire ambushing force. An investigation by the military confirmed the details of his story, resulting in military commendations and eventually being knighted for his deed.

To whomever is reading this journal, let it be known that this act of stolen glory remained a secret to all but Doyle, his greedy compatriot Reynolds, Holmes, and I, until this day. Please see this information is used to bring honor to the deceased Sergeant West and to bring justice to Arthur Doyle for his crimes against the British Empire.

Thus ends the Adventure of the Double-Sized Final Issue.

A VERY IMPORTANT NOBODY:
A THERAMIN JOULE MYSTERY

BY CHUCK REGAN

The magazine itself was unremarkable. The five-hundred-year-old copy of *Astounding Stories* was an original print, and not a molecular replica. It was brittle, but still legible despite the high lignin content of the cheap wood pulp pages. Some organization had gone to great lengths to preserve it. What Theramin Joule found remarkable was that the chronometric scans had confirmed his name and address had been written on the cover in 1936. Someone from that era had known that his address would be at 221-B, Indigo level, on the artificial satellite Jove's Halo in geosynchronous orbit over the north pole of Jupiter.

The first and only other time Theramin had felt this degree of existential angst was when he was eight years old and had discovered his parents dead. It had not been the fact that his parents were dead that had disturbed him, it was how he had felt about their deaths. More specifically, it was *how he felt about how he felt* about their deaths that had disturbed him.

They had spent most of their adult lives threaded deep into the virtual worlds of the digital network known as the Mesh. To his parents, Theramin and his brother, Danube, had been just two more apps—feed them the proper data and energy, and they would behave as expected.

Danube and Theramin had fallen into line, behaving like

boys were expected to behave, absorbing their lessons in icon identification, learning the history of popular memes through history, and investing into the appropriately kid-friendly brands, but after young Theramin discovered his parents dead—their bodies bloated, floating in cheap immersion pods, infected by substandard intravenous nutrients—he realized that not all that much would change for him, except the short-term inconvenience of having to arrange for their bodies' disposals.

It was not an expected reaction for a boy his age, and he understood this at the time. It merely affirmed what he had been fighting within himself up to that moment—there was a reason why he was annoyed by the vapid entertainment available to him, and there was a reason why he did not want to waste his time interacting with other children—he realized that day that knowledge was more important to him than people.

The death of his parents had clarified that for him. From that moment on, he shunned the pointless distractions of entertainment and used technology as a tool to give him as much access as was available to him, while his brother had invested himself into becoming as much an important part of the system as he could manage.

Now, a vibrant forty-five years old, Theramin Joule felt that existential disruption once again, but this time it was refreshing, and nostalgic, and infuriating, and invigorating. He had become bored by what the System had to offer him. There was nothing new to interest him. This world had nothing else to teach him.

Joule began to question the firm rule he had set for himself at eight years old: that he would never have his mind digitized. The taboo of transhumanism created a palpable tang in the back of his throat, nagging him like a gravity field, and just as he was contemplating the next stage in his life, expanding into a new universe of evolved digital minds that were not constrained by synaptic conductivity, nor time itself—this magazine arrived.

The core timeline could not be corrupted. It was a law of physics.

The very existence of this magazine confirmed as truth the ridiculed conspiracy theory that his reality existed within a corrupted timeline—a splinter universe created by some hidden cabal of transhumans, and at this moment, rereading the results of the chronometric scan of the ink on the magazine, he realized he had been ignoring that trampled path of cross-logic and pseudoscientific nonsense. The conspiracy theories were right.

Laying on the scanning bay was an antique publication which defied the laws of time travel. Nothing from the future can affect the past. The existence of this magazine all but proved that his reality was a lie.

• • •

After the Absolute Grand Unified Theory had been worked out by incorporating *consciousness* into the equation, the patterns of matter, energy, time, and conscious thought had fueled a revolution in science, philosophy, sociology, psychology, history, and time travel. The System had responded they way they always did with a new technology—they turned it into entertainment.

Timejack Temporal Vacations made it possible to "rent" a splinter universe and manufacture an alternate history. A timejacker's consciousness was projected into a native host body of that splinter universe, and would *puppet* that native, sensing what that body could sense, driving its movements, and speaking through its mouth.

It was discovered that it was very difficult to radically alter any timeline unless entire armies of timejackers acted in unison toward generating a specific goal. The temporal patterns tended to reorganize themselves to *smudge out* any single act—even the assassination of a key individual had little effect long-term. It took a lot of conscious effort to divert the path of a temporal river using technologies of that timeline, but it was all reduced to the hundredth monkey principle.

Once a tipping-point percentage of the population performed

an action, spontaneously, all the people of that population spontaneously performed, or attempted to perform, that act, given similar circumstances. Temporal Translocation was the culprit. When enough conscious energy is focused on one thought at one point in time, it acts like a bell ringing on the quantum level, which every mind could hear. If enough minds believed the Moon was a space dragon's egg, it became a global myth for that splinter timeline.

Once the philosophers and social scientists began to use Temporal Translocation in their formulas to alter splinter timelines, the System reacted as it always had—by exploiting any verdant new territory with capitalistic vigor.

World-changing wars of the past were repackaged as fully-immersive first-person shooters. Intimate trysts with important historical figures and celebrities became a standard package. Fortunes were made creating designer timelines. A popular timejack meme involved teaching advanced technologies to ancient peoples and watching how the anachronisms pulled their civilizations apart—Romans with ray guns, Mongolia as world super power, Victorian-era Moon bases. There were countless variations of World Wars I and II, many involving nanite-enhanced zombies.

Ethical discourse of these practices was quickly ignored for the sake of commerce. Comforted by the incorruptible laws of physics, the System flourished, and the corporations raked in the profits. The timejackers were guaranteed that no matter their actions, the core timeline could not be affected.

Yet, there the magazine lay, written by a hand that had foreknowledge of a person and place that would not exist to them for five hundred years.

"Anne?" Joule said to his synthetic assistant. "Call Dr. Andwhinge."

• • •

Joule tabbed through the data on his tablet as the rest of the passengers in steerage slept or made quiet chatter over the hum of the engines. It was hour fifteen on a thirty-six-hour trip to his first stop on the asteroid Ida, then a quick five-hour skip to the Timejack center. Joule used the uninterrupted time to pore over one other unsolved cases of a possible temporal corruption.

A month ago, Chlör Byzantine, a third-rate Mesh celebrity, had timejacked to 1955 to pick a fight with the writer Ayn Rand. His fight with her was meant to become an obscure meme, reinforcing Byzantine's esoteric sense of humor, but when Rand admitted that she had been forewarned of the impending attack twenty years earlier, and had since been training in esoteric martial arts, it opened up the floodgates to conspiracy theories. If it were true that someone had warned her, that meant Joule's own core timeline had been corrupted. Joule had watched an un-edited copy of Byzantine's timejack session and had dismissed the event as an elaborately staged hoax.

Hundreds of thousands of other researchers had timejacked into Ayn Rand's past to trace where the possible corruption had occurred. Either there had been no temporal corruption to be found, or some greater power was conspiring to hide the information. This, of course, was the fallback of all conspiracy theorists—*the absence of evidence only confirms it has been covered up*. Joule had assembled all the results of their research but had never invested much credence in the subject, having already dismissed this supposed Rand Paradox as merely a desperate publicity stunt confabulated by a declining Mesh celebrity. This "mystery" hadn't been worth any more of his time.

The year in which Ayn Rand had been warned was the same year as the publication of the magazine—1936.

The giggling of an infant broke the silence. A man played peekaboo across the aisle from the child in its mother's arms. Smiles ricocheted around the cabin. Although Joule could have afforded to rent a sleeping pod, or travel in the luxury of an Indigo-level suite, the Green section of a trans-system shuttle was much cheaper, and the white noise drone of the engines helped him focus.

As he breathed the same air as the migrant workers, he

wondered how little had changed for them since the times of serfdom in the ancient past. Skilled only in the kind of tasks robots were deemed too expensive to maintain to perform, these people barely earned enough for food. Greens rarely lived past the age of fifty.

Trace radiation in the water they drank and the dust in which they bathed poisoned them slowly enough so that blame could not be directly traced. Their faces were gray and crusty from the dust, and suffering weighed heavily in their eyes. And yet, these were the last true humans left in the System—no enhancements, no nanophores, no synthetic organs. Joule felt safe among them.

In his expensive suit, fiddling with his tablet, it was clear to them that he did not belong there, but when the mother of the infant made eye contact with him, she smiled. He attempted to return the gesture, but his sharp, self-conscious smile always seemed disingenuous. Before he could witness her reaction, he returned to his tablet.

His scans of the *Astounding Stories* magazine cover showed that it had been impregnated with several sets of fingerprints, but one thumb print in particular had been pressed very purposefully into the lower right corner, as if its owner had wanted to make their presence known. Over the ages, the oils in the thumbprint had darkened and blurred, but Joule was able to trace its swirl patterns through historical files to an orderly at a New York City mental hospital in 1936.

Once Joule could timejack into the orderly's body, he would be able to sift through that mind and extract how he could know Joule's address five hundred years in his future.

"Anne, open my account."

An emitter on his tablet projected the data onto his retina. His sponsors had deposited their credits into his account. What these sponsors all paid him to investigate was what had actually happened to Godzillah Glitch, the musician. For his own edification, Joule had already solved the case days ago, but had not bothered to reveal his findings. Godzillah's body had burned up when a microtear in his freefall suit turned him into a fireball in the thin atmosphere of Mars, but what Godzillah had kept secret from the public was that his mind had been digitized and transmitted out of the body long before his body's conflagration. Joule had followed the sale of a planetessimal's weight in osmium to a facility in the Hildas asteroid grange, where Godzillah's consciousness had been transferred.

Oddly enough, Godzillah had harbored a strong interest in the Rand Paradox. He believed that his existence was synthetic, but he came to these conclusions through altered states of consciousness via self-inflicted torment, all for the sake of his "art."

The trail of the osmium sale had been sloppy, and although Joule cared nothing about his style of "music," nor the subculture of self-abuse that his "Shatter" scene inspired, his fans deserved closure, and he welcomed the money they would otherwise have spent on useless medical enhancements and absurd body modifications. Once he returned from Timejack, he would transmit his findings. The message had already been composed to his synthetic assistant.

The money was all there in his account. He transmitted the agreed-upon amount to Dr. Andwhinge, the only person in the System Joule trusted to monitor his Timejack excursions, and sent the details of the host body, its location, and the date in 1936.

Dr. Andwhinge confirmed receipt and transmitted, "I know well enough not to ask, but what does this have to do with Godzillah Glitch?"

Joule responded, "Meet me at the dock, and I'll tell you."

To which Andwhinge replied, "Of course you will. See you then."

Dr. Wheedle Andwhinge had been Joule's trusted ally for over fifteen years, and in that time, Joule had rigorously tested the man's reliability and earnestness. Consistently, Andwhinge had remained forthright and honest, never violating any words spoken in confidence to either his Timejack superiors or to Joule's meddling brother, Danube, who often threatened to have Joule's temporal excursions audited. Andwhinge had stood his ground each time. He was a good man.

Joule was not surprised when he felt a gentle warmth arise in his chest. Despite Andwinge's augmented brain, he was still very human at his core. Andwhinge demonstrated no interest in those artificial experiences of "Viro," nor any of the other childish distractions in which lesser transhumans indulged. Joule felt the prerogative of any enhanced mind should be to help evolve and sustain one's own species. In his eyes, transhumans were obligated to raise up those who were less fortunate than they, not seek to escape deep into the chimerical, self-indulgent illusions of empty neurostimulation like his parents had.

It was all a macrocosmic parody of Joule's parental issues playing out across the System. These 2.0 people were as useless as his mother and father had been. Joule empathized with the Human Purity Movement, and their struggle to empower all 1.0 humans like these migrant workers, the Greens. Had Joule not have been able to insulate himself in wealth and prestige, he would be just another human struggling for resources, just like these families surrounding him in the shuttle.

Although Joule recognized the Human Purity Movement's struggles for equality as legitimate, he despised their use of brutal mind-hacks on transhumans—those acts were inhuman, and their leader, Antioch Krell, was the worst of all the Purists. He was an ideologue whose rhetoric had radicalized a quarter of the 1.0 humans to act on fear, bigotry, and violence. Terrorist actions against transhumans had increased a thousandfold within the last few months. Joule wondered what they would do once he revealed the truth that they all lived in a splinter reality. For now, Krell and his Purists were helping Joule's career, providing a contrast, making Joule the perfect role model for what they called true humans.

The main door to the passenger area opened, startling everyone. Three men in blue coveralls swaggered onto the floor as if they owned the shuttle. Three different company logos were stenciled on their backs and sleeves. Odd. Blues were very tribal about staying within their corporate brands. They rarely commingled.

The look in their eyes revealed everything. These men were not there to intimidate the Greens. Joule had witnessed too many times the belligerent bigotry of Blues against Greens. It was a primitive rite on display whenever those of slightly more privilege kicked those beneath them. Blues received the same treatment from the Indigo-level managers, and all were under the heel of the Gold-level overseers of Seyopont, like Danube and the other Oligarchs of the System. These men had a glassy sheen to their eyes. They were under the influence of the mild hallucinogenic twilight gas supplied to the Blue section of the shuttle. They should be happily numbed and half-asleep, not marching into Green sections.

These men were being *puppeted*.

The men spotted Joule and weaved through the Greens toward him. Joule casually placed his tablet in the storage area under his seat and stood.

"What can I do for you, gentlemen?"

The closest of them took a swing. Joule stepped into it before it reached the apex of its power. He deflected with his forearm, then kneed his attacker square in the solar plexus. Joule knew the cheap gray-plating in the Green section was shallow, only simulating gravity for the first quarter-meter closest to the floor. Joule's strike lifted the man out of this zone, and the attacker flew into one of his companions, knocking him backward. The third ducked and lunged in. Joule leapt off the floor, flipped, and kicked off the ceiling, dropping an elbow to the nerve bundle behind the third man's neck, knocking him out instantly.

The other two Blue thugs recovered and scurried between the cowering Greens. Joule watched the way they moved, and gauged what fighting apps might've been forced into their puppeted limbs. The two Blues were making use of the grav-plate effects, skating the soles of their shoes close to the floor. It would be easy for someone to trip them, but Joule could not expect a Green to risk a black mark on their record for attacking a member of a higher order. The Greens tucked their legs close to their seats and looked away.

Joule wedged himself into the corner of his seating area to force one attack at a time. He feigned a kick to the chest and, as the man shot out his hands to block, Joule's foot arced up to connect with the man's chin. His head snapped back and he drifted backward. The last attacker had crouched out of the way and crept forward. It was the stance of an assassin trained specifically for grav-plate combat. He kept his center of gravity low, but his thighs trembled—the body was not accustomed to the demands of the combat app. Whoever was behind the eyes of the Blue worker had not chosen his host wisely. Most Blues have enough enhancement to receive training apps to perform their specialized tasks, but it was clear that this worker had spent most of his life in Mars-standard one-third gravity. The fibers in his leg muscles were not dense enough to maintain the stance. All Joule had to do was show that he was ready to match his fighting style and keep the combat app on the defensive, trying to formulate a way through Joule's calculatedly confusing microgestures and feigns. The Blue's thigh muscles would eventually build up too much lactic acid, and he would collapse. The only variable Joule could not be sure of was how long it would take.

Not long.

Desperate, the man dove for Joule's midsection, and Joule drove his knee into the man's larynx. As he coughed and gasped for air, Joule pinched the base of the man's neck with one hand, and grabbed his tablet out of the compartment with the other.

Within three seconds, he locked onto the signal puppeting the Blue worker, but Joule could only trace it as far as the shuttle's relay before the signal was killed.

• • •

"Anything wrong?" Dr. Andwhinge said when he greeted Joule at the dock.

"No," said Joule, smiling and shaking his old friend's hand, defying the hygiene protocols. "This case has gotten interesting."

Joule watched the departing Blue workers and saw one of his attackers, now fully recovered, and fully himself. He appeared confused, as if he were not sure why he had been hurt while he should have been safely dreaming in his Blue sleeping pod. The man noticed Joule and a sharp sting of concern crossed his face.

"Someone you know?" said Andwhinge.

"I just bumped into him during the flight. Let's get to work."

• • •

"I still don't understand. What do you expect to find in 1936 about a dead musician?" Andwinge's comment fed into Joule's sensorium. A simplified avatar of Andwhinge's face floated in Joule's periphery. "Don't tell me you're investigating that Rand Paradox nonsense."

Joule continued to deep breathe in preparation for the timejack. "Then I won't tell you."

"Joule, you know about Temporal Translocation. There's been too much timejack activity in that era. You'll be getting a lot of whispers."

"I'm aware."

"I thought you considered the hacked timeline a silly conspiracy theory."

"I did, until someone sent me a five-hundred-year-old magazine."

"Who did?"

"That's what I plan to find out. The chronometrics confirm the ink on the cover was written in 1936. They had written my name and address."

"But…how could…?"

"Precisely. Either someone has found a way to timejack into the core timeline's past, or it's true that we are living inside a splinter timeline. In either case, someone is trying to point me toward the truth."

"Temporal physics cannot allow jacking the past. It's... *impossible*. I mean, this goes beyond brainteasers about paradoxes like killing your grandfather. It comes down to math. It can't happen no matter how much energy you throw at the problem. The paradox collapses in a quantum blurp."

"I read your doctorate, old friend. Although, I don't recall you using the term *blurp*."

"It's highly technical. It would take too long to explain. Three minutes until jack time."

"You're sure this splinter is clean?"

"I sifted through the code like you asked. No anomalies. It's as clean as I've ever seen, aside from the translocation noise."

"Can you keep it sterile?"

"I locked it off as a Black operation. You'll be alone in there."

"Good...I've already received some unwelcomed attention."

"...that man from the shuttle?"

"He was one of the three men who attacked me right after I sent you my agenda. They were hastily puppeted. Someone else doesn't want me to find out the truth."

"Sixty seconds. I'll set up three more empty Black lock excursions to throw anyone else off your scent."

"Thank you...and although I trust your due diligence implicitly, Andwhinge, I'm going to need you to watch closely for any incursions."

"If someone at Seyopont wants in, they have the equipment to break in and cover their tracks, but...I have some work-arounds. I got your back, Joule."

"You're a good friend, Andwhinge."

"Downstreaming in ten...nine...eight..."

• • •

The asylum staff doused the floors regularly with ammonia, bleach, and camphor to cover the stench of urine and feces seeping out from the seams in the tiles. Repetitive, wordless screams and gibbering chatter echoed down the hallway as Joule sorted through his host body's memories.

This orderly at the asylum, James Ortmeier, had wrestled so many patients into their restraints and straightjackets that, as a defense mechanism, he had bleached his own memory of any human traits those patients might have had, remembering only their gnashing teeth, blood-scraped fingernails, torn-out hair, and feces-smelling breath. Ortmeier had wrangled the most disturbed patients at that asylum, but remembered only enough of their gibbering words to know how to retaliate against the wounds they had inflicted on him.

Ortmeier was almost as bad as the worst of the patients—he himself struggled with an obsessive compulsion of his own thoughts. He feared the patients' ideas could somehow infect him, so he tormented them, exacerbating their conditions by playing to their paranoid delusions. Joule felt the mnemonic bleed worm into his mind—the orderly's thoughts and affectations flooded into Joule's sensorium, tainting him with twisted, sadistic ideas. Joule pushed back, using his lifetime of mental discipline to reassert his personality. The orderly's thoughts gnashed like a rabid beast.

To a female syphilitic patient in restraints, Ortmeier would whisper that beetles were eating her alive from inside. To a paranoid schizophrenic with religious persecution delusions, Ortmeier would use details from the patient's case history to describe what tortures awaited him in hell. The orderly took great steps to hide his sadistic behavior from the other staff and doctors, and Joule had all of it at his fingertips. Joule squeezed Ortmeier's mind like a grapefruit in a vise, but each drop of the orderly's memory juice taxed Joule's sense of self. Each extracted thought held the danger of taking root and infecting Joule with Cross-Consciousness Psychosis. Joule's sensorium flashed warnings. One by one, the firewalls protecting him from mnemonic bleed were failing.

And there it was—a memory of this orderly listening to a patient jabbering to a psychiatrist about how his mind had been taken over by someone from the future. This had fascinated Ortmeier. He had

recently read something similar—a flash of the magazine cover—
Astounding Stories—the same magazine Joule had been sent—and
the story, "The Shadow Out of Time," described the experience of
someone being timejacked.

Joule pulled back from the interface and let his systems
rebalance.

"You were deep into the red," said Andwhinge's avatar.
"Another few seconds, and I was going to yank you out."

"What do we know about this author, H.P. Lovecraft?" Joule
said mind-to-mind. It struck him as odd that he had never before
heard of this writer.

Andwhinge downstreamed all the data on file about the
author. Joule's tablet filtered the information and reparsed it into a
shorthand mental notation system of Joule's own design, tailored
to his synaptic architecture. Joule immediately understood. H.P.
Lovecraft had been very sensitive to temporal translocation—it
was a rare, but well-documented phenomenon—and, inspired
by the other splinter timelines which he experienced in dreams,
Lovecraft had constructed an elaborate fiction of alien gods and
occulted, ancient histories.

Joule was also surprised to learn that there existed many
artificial splinter timelines which attempted to reconstruct
Lovecraft's fictional creatures for the sake of fandom. It was as
if they had been consciously hidden from him. Thousands of
timejacking fans had created genetic labs deep underwater off the
coast of Massachusetts in the late 1920s, and had successfully bred
into existence hybrid human-amphibians and other monstrosities.
The technology had to have been developed in secret, based on
early twentieth-century resources.

If people like them had put as much energy into transforming
the real world as they did toying with these splinter timelines,
the real world could be transformed into a viable utopia. This
reinforced to Joule how distorted his world had become, with its
absurd imbalances of equality.

Most intriguing, these many bizarre curated splinter universes inspired by Lovecraft's writing had caused a feedback loop into the richness of the author's imagination, creating resonances in his fiction for hundreds of years after his death. According to the Absolute Grand Unified Theory, ideas had energy, and with enough energy, these dark gods might gather the temporal translocation energy impregnated with their fiction-made-flesh realities and manifest across all splinter universes.

It was the orderly's thoughts seeping through. Joule had dropped his guard. He tightened the reins on his host body's mind and dug deeper.

The orderly had given this patient a copy of the same *Astounding Stories* issue. The patient had written notes in the margins about people in the future taking over his mind. This was the evidence he needed.

The magazine had been locked away in a filing cabinet in the patient's case file. If Joule could send that evidence back to his present, it would prove that the timeline had been corrupted. But first, a conversation with the patient was in order.

• • •

Joule turned the key and unlocked the isolation room, which smelled like cottage cheese and rubbing alcohol. The patient kept his face to the wall as Joule stepped inside and closed the door.

"I got nothing to say to you, Jimmy," the patient said, defeated, curled on his bed, his back to the door. "Don't take my tray, I'm saving it for later."

On the hospital table, a bowl of cold lentil soup had solidified into paste.

Joule paused the timejack stream and scrolled through the data on the man on the hospital bed, Christopher Spark. The latest information on him was spotty and generic. Usually, the quantum flux linking every splinter reality collapsed quickly into an ocean's worth of details. The more pure the timeline, and the closer in proximity to the person, the more consistent the details should be, but it was as if the fabric of Mr. Spark's existence after 1935 had been mauled by a rabid animal, and large chunks of his psychic pattern were missing.

Prior to 1935, the patient had been an accountant, and not at all prone to wild imaginings. He began to have blackouts and would disappear for weeks on end. He would return, confused and afraid that his body had been possessed by demons.

His family had him evaluated by a psychiatrist. He was committed soon after, and the patterns frayed dramatically after that. Too many timejackers must have been kicking around in his head. The intense temporal translocation energy had annihilated Spark's personality until he no longer was sure who he was.

Joule un-paused the moment and cleared his host's throat. "What do you remember about Ayn Rand?" Joule said through Ortmeier's mouth, but using Joule's paternal voice—the specific tones and inflections that tended to garner the most cooperation from people he questioned.

Spark rolled over and looked into Ortmeier's eyes. Playing on Joule's periphery had been Ortmeier's memories of the many encounters between this host body and the patient. Ortmeier had consistently spoken to Spark with mocking condescension. This paternal voice was different.

"Jimmy?" Spark said, sitting up, the plane of his eyes locking on to Ortmeier. "What's wrong with you?"

"What do you remember?" said Joule, maintaining his soothing delivery.

Spark's breath snagged in his throat. He swung his feet to the floor. "It's you!"

Joule held back Ortmeier from grabbing the billy club at his side. "Who do you think I am?" Joule said.

"You're the one from the future! You did this to me! Why?" Spark stood.

"Sit down!" Joule barked, taking a step forward. Spark was in a fragile, manipulative state from a combination of the drugs in his system and the abuses by the host body who had barked the words. "Now tell me what you remember," Joule said, returning to his paternal tone.

Spark eyed him suspiciously for several moments. "You testing me? Because I said too much already?"

Joule weighed the intelligence of the patient against the trauma of his experience. He decided to try the truth. "Mr. Spark, I'm investigating a crime, and you would be helping a lot of people by telling me what you know."

"Got tired of poking around in my brain, so you decided to talk now?"

"You remember speaking to Mrs. Ayn Rand, the writer?"

"Yes."

"And you warned her about an attack in her future?"

Spark chuckled. "Yes, you did."

"And…the person controlling you told her how important she would be for the future of civilization."

"My mouth said that. I didn't. I didn't know who she was."

"You believe you were possessed by someone from the future?"

"I don't know what else to call it. Something took over my body. All I could do is watch it happen. I thought it was you who…turned me into a puppet. You talk like he did."

"I can only give you my word it wasn't me, but I'm trying to find out who it might have been. What can you remember about the entity that made you speak to Mrs. Rand?"

"He had a strange name."

"Take your time."

" …Vitamin."

"Vitamin?"

"No. Not that. And something about gemstones, but…made out of electricity. It's difficult. I wasn't…talking *to* him. I just heard what he said, and I could get some of his thoughts." Spark pointed to his skull. "So many ideas in my head now, I don't know what to trust, even my memory. All I remember was trying to…" His eyes opened wide. "Jewel! Vitamin Jewel! But, wait, not *vitamin…*

it was a word I never heard before, but sounded like Vitamin. Thetamin? Something like that."

"Theramin?" Joule said.

"Yes! That's it!"

"The person who timejacked you was named Theramin Joule?"

"Do you know him?"

• • •

Joule picked the lock on the records room and thumbed through the case files of Christopher Spark. In it, he found a copy of *Astounding Stories* with notes scribbled in the margins.

Joule had often entertained the possibility of living in a splinter timeline, as he had done with other absurd beliefs, so as to keep his mind pliable and nimble, not fossilized upon "facts," the state of which, like electrons, depend upon the observer's expectations, according to the Absolute Grand Unified Theory.

Had a future version of himself created the splinter timeline? Why would he need to perpetuate the lie that the world existed within a splinter timeline? Maybe the news destabilized the splinter, causing systemic ontological shockwave throughout. Maybe the magazine in his hands had some answers. He prepared himself by opening himself up to the options.

Joule opened the magazine and read the scribbled notes. It looked like his handwriting—frenzied and jagged, but it was his handwriting. It mentioned a cracked timeline and too many pasts at war with the future.

Temporal chaos in the core timeline. Must fix. Need soldiers. Tactical Capitalism must succeed to create superior strategists. Professional mindfuckers. Nothing else worked. When the core timeline is filled with one consciousness (atonement), temporal translocation will be fixed. Lovecraft was warned. Rand was warned. Others must be warned.

Joule had to think. He paused the timestream.

The creak of rubber soles on hall tile. The timestream hadn't paused.

"Andwhinge, get me out," Joule said aloud.

There was no answer. Joule couldn't pull up the controls. His feed was locked in. Had he succumbed to Cross-Consciousness Psychosis? Joule recited a passage from the Timejack user's manual about mnemonic bleed. His host's body could not know those details. He was of his own mind, that was certain, but he was locked into 1936.

The shoes in the hallway stopped at the door and jiggled the handle. A key in the lock. Joule pulled himself tight under a desk.

"Joule," a woman's voice whispered. "It's Andwhinge. It's me."

Joule crawled out and stood. He attempted to straighten his posture into a facsimile of his own body, but Ortmeier's hulking body made the act look absurd. Joule already felt absurd, hiding like a child. Andwhinge had timejacked into the body of a nurse—a burly nurse with a scowl like a bulldog. More absurd, imagining the frail doctor buried beneath that flesh.

"What happened?" Joule said.

"This comes from high up. They're locking down all Timejack ops. I created a back door, but there's little time."

"In different circumstances, I'd say what you just said was profoundly funny."

"Yeah. It's not though. Follow me."

Joule caught up to Andwhinge. "Who is doing this?"

"It's Danube. He sent an incursion team. I rerouted them to downstream into some kids in the Bronx. It'll be a while before they can get here. "

"So you…bought us some—"

"Yes, yes, very funny, Joule."

They stopped at the isolation room for Christopher Spark. Andwhinge unlocked the door. On the bed, lying with his back to them was the patient Spark, but his body was a faintly glowing flat silhouette of deep indigo.

"What is this?" Joule said, hesitating. He had never seen

anything like it. A profound wave of déjà vu swallowed him like a tidal wave.

"Emergency hack," Andwhinge said through the nurse's mouth. Her eyes could not meet Joule's. "It's one of my work-arounds."

"But what *is* it?"

Andwhinge's eyes flicked to the door—a millisecond later, the sound of a door unlocking at the end of the hall echoed through the room. "That's them. They're coming for you. You have to trust me."

" …what do I do, Andwhinge?" Joule said.

The nurse gestured to the prone body. "Lie down in that position. I can reroute you and pull you back home."

"You've done this before?"

"Yes."

"So it works?"

"Yes."

Joule noted Andwhinge struggled to maintain eye contact. Even though the two men looked at each other through two sets of alien eyes, Joule knew his friend well enough that he could see that something was wrong. He was lying.

"What did my brother say to you?"

"We don't have time for this, Joule!" Andwhinge said.

"What did he say?" Joule insisted.

Three children stood in the doorway, dressed in rumpled and dirty clothes. "Theramin Joule, you are to come with us."

• • •

Theramin Joule sat in a holding cell in the Timejack facility, going over the details of the case when a telepresence android opened the door. On its face was projected the holographic image of his brother Danube Candor. He sat and crossed his legs in the seat next to Joule.

"Min." Danube managed to pronounce the syllable as if it were a condemnation, a taunt, and sad, parental shame all at once.

"Noob," Joule responded according to their fraternal tradition.

"What are you doing messing about in 1936? You know that era is dangerous."

Joule crossed his legs to mirror his brother's posture. "We are living in a corrupted timeline, and you and Seyopont are covering it up."

"Ah," Danube said. The android picked nonexistent lint off of his polyalloy ankle. "That. Yes, I wondered when you would get around to noodling into this." He looked up and cocked his head, folding his hands in his lap. "Hypothetically, say it is true. How would it benefit the System if you revealed this information?"

"They probably wouldn't believe me."

"With your reputation, most would."

"And with your reputation, whether or not it were true, you would try to discourage me from revealing it, or resort to discrediting me."

"Theramin, you are my brother. I know you would see reason before I would have to resort to such measures. Let's continue this conversation in person. Will you be willing to come to Luna 2?"

"We can talk here. My last shuttle experience was not so pleasant, and it's a long way to Luna. Too many variables."

"I can't understand why you insist on traveling with the Greens. I'm surprised you haven't encountered more unsavory characters. I can book you in the best Indigo suite."

"What do you know, Danube?"

The android approximated a sigh. "Our timeline is stable."

"But we are not living in the core timeline."

"No. We exist in a prime splinter off of the true core timeline. We are the result of hundreds of years of social engineering. If it were revealed that we were not the true core timeline...well, I'm told there are numerous emanations."

"Such as?"

"Antioch Krell brings down the System in a great war against transhumans. Technology is shunned. We never leave Earth again. The Sun goes nova. The end."

"And if someone kills Krell, he is painted as a martyr, and the pattern is not broken," volunteered Joule.

"Precisely. There are many variations, but it all ends up the same."

"And me? Why get me involved?"

"I have no idea, Min."

"I can always tell when you lie, Danube. Even in telepresence."

"The point remains. This information cannot be revealed to the populace."

"Yet someone takes great efforts to send me a pristine, preserved copy of a five-hundred-year-old magazine with my name and address on it."

"I know," said Danube. "It's a conundrum."

"It's a trap," said Joule. "Just before your agents came for me, I received a powerful wave of déjà vu. I had been there before."

"You should be tested for CCP. You sound as paranoid as that orderly."

"Temporal translocation can manifest as déjà vu. In another splinter timeline I must have gone through that backdoor hack. What is it?"

"I'd tell you to go ask Andwhinge, but he's been transferred to Ceres. He'll never come near Timejack equipment ever again, and neither will you, brother. I'm afraid you've earned one too many black marks."

"I see."

The android stood, his hexiplas palms smoothing out phantom creases in his jacket. "You've brought this on yourself, Min. It's out of my hands. I can keep this incident from getting into the Mesh. You have your reputation to maintain, but I suggest you follow through with your investigations of Godzillah Glitch and leave this Rand Paradox business to the halfwits."

"So I'm free to go?"

"Yes. Oh, and I'm afraid your tablet had to be destroyed. Too much incriminating evidence, I'm afraid."

"Of course."

•••

Back at home at Jove's Halo, Theramin Joule tabbed through a clone of his tablet and ran updates. He suspected his brother had already analyzed Joule's coding on his old tablet in order to design a hack, but he couldn't behave as if he suspected it. Joule dictated his experiences over the last week to Anne and saved them as he normally would. He followed his own protocols of planning next steps, weighing pros and cons, laying out all the details he recalled, expecting Danube and his minions at Seyopont to be listening in. His brother knew him too well. Any deviation might tip him off to what Joule was actually planning.

He had to find a way into the core timeline, and the only way to do that would be to do something nobody ever expected him to do—go full transhuman.

Joule sent all the information he had on Godzillah Glitch to his MeshMash account and watched the trend ratings stack. The nouveau-2.0s celebrated Glitch joining their ranks and looked forward to a new, upgraded release from the musician. No love was lost on Glitch from the Human Purity Movement. His form of entertainment was considered an abomination by Antioch Krell and his followers. Joule privately agreed.

What Joule did not reveal in his message was the final resting place of Godzillah Glitch's consciousness and, despite being offered astronomical amounts of money, Joule added to his MeshMash account that he was actively seeking sponsors to fund his investigations into the Rand Paradox.

•••

Like Joule's mental exercises entertaining absurd conspiracy theories to their logical limits, Joule had entertained the inevitability of having to embrace transhumanism as the only means of survival in his rapidly changing world. The most viable of his contingency plans relied upon a company called MetaPhore. Joule had nurtured a relationship with one of its developers.

The money that had flooded into his account sponsoring his investigation into The Rand Paradox had afforded him the most advanced processor—a prototype 3.0 digital medium for his mind. The digitization process was simple and fluid. He raced through the adaptation exercises with unprecedented speed and marveled at the options available to him, but Joule remained focused on his plan.

He would find a way into the true core timeline.

• • •

The Mesh spread out before his senses as if he were in the guts of a Jupiter-sized jellyfish. Ten thousand cities of lights pulsed and glittered around him—each flicker was a mind connected. Joule floated in one position, observing the patterns, letting his mind process the data in its most raw form as the lights flicked from point to point, lingering with other lights, whispering.

He watched and listened and remembered.

Joule's 3.0 mind stored it all. He had instant recall of the most minute of details while simultaneously absorbing more data in one second than his Human 1.0 mind could gather in a year. The nodes accumulated in patterns like coral growing on a high-gravity planet—densely packed layers—and within each layer were the history of each interaction.

The Mesh was a meta-mind, just as he had suspected, but what was it thinking, and how could he access its core program?

Joule recalled his ten-dimensional math equations and unscrolled the Mesh into a polyhedral two-dimensional map like the "orange peel" projection of the Earth. The lights and nodal synapses of the Mesh uncoiled around him like fractal spaghetti, collapsing to twelve points of infinite density. Joule then smoothed this map onto the Calabi-Yau manifold—an undulating, twisting sphere which was used to map ten dimensions the way a Moebius strip mapped three.

Joule felt a wave of existential dread rise in him—he had read it was something all transhumans faced—the sense of a mind unleashed, where limitations were restricted only to one's will and imagination. Floating outside of any previous context, Joule had no body, and no baseline state. He could become anything here in the place where people became gods, and one femtosecond later collapse into an eternal loop of self-reflection—who am I? What am I? Do I truly exist? As if summoned, hundreds of thousands of stone buoys floated up from the undulating map—these were the ancestors of all transhumans. These were the fallen heroes who dared to attempt the impossible and had failed. Cocooned within inert crusts of self-doubt and fear, they remained fossilized for eternity.

They were a warning. They were also a reminder to Joule to stay on his path.

As he was distracted by his own thoughts, some of the corners had peeled up from his model of the Mesh. He smoothed them down again and descended into its folds. The Mesh skittered and pulsed around him as he followed the ribbons into the center of the maze.

At the core, where the ten dimensions collapsed into an infinitely dense point of probability, Joule hesitated. Was his own life less important than knowledge?

Yes.

* * *

"Theramin Joule?" said a familiar voice.

Joule opened his eyes, was momentarily surprised that he once again had eyes to open, then was more surprised when he saw his own face—an older, smiling version of himself.

"You made it! Congratulations and all of that. You've reached the core timeline."

"You're..."

"Yes, I am you. And now, you will become me. Your job is to maintain the splinter universe you just left."

Joule sat up from an immersion bay and looked at his own hands—he had the same calluses and freckles in the right places.

"This is your hero's journey," the older Joule continued. "You've sacrificed yourself for knowledge, now use that knowledge to bring through the next you. We'll be starting you off in a time and place you're already familiar with..." Older Joule paused.

"1935, New York City?" Joule said. Outside his immersion pod were a sea of other pods. The floor gently curved up to meet the ceiling. He was inside a massive space station.

"Of course," said older Joule. "We've prepped all the files you'll need for reference, but you already know what we're doing. You always do..."

"The core timeline must become stable, so we must populate it with one consciousness," said Joule.

"Never play with time travel is the moral to the universe's story," said Future Joule. "That said, we have to use timejacking to create more Theramin Joules. We have over seven hundred billion working on it already, but we'll need a bunch more to obtain singularity."

Joule looked into his future-self's eyes. He had so many questions. "We need to populate the universe with...me?"

"So much for being a unique snowflake, hey Joule? Now. Time's a-wasting. Go buy yourself a copy of *Astounding Stories*." Future Joule gently pressed on Joule's chest, guiding him back down. "And don't be too hard on Dr. Andwhinge. He's a good man."

HO HO HOLMES

BY NAT GERTLER

The boss tapped his pipe impatiently as he glowered at the topmost letter in the stack. These notes, piled on the lap of his red velvet smoking jacket with its white fur trim, were written in a plethora of languages and addressed to a variety of names. Some letters addressed the boss as "Kris Kringle," others "Santa Claus," still others "Father Christmas," or "Sinterklaas," "Saint Nick," "de Kerstman," or any of dozens of other names. Few if any used his original name, but that was the name we knew him by around the North Pole—not as the legend, but as the real man behind the myth, the man whom it was our honor to serve.

"You called for me, Mr. Holmes?" I asked. It was more statement than question. I knew that he had called for me, but I also knew that his ability to intensely concentrate on any matter sometimes obscured in his mind all else, including things he himself had done a moment before. I did not need to make him aware of my presence (the bells on my shoes surely did that sufficiently) so much as remind him that he had, apparently, some reason for that presence.

"Why didn't someone bring Sandeep Hawthorn of 2629 Billings Street, Dekatur to my attention?" he demanded, looking not at me but at the letter. "He is asking for the Bloozy-Blu Ultra Pony Squad figure this year."

"And wowzers, we shall get it for him and make his Christmas won-dun-dunderful!" I said in my default spirited manner.

238

"But he asked for it last year as well…and, no, don't bother checking, I remember, he got it. So he should've been asking for Tickeldy-Pink, or Mizz Scarlett, or any of the three mega-ponies. But instead, he asked for Bloozy-Blu, a baseball bat and glove, and a remote control truck, a year after asking for and getting the Bloozy-Blu, an art set, and a toy oven."

"Perhaps the poor li'l feller broke his Bloozy-Blue?"

"Perhaps, my dear Wuzzin, but no. Dani Roland of 2622 Billings Street, Dekatur this year asked for Tickeldy-Pink and Mizz Scarlett and all three megas."

I looked up Dani Roland in the ledger. "She's certainly not going to get all of those things…perhaps not any of them, she's been naughty-listed in the past, but I see your point. You think Dani stole Sandeep's Bloozy-Blu."

"Wuzzin, you have a wonderful ability to pinpoint the obvious. No, no, that's a compliment," he said, waving away the rejoinder that I was definitely thinking but might not have chosen to voice, "so many of your fellow elves skip gleefully past the obvious without a lick of attention. But while noticing what's interesting about what Dani asked for this year, you missed the clue in the other things that Sandeep asked for."

"Baseball items and a truck? That's grand and great, but not particularly interesting, a large portion of boys that age will happily ask you for sports equipment or a truck."

"Yes, but look the year before. His tastes weren't so gender-specific. It's like he's trying hard to prove his boyness now. So what made him change?"

"Perhaps it's just a phase, nothing to explain."

Holmes look exasperated. He is, of course, an amazing man, but far from perfect. While he is quite aware that he is amazing, he has never accepted that the rest of us simply do not have the brainpower to work on his level. "Why look for a lack of explanation when one is staring you in the face? He's going for the boys' toys because he's been made to feel there's a problem if he doesn't. The girl across the street didn't *steal* Bloozy-Blu…she *blackmailed* him for it. Probably caught him playing with a toy oven or somesuch and threatened to tell the other boys at school."

"That's mean!" I said in a shocked tone, proving that I too had trouble adapting to the truth. I knew intellectually that humans had far more cruelty built in than elfin society did, but examples still always came as a surprise.

"Change Dani's schedule for this year to *three* pair of pajamas, all gray. I want the point to be clear. You may want to put that down as her default delivery for the future. I would love to be wrong, but I suspect she'll be earning fresh pajamas annually for years to come. Meanwhile, tag Sandeep's account. If he asks for anything even a bit away from the norm in the future, make sure he gets it."

I was entering those details into my ledger when the door flew open. I was ready to take whoever came through to task for such a gross violation of protocol, entering Mr. Holmes's office without so much as a knock, when I saw Frazzen's face and realized that whatever was happening, it was more important than protocol.

"Mr. Holmes, sir," she said, out of breath and her usually musical voice strained. "Brizzen's sent me to tell you—Dancer has been found out in Livingstone Field, dead."

"Golly! That's horrible," I opined. "I knew she was getting on in years, but I thought she still had a couple decades…"

Holmes held up his hand to stop me. "No, that's not what Frazzen is saying. Go on, please, Frazzen."

"She was killed. Slaughtered. Smashed in the noggin."

• • •

It took us half an hour to get out to Livingstone Field by snowmobile, which gave us time to get what little information Frazzen had, shouted over the whine of the engine. Brizzen had found the dead reindeer several hours earlier, while out on a hike. On snowshoes, it had taken him hours to get to the nearest shack, where he found Frazzen and sent her to talk to us, while he himself went to alert stablemaster Grizzian.

Livingstone Field is a vast, flat expanse, largely featureless unless you consider snow to be a feature. When we got within a quarter mile of where the reindeer carcass lay, Holmes stopped the snowmobile and he and I walked the rest of the way, leaving Frazzen with the vehicle not because it needed any guarding, but simply because she was too stressed and would not likely be useful in examining the scene. I was momentarily surprised he even took me along, but he needs someone to talk to when working things through. At times, I'm helpful because we have a rapport, although at other times, he'd do as well just talking to a Dancin' Betty doll from the toy storage shack.

We walked the last quarter mile, he explained, to ensure that we weren't damaging any potential evidence with the snowmobile nor overlooking anything in our haste. I was fine with that slow entry, being in no rush to see the remains of this once beautiful creature, a feeling that only increased as we grew closer and I could see a wide bloom of blood-stained snow surrounding the spot where she lay.

• • •

The scene when we finally reached Dancer was even more heartrending than I had anticipated. The body was drenched with blood, and there was more blood tainting the clean white snow for yards around. Dancer's skull had been utterly pulped at the top, with chunks of brain, bone, and antlers scattered. While I instinctively drew away from the gruesome sight, Mr. Holmes leaned in closer. "This wasn't just one or two blows, it was many. A dozen or more, probably. Had it been fewer, I could get a good outline of what struck her, but this? Each blow destroyed the marks of the previous ones, and by the end, it was like it was hitting soup."

I could not respond to what I saw nearly so dispassionately. "Gosh, such a senseless tragedy!"

The boss shook his head. "We must not believe that. Tragic, yes, of course. But not senseless."

"You see sense in smashing a reindeer's head in?"

Sherlock Holmes let out a sigh that filled the chilly air in front of him with a fog, giving physical form to his disappointment. "It doesn't matter whether *I* see sense in it, dear Wuzzin. What is important is that we remember that whoever perpetrated this saw sense in it. Things are not done without reason. Find the person for whom this killing made sense, and you have found your killer. Believing that it cannot make sense is, in practical form, giving up. The killer has a motive, even if we cannot yet suss what that motive is."

"Obviously, the killer was trying to stop you from making your deliveries and bringing joy to all the wunnerful li'l kiddies of the world this year."

Holmes cocked an eyebrow. "Obviously? Likely, perhaps, but obviously?"

"Well, shucks, the other reasons for killing that come to mind certainly don't apply. I doubt anyone would kill a reindeer to rob them, or out of revenge for a love affair gone wrong."

"If that's all that you can come up with, you have a limited knowledge of killing. Which is, I suppose, a good thing. It's not something that the typical man nor elf need be too well versed in. But you leave out such motives as protecting secrets—the dead tell no tales."

"Nor do reindeer, even when alive."

"Deceased reindeer make excellent stew meat, I am told. No, no, don't bother telling me that this one hasn't been eaten. I am merely demonstrating that there are many reasons for killing, and we can waste our time eliminating all those that do not apply, or focus on finding the one that does."

"I still reckon it was to stop your oh-so-magnificent deliveries."

Holmes did not respond. He just scanned the snow surrounding the corpse.

"Did it work? Will you be able to deliver the gifties without

Dancer? Or do we have to…" I trailed off, unable to bring the words "cancel Christmas" to my lips.

"What? Oh, yes. I've done it before with seven. Remember a few years back, when Vixen was pregnant? Couldn't risk having her on the team."

"Vixen's daughter! Zephyr! Can she take Dancer's place?"

"Not this year. Zephyr has started to fly, but she hasn't the necessary range or control yet, last report I got from Grizzian. She's got at least two years before she's mission-ready."

"Then gee whiz, it sure is good that you can make it with seven." I said, for once having to force a smile onto my face.

"Yes, but it's a tight fit with no room for error. The calculations show that it would all fail if I had to take even a few more pounds… if, for instance, I weighed as much as those ludicrous pictures that the publicity elves distribute. Egad, they make it look like I've never turned down a cookie in my life. I do wish they'd stop promoting that image of me."

"No, you don't sir, and you know quite well why they do that. You realize the success of your operation depends on you not seeming threatening, as safe as everyone's jolly ol' grandpa. If people knew what you really looked like…well, you might be okay to pass on the street, but if people started thinking of your bony self with that talon-like nose of yours, sneaking into their house through their chimney and tippy-toeing around, it'd give the kiddies nightmares! They would think you were there with the intent to murder, and your motive would be stew meat! And furthermore," I emphasized, trying to find a tactic that would keep this conversation from recurring ever again (yet knowing I would fail), "you know all this to be true. You know that image to be necessary. And I can prove that, because I have heard you say a hundred times, a thousand times that you wish they would stop doing that, but you have never once gone to the publicity shack and told them 'stop doing that.' That's all it would take. Three words from you and it stops, because by golly, you are loved, you are worshipped, you are respected, and you are obeyed. Yet you do not take that step, because you know they are right, sir."

Holmes let what passes for a smile in his facial repertoire pass his lips (no, he could never even fake being the man you see on the posters). "You are," he said, "very good at telling the truth. Not that any of you elves have any talent for lying. Few of you even seem to see it as an option. But you in particular, when you see the truth, you like to put it all out there, straight and bare, don't you? Sometimes, I wish you'd stop that."

"No, you don't," I responded, in my usual chipper tone.

"No, I don't."

• • •

Holmes examined the snowy plain surrounding the carcass from all angles, trying to find any trail of the attacker, but to no avail. The only tracks that he could see were Dancer's and some faint outlines of the snowshoe tracks left by Brizzen, and, more recently, by ourselves (and even those were quickly being lost to the wind). "So the killer left no tracks?" I asked.

"Or the wind has long since brushed them away," Holmes explained. "If the perpetrator approached the scene on snowshoes, the track would be gone. But snowshoes would make it impossible for the killer to have chased Dancer, yet by the spacing of her hoof prints, she was clearly running."

"And a person couldn't run that fast in snowshoes."

"A person can't run that fast through snow no matter how they are shod. Even an aging reindeer like Dancer should still be able to do bursts of more than twenty miles an hour. The attacker would need a vehicle of some sort, if he were chasing after her."

"If? Surely, Dancer was fleeing from whatever nasty ol' fiend killed her."

"Again, Wuzzin, you fail to see all the options. What if Dancer was not running *from* something, but *toward* it? If the killer presented some sort of a lure or bait that drew her in, then there was no need to go fast at all. He could have come in on snowshoes and stood there for hours, for all we yet know."

• • •

Our trip to the stables was, if not silent thanks to the engine, certainly devoid of conversation. Holmes was deep in concentration, and Frazzen clearly did not want to hear the details of what we had seen, and for that I could not blame her; if I could unsee it myself, I would. As we approached the stables, we could see many reindeer in the pen. I could not quickly count to see if they were all there, and even if I could, I was unsure how many there were supposed to be. (I dealt mainly with delivery planning, and leave things like toy production, reindeer care, site maintenance, and the various sundry aspects of our North Pole operation to the capable hands of other elves.) I could see there were at least some of the flyers, all female (because that's where the flight ability lies), and some of the breeding studs (recognizable during this season by their lack of antlers). And I recognized Zephyr, more mature than when I'd last seen her but still slightly smaller than the flight team. There were clearly other reindeer who were somehow necessary to the operation in some way, but again, this was not my department.

Upon hearing our approach, stablemaster Grizzian stepped away from a bit of grooming she'd been doing and rushed toward us. She was old even for an elf, but showed no sign of having been slowed down by it. "Hello, sir. Have you been to see Dancer?" she asked. When Holmes nodded, she launched her next question. "Is it as bad as he says?" he said, gesturing toward Brizzen, who stood slumped against the open doorway of the stable.

"Yes, it is oh-so baddy-bad indeed. Are all the others account-ed for?"

She nodded. "They're all here."

"What was Dancer doing so far away?" I asked.

"Golly, this time of year, they're all usually out," she said, gesturing with her hand. "This close to delivery time, they're wandering or flying or doing whatever it takes to stay calm. They only come home when they need food or when I blow the horn to call them in. I blew the horn the moment Brizzen told me the news."

Holmes shook his head. "They're not calm, though."

"Nope."

"What does that mean, not calm?" I asked. "Are they frightened, are they angry, are they…"

A mitten-clad hand came down on my shoulder. "You're looking for a more complex range of emotions than these reindeer exhibit," Holmes explained. "They are fairly simple creatures, with two visible emotional states: calm, and agitated. Agitated can be happy or angry or frustrated or sick or ready to mate or any state other than calm."

Grizzian concurred. "I've been tending this wonderful herd for over a century now, and even I still need to know the cause of agitation to have a good guess at what form of agitation it is. They aren't at all stupidheads, and they have some form of communication among themselves but they aren't expressive in any way an elf can read. Mister Holmes, if you ever come up with a reindeer decoder, put that on my Christmas wish list."

• • •

We approached Brizzen, who was still morosely leaning on the stable door frame. He didn't snap into alertness the way that most of us elves do when the boss looks our way. I tried to find cheery words for him, but all the usual greetings seemed so hollow in the moment, so I just said "Brizzen" to acknowledge his existence. His eyes turned toward me for a moment, then went back down to the ground.

"Don't worry, I'll calm things down with Huzzin," Holmes said to him, in a tone more matter-of-fact than reassuring. "Things will be okay if you just clown around a little less. Now if you could…"

This grabbed Brizzen's attention. "Is that what Huzzin called it? Clowning around?" he demanded, in a tone that I had never previously heard any elf use with the boss.

"No, not to me, anyway," said Holmes with a shake of his head. "I've not spoken with Huzzin lately."

Confusion crept across Brizzen's face. "Then how in the widdly-wide world did you know that he was mad at me for fooling around?"

Holmes sighed. "Most elves don't go out on a several mile hike for no reason…and particularly not production elves so close to the Christmas deadline. For you to choose to go out—or for Huzzin to let you go—there must've been some conflict at hands. Now, looking down at your pants, I see a line of grease just above the cuff. That's the familiar mark on loose pants. You've been riding bicycles, I presume."

"Testing them out, yes, that's part of the job," the elf replied. "The kiddies would be sad sad sad if their new Christmas bikes'n'trikes didn't work."

"Of course," said Holmes, "but the chain is on the right side of the bicycle. You have grease marks on both cuffs, albeit fainter on the left. You've been mounting bicycles backwards at times… that is to say, trick riding, showing off, fooling and/or clowning around. Now, I know Huzzin well, and he loves merriment as much as the next elf for ten, maybe eleven months of the year. But in the final weeks before deadline? You should know better than that, and I'm sure you will, next time."

"Oh, it was obvious then," said Brizzen, apologetically. "I should've known immediately. I'm just a bit too upset."

"I understand. So, did you just happen to pass right by Dancer's body?"

"I wasn't going to go right by it. In fact, I was just about to turn around and head back to the toy production shack, but I saw it…her…in the snow from a while away. My peepers, they see pretty good. I wasn't sure at first just what that thing in the snow was, but I thought I ought to check."

"And when you got close, when you could tell it was a reindeer, how'd you recognize it was Dancer?" said Holmes, staring intently at the elf's face.

"The fur pattern, I suppose mostly the amount of white on her rump. She has the most whiteness of any of them."

"You've spent a lot of time with the team?"

"Not really. Which is good, they scare me, so big." Brizzen gave a little shiver. "But a few seasons back, we were assembling stuffed reindeer, for the kiddies. Had to get them right. Kids can tell!"

"Did you see or hear anything else unusual around the scene?"

"No, no, just the body. And the blood. All the blood…" He trailed off, his attention turning back groundward.

"Were there any other tracks," asked Holmes, "besides Dancer's, near the body?"

"I didn't see any," Brizzen mumbled.

"But would you have?"

"Of course. I told ya, my peepers are good."

"You might have seen, but would you have noticed? Is it something that your mind would have called attention to?" Brizzen looked puzzled, so the boss continued. "Close your eyes for a moment. Just try to pull up in your mind a picture of what you saw. Now look around that picture, not just at the body, but around it, the land next to it. Think about the sounds you heard, the…"

He stopped when he saw that Brizzen had broken down in tears.

"He's thinking about all the blood again," I said. "You've lost him."

As we headed back toward the snowmobile, I asked, "Did you really need to bring up his trick riding? That seems like a little bitty matter at this point."

"I needed to do something to get his mind off the crime scene," Holmes explained, "just for a moment. To distract him from the immediate tragedy, just to clear the shock so that I could get some answers."

"That didn't last long. You got some answers, did they help?"

"I won't know that for sure until I get the big answer."

• • •

We were heading back toward the information shack, planning to check the recent satellite imagery and radar data to see if there was any sign of an outside interloper, when the boss looked back, slowed for a moment, then changed course. I tried to signal the way to the information shack, just to make sure that there wasn't some error, but we headed towards the toy production shack instead. It wasn't until we were dismounting the snowmobile in the parking shelter just outside the shack that Holmes spoke.

"How could I have been so long blind, Wuzzin?" he said. "I spent so much time looking for the tracks that weren't at the scene that I failed to fully consider the tracks that were there."

I tilted my head, as if seeing the world from a slightly different angle would help me see his point. "You mean Brizzen's? Gee whiz, boss, I cannot think of why he'd've killed Dancer."

"Oh, he gets written off not even with a 'why' but with a 'how.' He's not a third as high as the top of Dancer's head. To lay blows where they landed, he'd have needed some sort of hammer with a handle twice as long as he is tall. Were he able to wield such a weapon, he'd had to have struck the poor creature with force and at an amazing rate to get in all that damage before Dancer fell to the ground. Not to mention his dragging the weapon to and from the location would have left a trail. No, it's not his tracks I'm talking about. It's Dancer's."

He paused a moment to let that sink in, as if giving me four seconds to dwell on it would bring to my little mind the understanding that it had taken his amazing brain an hour to achieve. As you can well expect, I proved a disappointment in this regard. "Dancer's?" I asked, to turn the conversation back over to him.

"Her tracks clearly showed the signs that she was running at a high speed, and indeed a reindeer has a reasonably high speed for a land mammal; not as fast as a gazelle or a coyote or a Mongolian wild ass, but fast nonetheless. But the land speed of a reindeer has nothing on the airspeed of one who can fly. Whether rushing toward something or fleeing some attacker, Dancer would have done it much more quickly had she flown…and in the case of an attacker, heading to the sky would have taken her where most attackers could not possibly have followed. But she didn't fly, and that leads me to only one conclusion:

"Dancer was not a flying reindeer. Not anymore. At least, not reliably. Age had finally taken her ability, as it will eventually take abilities from most of us.

"Once we accept that, the rest of the picture becomes instantly clear. Why were the other reindeer acting more on edge than usual? It surely wasn't just Dancer's absence; the members of the team are apt to be wandering off at any given moment, so her not being there was not unusual. No, they knew what had happened because they had done it. It may have been one of them or some of them or all of them that had done it, but they all knew it had been done. The objects that had smashed Dancer's head were the flailing hooves of reindeer. That is, logically, how a flying reindeer would attack an earth-bound one, from above."

"But Holmes, that's icky! It's…it's…it's not 'cannibalism,' but there must be a word for killing a member of your own species," I said, floundering in my hunt for language.

"Of course there is. It's 'murder.' We don't use that term when a man kills a bear or a bear kills a man. 'Murder' is an intraspecies concept."

My heart was racing as I felt a surge of panic take me over. My speech became more rapid and higher-pitched than even my normal elfin tones. "Oh, this is a disaster. This is ruination. The mission will be scuttled! The deliveries will not happen! No gifties for the kiddies! This is unprecedented!"

"Calm yourself, Wuzzin. The mission will go on as planned." Holmes hung his goggles over the handle of the snowmobile.

"You won't have the seven reindeer you need! Even if just one of them committed this foul deed, removing the murderous individual leaves you with an insufficient team!"

"I will not be removing anyone from the team, Wuzzin. You are acting as if this was a case of human or elf society, where what we most value is protecting the individual, and thus must condemn the killer. But that comes because the biggest danger to our societies come not from outside but from within—more true of humans, with our range of base and vile instincts, than of you elves, of course. The animal kingdom is different. They haven't overcome their outside predators the way that humans have. Animals will protect the group even if it requires sacrificing the individual, as it did today. And to my team, the group is the mission and the mission is the group. The team exists to help me make the annual deliveries. Anything that interferes with that is a challenge to the group.

"You assumed from the very beginning that this attack was done in order to scuttle my mission this year, yet nothing could be farther from the truth. Had I hitched up the full team and Dancer had become dead weight, the mission would have failed; not immediately perhaps, but before most of the deliveries had been done. Do I wish that the reindeer had had some way to communicate to me or to their handlers that there was a problem, so that we could simply have removed Dancer from the team and let her live out the rest of her natural life as a no-longer-flying reindeer? Most certainly. But I cannot hold judgment against animals for seeing the problem and addressing it in a way that was within their abilities."

This was a dark moment for me, knowing that our mission of joy had such a bloody cost attached, but the boss would not let me linger on it.

"Come now, Wuzzin! Christmas Eve rushes ever closer, and there is still so much to be done. As sad as Dancer's death is, it would be sadder still if her death were in vain. There are toys to be checked, and Huzzin's one elf short at the moment!"

With a clap of his hands, Sherlock Holmes rushed into the toy production shack, and I followed along as well as my shorter legs would allow.

ABOUT THE AUTHORS

DEREK BEEBE is the author of the fantasy novel *It's a Wonderful Death*, and his short stories have appeared in the *Tales of Fortannis* collections. His web page is **www.DerekBeebe.com.** He is a regular contributor to the podcast network WhenNerdsAttack. com. He lives in Pennsylvania and spends far too much of his life on television, movies, and books.

This is **KEITH R.A. DECANDIDO's** second story with Shirley Holmes & Jack Watson, following "Identity" in the previous *Baker Street Irregulars* anthology. He hopes they will have many more adventures. He's written more than fifty novels, more than seventy-five short stories, more than fifty comic books, and a metric buttload of nonfiction that he hasn't even attempted to count. His oeuvre ranges from media tie-in fiction in dozens of different licensed universes (among them *Star Trek, Supernatural, World of Warcraft, Doctor Who, Aliens,* Marvel Comics, and tons more) as well as original fiction in both the fictional cities of Cliff's End and Super City as well as the somewhat real locales of Key West and New York City. Find out less at his website at **www.DeCandido.net**.

NAT GERTLER is a professional *Peanuts* nerd, as well as the publisher of the *About Comics* line and the creator of Licensable Bear™. A graduate of Simon's Rock Early College, he's written or co-written about two dozen nonfiction books (winning a Ben Franklin Award in 2016), various short stories, over a hundred comic book tales, and a TV episode or two (well, one). He lives in

Camarillo, California with his wife Lara and however many kids they have.

NARRELLE M. HARRIS writes crime, horror, fantasy, and romance. Her thirty-plus works include vampire novels, erotic spy adventures, queer romance, traditional Holmesian mysteries, and the Holmes/Watson romance *The Adventure of the Colonial Boy*. In 2017, her ghost/crime story *Jane* won the Body in the Library prize at the Scarlet Stiletto Awards. **www.narrellemharris.com**.

GORDON LINZNER is the founder and former publisher of *Space And Time* magazine. A lifetime member of SFWA, he is the author of three published novels and dozens of short stories in publications such as *The Magazine of Fantasy and Science Fiction*, *Rod Serling's Twilight Zone Magazine*, *Eerie Country*, *Tales By Moonlight*, *Swords Against Darkness*, *100 Wicked Little Witch Stories*, *Bruce Coville's UFOs*, *Museum of Horrors*, and *Altered States of the Union*, among other magazines and anthologies.

DANIEL M. KIMMEL's book on the history of FOX TV, *The Fourth Network*, received the Cable Center Book Award. His other books include a history of DreamWorks, *The Dream Team*; *I'll Have What She's Having: Behind the Scenes of the Great Romantic Comedies*; and *Jar Jar Binks Must Die…and Other Observations about Science Fiction Movies*, which was shortlisted for the Hugo Award for Best Related Work. His first novel, *Shh! It's a Secret: a Novel about Aliens, Hollywood, and the Bartender's Guide*, was a finalist for the Compton Crook Award. His latest book is *Time on My Hands: My Misadventures in Time Travel*.

STEPHANIE M. McPHERSON is a writer whose work has appeared across a spectrum of media, including *The Boston Globe Magazine*, the PBS NOVA website, and the national radio show *Living on Earth*. She earned her Master's degree in Science Writing from MIT in 2011 and has since written about everything from diabetes to 3D printers in space. This is her first published piece of fiction. She lives in the Greater Boston area with her husband, daughter, and calico cat. You can read more from her at **www.stephaniemmcpherson.com**.

JODY LYNN NYE lists her main career activity as "spoiling cats." She lives northwest of Chicago with one of the above and her husband, author and packager Bill Fawcett. She has written over forty-five books, including *The Ship Who Won* with Anne McCaffrey, eight books with Robert Asprin, a humorous anthology about mothers, *Don't Forget Your Spacesuit, Dear!*, and over 160 short stories. Her latest books are *Rhythm of the Imperium* (Baen Books), *Moon Beam* (with Travis S. Taylor, Baen), and *Myth-Fits* (Ace). Jody also reviews fiction for *Galaxy's Edge* magazine and teaches the intensive writers' workshop at DragonCon. Her web page is **www.jodynye.net**.

CHUCK REGAN is a big geek who writes a lot of pulp genre crap. **www.chuckregan.com**.

R. ROZAKIS has the amazing superpower of causing professors and technicians to stare at her lab equipment and say, "I've never seen it do that before!" Her current job in marketing in New York City seems so much safer, really. Her biggest argument with her exceedingly patient husband is in what order they should show *Star Wars* to their preschooler. Previous work has appeared in *Daily Science Fiction*, *Andromeda Spaceways Inflight Magazine*, *Allegory*, *Liquid Imagination*, *Every Day Fiction*, and the anthologies *Substitution Cipher* and *Clockwork Chaos*.

HILDY SILVERMAN is the publisher of *Space and Time*, a five-decade-old magazine featuring fantasy, horror, and science fiction (**www.spaceandtimemagazine.com**). She is also a short fiction author whose most recent publications include, "The Great Chasm" (2016, coauthored with David Silverman, *Altered*

States of the Union, Hauman, ed.), "A Scandal in the Bloodline" (2017, *Baker Street Irregulars*, Ventrella and Maberry, eds.), "The Show Killer" (2017, *TV Gods 2: Summer Programming*, Young and Hillman, eds.), and "Invasive Maneuvers" (2017, *Love, Murder and Mayhem*, Colchamiro, ed.).

SARAH STEGALL writes science fiction, fantasy, and mysteries. Her latest novel, *Outcasts: A Novel of Mary Shelley*, is about the night Mary Shelley sat down to write *Frankenstein*. She is the author of the Phantom Partners series, as well as the novel *Chimera* and the YA novel *Farside*. Her most recent short stories have been published in *Deadworld: A Tribute Anthology to Deadworld and Comic Publisher Gary Reed*, and *The X-Files: The Truth Is Out There*. She researched and helped write the first three *Official Guides to The X-Files*. Sarah lives in Northern California because the fog hides her better.

MIKE STRAUSS is a graduate of Carnegie Mellon, currently living in Pittsburgh. He works as a full-time freelance writer and content marketing specialist. He has had four stories published in the *Tales of Fortannis* anthologies, as well as in the previous *Baker Street Irregulars*.

ABOUT THE EDITORS

New York Times bestselling author **JONATHAN MABERRY's** latest series *Rot and Ruin* has just been optioned for film, and other works of his are heading for the big screen as well. He's a multiple Bram Stoker Award winner and has written for Marvel comics as well. He's been named one of today's top ten horror writers. His website is **www.jonathanmaberry.com**.

MICHAEL A. VENTRELLA's humorous novels include *Bloodsuckers: A Vampire Runs for President* and *The Axes of Evil.* He edits the *Tales of Fortannis* short story collections, and has had his own stories printed in many anthologies, including Janet Morris's *Dreamers in Hell, Rum and Runestones, Twisted Tails*, and *The Ministry of Peculiar Occurrences Archives.* His web page is **www.MichaelAVentrella.com**.